# SOMETIMES YOU COULD DIE

Anglo-Italian private detective Tommaso Ronald Hogget excels at finding missing things and missing people – sometimes when they're dead. Hogget enjoys fine wine, good food and always travels first class – when he's on expenses. He's not necessarily the most honest detective and certainly not the bravest, but he has a back-up man for the violent bits: Dave Baxter, ex-paratrooper and intellectual mini-cab driver. When Hogget is asked to find the murderers of a millionaire's wife and the trail leads from New York to Paris to northern Italy, expense is no object but both he and his minder Dave will earn their fees the hard way.

# SOMETIMES YOU COULD DIE

# SOMETIMES YOU COULD DIE

*by*

James Mitchell

**Magna Large Print Books**
Long Preston, North Yorkshire,
BD23 4ND, England.

British Library Cataloguing in Publication Data.

Mitchell, James
    Sometimes you could die.

    A catalogue record of this book is
    available from the British Library

    ISBN   978-0-7505-4302-6

First published in Great Britain in 1985
Published by Ostara Publishing Ltd. in 2015

Copyright © James Mitchell 1985

Cover illustration © iArt Images by arrangement with
Alamy Stock Photo

The moral right of the author has been asserted.

Published in Large Print 2016 by arrangement with
Ostara Publishing

Magna Large Print is an imprint of Library Magna Books Ltd.

Printed and bound in Great Britain by
T.J. (International) Ltd., Cornwall, PL28 8RW

For Christina and Alberto
and Maria-Pia and Willi

# 1

Sometimes they call it Business Class; sometimes it's Executive. Not First. Nothing so grand as First, with its endless champagne and infinite space, but not Tourist either. I wouldn't have gone if it had been Tourist. I honestly wouldn't. I'd had enough of that when I flew to Hong Kong to deliver some diamonds back in '77, and I'd told myself at the time, never again. Not when somebody else is paying. If they want me they must buy me a Business Class ticket. Even if it's only as far as New York. It's the principle of the thing. I'm a business man after all.

What I do is I find things, and sometimes I deliver them as well – in what you might call an informal sort of way. No rough stuff. Nothing like that. If you look me up in the Yellow Pages you'll find me among the Private Detectives, but finding and delivery's what I really do. Servicing the client. A business man ... I've sought and delivered all sorts. Diamonds, like I said. An icon one time. Another time it was a shih tzu and nobody was more surprised than me when it turned out to be a dog. It's often a kid. The parents have split up and one of them snatches the kid and the other one comes and sees me. I hate that job. I've done it in England and Ireland and Canada and France and Italy and I hate it. But all the same I do it. I have to. It pays the bills.

But going to New York on the Jumbo and watching Streisand and Redford and drinking bourbon, that was different. I was enjoying myself. I'd found what I'd been sent to find and now I was delivering and I was happy – that's how big an idiot I was – because it wasn't kids.

What it was, it was a coin. An Athenian deodrachm of 470 B.C. Silver. Weight 42.78 grams, found in Corinth 1929. One not quite so good was sold at auction a couple of years back for $275,000. The most valuable coin in the world that wasn't American. Or number eight in the league if you include the ones that were... Obverse was a head of the goddess Athena, reverse an owl. I liked the owl. Clever, but not conceited about it. And just a little bit cocky. Those days I liked to think I was like that...

Finding it had been a problem – but then like I say, I'm good at finding things. It's what I'm for. That and delivering. Even when I was a kid – if my mother lost anything – like a brooch say or a ten-bob note – she'd just turn me loose and I'd find it. Every time. Same with the Athenian deodrachm of 470 B.C. Only that was a bit more complicated. Just a bit. It had been in the Corinth Museum until the war, when a bloke from the Gestapo nicked it, and all I had to do was find out which one. There had only been forty-three Gestapo blokes in the Corinth area at the time. And when I did find out which one, I put the job out to tender with what you might call a sub-contractor, and he nicked it from the Gestapo bloke, who by now had become very respectable and managed a factory and went to church on Sundays –

Lutheran he was – so he wasn't in much of a position to make a fuss, any more than I was if somebody nicked it off me. Like I say. Informal. Like the delivery. No use declaring the thing and having the Customs find out it belonged in a museum in Corinth. They might give it back and then I'd have the whole thing to do again. Better just to hand it over to Mr Black...

The touchdown was nice. No judder, no bounce. Sky became ground and we taxied into the terminal and that was that. I picked up my hand luggage – the plastic zip contraption that's supposed to hold soccer boots and actually holds duty-free booze – and waited to be herded off. Take it as it comes, that was my motto. No use in shoving, no use in trying to get to the head of the queue – if there was a queue – this was New York in July, and the hottest summer in years... Take it as it comes... Out along the covered walkway and into the terminal where the air-conditioning's shortcomings were already becoming apparent, so that my shirt was pasted to the small of my back. Out I went to pick up my baggage, one two-suiter, one suitcase, and on to the immigration and passports, and the surliest collection of manic-depressives you could meet in a day's march. And then on to the master-class, US Customs.

The geezer I got didn't like me. But that was OK. He didn't like anybody. He went through my two-suiter and my suitcase and my duty-free bag, and he didn't like *them*. Then he stepped back and looked at me. I wore a pair of tailored jeans, a cotton shirt by Turnbull and Asser, a gold ID bracelet and a gold chain, and he didn't like them, either. So he asked to see my passport. Don't ask me why. I doubt if even *he* knew why. It was just something to do that would increase the tension. I handed it over and he leafed through it, then went back to my personal details: age thirty-three, height five feet nine, eyes blue... All that. But what really got him was the space that said 'Occupation'.

'Demolition contractor, humh?' he said.

That's what it says, because over the years I've found it's a good thing to be. Demolition contractors make money, so they'll never be a charge on the countries they visit. Also they smash things, and all the world loves a wrecker. My friend from customs certainly did.

'Must be interesting work,' he said.

'Oh it is,' I told him.

'You really knock things down?' he said.

'I flatten them.'

He sighed. 'Man, that's some line of business.'

'It's what I'm paid for.'

'Hey,' he said. 'Hey, that's right. You get paid for doing it.'

He made me sound like a nymphomaniac prostitute, but I smiled anyway. 'Have a nice trip,' he said, and waved me into the maelstrom, which my dictionary says is 'any turbulent confusion.' Kennedy Airport was all of that, and not a porter in sight. Maybe now is the time to sample the delights of a helicopter ride into Manhattan, I thought. But I was wrong. Mr Black was waiting for me.

Mr Black was a go-between – he told me so himself – but he was the kind of go-between who

12

stays at the Grosvenor House. And not just any old room, either. Mr Black had a suite. He had the look of an Ivy League graduate who had done well as an athlete and was now going very slowly to seed, though there was still a lot of muscle left. He had the confidence of a man who lived very closely to a source of great power, and who enjoyed the experience. Which was fair enough. He handled the negotiations well. Better than I did. The job had paid OK, but not well enough to compensate for the possibility of an ageing *gauleiter's* revenge, or a Greek prison.

In England he'd worn a suit on each of the three occasions I'd met him, and at Kennedy Airport he wore a suit once more, though the air-conditioning was dodgy and the outside temperature was 92°. His was the only jacket I'd seen since the plane landed.

'Mr Hogget,' he said. 'It's good to see you.'

'Good to be here,' I said.

'I hope our little venture was successful?'

Over a quarter of a million dollars' worth, and he called it little.

'Of course,' I said, and if I sounded surprised who can blame me? Nobody in their right minds would fly the Atlantic to report failure to Mr Black. 'Great,' he said, and only then did he reach out his hands and take my cases, lead me to where a second man stood waiting.

'This is my associate, Mr White,' said Mr Black.

Mr White also wore a suit. He too had the air of an educated athlete going cautiously to seed, the confidence of a man who lived close to great power. The only observable difference was that Mr

White was a negro. He looked to Mr Black.

'He's got it,' said Black.

The negro let out his breath with a sigh.

'It's good to see you, Mr Hogget,' he said. 'Right this way. The transportation's all fixed.'

More maelstrom, and sticky, humid heat, but the transportation was indeed all ready and waiting, a Rolls Royce Corniche with a chauffeur in a shirt of dazzling white, a neatly knotted black tie... Black and White bothered me. Or rather their coats did. The Roller's air-conditioning was much more efficient than the airport's, but the coats bothered me even so. And then the penny dropped. Mr Black and Mr White had to wear coats because somewhere on their person they carried guns – and that bothered me even more.

Mr White sat beside the driver, Mr Black kept me company in the back. Neither of them seemed in the mood for conversation since I'd told them the only thing that they wanted to know; that I'd got the deodrachm. All the same I wanted to talk. I always do: silence makes me nervous.

'Where did you book me in?' I asked.

'The Plaza,' said Black, but that was OK. Black's boss was picking up the tab. Somewhere near the Holland Tunnel, White cleared his throat.

'You better tell him,' he said.

'OK.' Black turned to face me. 'Before we go to the hotel we want you to meet our principal.'

'Hey,' I said. 'That's great.'

'I think you'll find it so,' said Black.

'Who is he?'

'Martin Donner.'

And that was the source of power that warmed

14

Mr Black and Mr White. Martin Donner. A bit like the Athenian coin I'd had nicked for him. I mean, just like the deodrachm was the most expensive coin that wasn't American, so Mr Donner was on his way to being one of the richest men in the world who wasn't an Arab – or so I would soon be told... And he collected coins. A bit of a laugh when you think about it. I mean if he could've converted his holdings into silver dollars he'd have over sixty million of them. Yet he still collected coins... And there was T. R. Hogget going to meet him. Little Ronny Hogget whose dad used to keep the grocer's shop, on his way to meet Martin Donner, widower and multi-millionaire.

It was a 1940s castle in the Upper Eighties, on the corner of Fifth Avenue. Narrow entrance with a guard room attached, more guards in the court-yard and lobby. When I got out of the Rolls they gave me the hard eye, but only until Mr Black and Mr White got out. After that, it seemed, I was no longer the guards' problem: just Mr Black's and Mr White's.

Donner owned the penthouse – for all I knew he owned the whole building – and it was full of sur-prises. Black let us in with a key, and as I stepped through the front door a bell clattered. The front door was wired up for electronic screening.

'Just a notion of Mr Donner's,' said Black. 'He's seen so much unpleasantness in his life. You must be carrying metal.'

'Well of course I am,' I said. 'Nail-file, pen-knife, money-clip. I always carry metal.'

'Just the same,' said Black. 'If you wouldn't

mind my colleague searching you? Just to be sure? Mr Donner really would prefer it.' Which meant it had to be.

'Unless you have any objections to being searched by someone in my ethnic category?' said Mr White.

'Not at all,' I said. 'Humiliation comes in all colours.'

It was humiliating all right, but at least it established one thing. Mr Donner had nothing to fear from me except assault with a Swiss Army knife, or maybe a nail-file.

We were taken into the presence, to a room only slightly larger than the ground floor of my house in fashionable Fulham. Donner was seated in an armchair, reading a book. He wore a suit of Donegal tweed and a log fire burned enthusiastically. And just as well. The air-conditioning had been turned up to the point where I shivered as I crossed the door.

'Mr Hogget,' Donner said. 'Come in, come in. You don't mind a little cool air, do you? I mean who needs sunshine? Come on up to the fire.'

I'm so rich, he was telling me, that I can even make my own weather. I went up to the fire. Black and White, I noticed, hadn't been invited, so they stayed where they were...

'You brought me the deodrachm?' he asked.

'I did.'

'May I see it please?'

My hand moved, and his whole expression changed. He was a slim, elegant man, perhaps forty, certainly no more, with the look of an actor who specialized in snide remarks, but when my

16

hand moved to produce wealth he became different. And frightening. He looked like a bird of prey.

I took the gold chain from round my neck, opened it, slid off the gold ornament that was suspended from it, and opened it too. Inside was the deodrachm. I gave it to Martin Donner and he held it in his cupped hands. His eyes were loving.

'Oh boy,' he said. 'Oh boy.' He looked up at me then, and saw that I was shivering. 'Get him a coat,' he said, and Black went out at once.

'I have a hundred and eighteen coins,' Donner said. 'This is the most valuable of them all.' His hand closed round it, then he put it down, handed me a cheque and at once picked it up again. 'You did well. I guess you know that. Four weeks to track down a coin as rare as this.'

Actually it was three, but who am I to argue with so much money?

'You're all right, Hogget,' he went on. 'I really mean that.'

Then Black came bustling in with a coat. It was cashmere, and I still wear it.

'Finding things,' said Donner. 'It's a knack. Some of us have got it, and some haven't. You've certainly got it... You want to have a crack at finding something else for me?'

'If I can,' I said.

'Sure you can. You could find one twig in a forest.' He opened his hand, looked at the deodrachm again.

'My wife was kidnapped and then murdered,' he said. 'I guess you know that.'

'I read about it,' I said.

'Sure.' The fact didn't surprise him. Half the

17

world had read about it. 'I want you to find the one who killed her,' he said.

That should have been my big scene, I suppose. Me the sworn enemy of organized crime, the avenger of the weak and the downtrodden – and if you've been murdered then you're both, no matter who your husband is – but instead, it developed into what my friend Dave described as an unseemly haggle about money. You see, I'm not a violent man. Never have been. When there's violence I sub-contract to Dave, because he's good at it. But this looked like being violence all the way. I mean this was a kidnapping and a murder. And it had been done in a place called Riva del Garda in Italy for God's sake. And that meant it was either professional criminals – Mafia as likely as not – or it was terrorists. And either way it was guns. And blokes being shot at. Or more precisely me being shot at. I didn't fancy it. Not a bit. And I said so. And then he offered me fifty grand – dollars, not pounds, and I turned him down without even pausing for thought as they say.

'She was my wife,' said Donner. 'She was young – and beautiful – and she died alone. Stabbed with a knife. Just like that. Then they cut her head off. Don't you think I'm entitled to find the bastards who killed her?'

'Well of course you are,' I said. 'And I wish you luck. But it won't be done by me.'

'I wouldn't want you to deliver,' he said. 'Not those guys. All I want you to do is find them. I'll take care of delivery. What do you say?' I said nothing.

'Seventy thousand dollars,' he said.

18

'Mr Donner,' I said. 'I just don't want to do it.'

'I need you,' he said.

'There's plenty of blokes do my job,' I said.

'Not like you,' he said. 'You're the best... And anyway you speak Italian.'

'Who told you that?' I asked.

He didn't look at Black, or White. He didn't have to. One of them had checked me out. Most probably Black. All he'd have to do was pick up a 'phone in the Grosvenor House...

'You speak Italian because your mother was Italian,' said Donner. 'You even know the place where my wife was last seen. Over by Lake Como. It's near Verona – where your mother's relatives live. You're the one, Mr Hogget. I know you are. I know you can find these guys – and I want them found.'

There was an urgency, a sense of passion in those last words that I hadn't heard in him before. I still said nothing.

'All right,' he said at last. 'You tell me how much.'

'It isn't the money,' I said.

'Of course it's the money,' said Donner. 'You're scared – that's your business. And anyway I like it. It shows me you're not a fool. But there's always something can make a man brave. With you I think it's money. So tell me how much.'

He didn't mean to be insulting, I'm quite sure he didn't. All he wanted was me – and a chance to make me deductible against his income-tax. So I mouthed numbers at him just to shut him up; to enable me to get away from an applewood fire (where had he got applewood logs in New

19

York in July for God's sake?) – and back in the maelstrom where I belonged.

'I want fifty thousand dollars now,' I said, 'whether I find them or not. And another fifty thousand the day I find them. Also I want all expenses paid.'

'It's a deal,' he said.

That floored me. It really did. He was the sort of geezer who would debate the price of a cab-fare – or hire someone else to do it, like Black. And here he was handing over fifty – maybe a hundred thousand dollars, just like that. He must really want the ones who took away his wife, I thought. I was right.

'You know it's interesting,' he said. The ransom they asked for Mrs Donner was a million. And here you are – asking ten per cent. Interesting. That's the legitimate finder's fee.'

'You didn't pay me ten per cent on the deo-drachm.'

'That wasn't legitimate,' Donner said, and smiled. Black and White laughed out loud.

'And anyway,' I said, 'you didn't say you wanted me to find the money – you said you wanted the kidnappers.'

'What I'd really like is both,' said Donner. 'But the kidnappers I've got to have.'

The heat of the fire was getting to me, and I'd had a long day, and my stomach thought it was breakfast time and I'd soon be eating dinner. And I was bushed. 'Can we meet tomorrow?' I said, 'I've got a lot of questions I have to ask.'

'Ask them now,' said Donner.

'I'm whacked,' I said. 'Jet lag I suppose. Tomorrow would be better.'

'Tomorrow I fly to Perth, Australia. Today is all there is.' He turned to Black. 'Tell them to fix some sandwiches and stuff,' he said, then to White. 'Phone the Plaza. Tell them Mr Hogget may be a little late. Then wait outside.'

They went like lambs, and I proceeded to start earning fifty – maybe a hundred thousand dollars. It was exhausting, but it was the only way I knew how to make fifty – maybe a hundred – grand.

Three hours later I'd eaten four tuna fish sandwiches, and drunk a third of a bottle of cheapish bourbon and two cups of instant coffee. Donner explained to me that he wasn't interested in either food or drink and therefore didn't see the sense in wasting money on either, but even so he let me pour my own drinks. Whisky was the only thing that would keep me going, and he knew it. So I asked the questions and wrote down the answers and three hours later I'd got all there was – or if I hadn't I was too whacked to find out. I said so.

'Yeah,' said Donner. 'You go on to the hotel. You've got it all.' The way he said it I'd just won the Academy Award for nosiness. Somehow I managed to get to my feet without falling over.

'I'll be running along then,' I said.

'Sure,' he said. 'Pip pip, cheerioh, toodleoo, and all that sort of rot.'

I gathered that he was not enamoured of English speech-patterns. He picked up a brown envelope and shoved it at me.

'You'll need to talk to people,' he said. 'Not just here. London. Paris. All over the place. I've written you letters of authorization. They're in there. And a few facts and clippings. Some photographs too. There's more at the old apartment.'

'Thanks,' I said. 'There's also the matter of a cheque, Mr Donner.'

'That's right,' said Donner, and wrote it then and there. Fifty thousand dollars.

'Thanks,' I said again, meaning it this time. 'Just one thing more. If you're off to the land of Oz – who do I report to? Mr Black? Mr White?'

'Oz?' he said, then: 'Oh I get it. Australia, right? No, Mr Hogget, Mr Black and Mr White are going with me. You talk to Cass.'

He spoke as if I should know exactly who Cass was, and bushed or not, I didn't ask for further enlightenment. I wasn't that bushed. Anyway it would be in my notes, and even if it wasn't I would find this Cass for myself.

'This Black and White lark,' I said. 'Is it some sort of joke?'

'I don't make jokes,' said Donner, and I believed him. 'I call them Black and White because they're names which remind them who they are.'

'Oh ah,' I said, and wondered what the name Hogget was supposed to remind me of. A hogget isn't a pig by the way. It's a grown lamb that hasn't been sheared, but probably soon will be. I should have remembered that.

And then the geezer who served the sandwiches came in. He wore a white jacket and looked like Mohammed Ali's successor. Silicon Valley was on the line, he said. Silicon Valley, California, is where the silicon chips are made. It is also where Donner made his last forty or fifty million. Donner was up and out in the time it takes to say goodbye, then the butler took me out to the lift, and a guard took me out to the Roller, and the chauffeur took me into the Plaza. The weather had broken, I remember. It was raining. Just as well I wore a cashmere jacket.

# 2

The next day, when I caught up with it, was bright and hot and cheerful. I sent the cashmere jacket to be cleaned, and ordered breakfast because whatever time it was, my day was just beginning, and then a bottle of Californian Riesling, because for some reason I didn't feel like bourbon. So first I ate, then I drank, and as I drank I thought of Mrs Donner, and what I had let myself in for... First the photographs. Elizabeth Jane Donner, known always to her friends as Jane. Tall... Tallish anyway. Five foot six. With any kind of heels she'd look me straight in the eye. A beauty. Or maybe that was too easy. Certainly the body was beautiful – there was a picture of her in a bikini to prove it – but the face: maybe beautiful wasn't the word. Nice hair. A rich deep brown with auburn highlights – natural or man-made, who cared? That was beautiful. And the eyes, the colour of amontillado sherry, they were beautiful too – but the nose was too snub, the mouth too wide, the chin too firm. And yet – with a dozen women in a room she was the one you'd look at. Every time. Maybe what she had wasn't beauty, but it was a hell of a nice thing to have, even so.

She'd been born Elizabeth Jane Gregory, daughter of Dr and Mrs Martin Gregory. Private school and Bryn Mawr. Bachelor's degree in English literature, followed by a master's. Journalism, the refined, egg-headed kind, and then marriage. No kids. I found that sad. She should have had kids, looking like that. Homes in New York and Paris and London. A great one for travelling, though usually not in the same direction as her husband. He flew towards money. For her the tug was culture. And yet in a way that worked out to be money too. She'd financed four little magazines and three of them had died in infancy. But the fourth had made money from the beginning. It still does make money... Same in the theatre. She'd backed plays in London, Paris, New York. Seven disasters in a row, then a runaway success that had paid off the disasters and still run into profit. And she'd enjoyed it all. The triumphs, of course, but even the failures had given her something. You could tell by her smile. When I told myself that, I realized that it must be love at first sight and I must pull myself together... The lady was dead.

Donner had seen the body – or what was left of it. So had Mr White. Up in the mountains north of Bolzano, just off the Merano road. Where the people all speak German and are cheerful, hard-working, religious – and somebody had knifed the almost-beautiful Mrs Donner, then cut her head off and hidden it in a place unknown and left her to the crows... She was dead all right, Mr Donner said, and it displeased him. She must

24

have been such a wonderful thing for him to possess, I thought. Maybe even better than an Athenian deodrachm. And then he'd paid a million for her, and the killers had reneged on the deal. Mr White had carried the cash to Italy, and done precisely as the kidnappers had said he should. Money in a suitcase. Rent a Fiat hire car and abandon it on a road in Verona with the money inside, then go back to your hotel and wait for a phone call. And it came. That was the weird thing. The terrible thing. The caller told Mr White exactly where to go, and he went. And found Jane Donner dead.

*If Mr White was telling the truth.* If not, he was worth a million, and still working for Mr Donner, because he was too smart to grab the money and run and have Mr Donner hire a bloke like me to find him, and a platoon of blokes like Mr Black to deliver him. Mr Donner hadn't mentioned any of this because it was too bloody obvious. Also it was up to me to check it out in case Mr White turned out to be one of the killers. Not a job I relished when I recollected what size he was. But fifty grand was fifty grand – and a hundred was a hundred.

Thought of all that money actually made me think of the wife. My wife, I mean. Not that Melanie's greedy. She just likes getting nice things. The only snag is she tends to like getting them at pretty frequent intervals... I thought I'd give her a bell and let her know I was still earning. I never do as a general rule. It costs too much. But this time Mr Donner was paying ... so I dialled the code and then the number and while it tocked and clicked I looked at the picture of Jane Donner again, the big studio portrait, head a little to one side – smile just beginning. Far and away out of my league, I told myself. But a lovely lady... And then the ringing tone, and then the sound of the receiver lifting.

'Hello?' I said. 'Melanie?'

There was a pause, and all I could hear was the space between us.

'Melanie?' I said.

'Ronny,' she said. 'Is that you?'

Clear as clear, and all done by satellites.

'Of course it's me,' I said. 'Who were you expecting?'

'But you never phone,' she said.

I could have done with a little more enthusiasm.

'The client's paying,' I said. 'He's happy because we're doing a very good deal – but of course if you're not interested—'

'Oh Ronny, you know I am,' she said.

So I told her a bit. Not much. No names, and nothing about what the deal was, especially not the deodrachm. She likes things legal, does Melanie. But she likes things nice as well. She likes me to make money... In the middle of telling her how clever I was, what a good deal I'd made, I thought I heard a match striking. 'Melanie,' I said. 'You're not smoking again?'

'Of course I'm not,' she said. 'Didn't I promise you?'

'I thought I heard a match,' I said.

'Not even you could hear a match across three thousand miles,' she said. 'But I'm not smoking. *Honestly* I'm not.'

When she says 'Honestly' she never lies. So I told

her I loved her and I'd bring her back something nice from Bergdorf Goodman's or maybe even Saks. Then I hung up and went back to Jane Donner...

Martin Donner had moved into his present fortress after Jane's disappearance and death. The one before that hadn't been nearly so secure, it seemed, and the thought made him nervous. But he still owned the old place, and it was where I'd have to start. It was empty, and all his wife's things were there... Just a matter of visiting the place, for which I had neither a key nor right of entrance... Which reminded me who Cass was. She was right there in my notes. Underlined. 'Cassandra Milligan'. Used to be Jane D's secretary. And a telephone number. I dialled it.

'Mrs Donner's office,' a female voice said.

'I'd like to speak to Miss Cassandra Milligan,' I said. 'This is T.R. Hogget.'

'I'm Ms Milligan,' said the voice. It was cool to the point of chilly. No joy to her to learn that T.R. Hogget had entered her life.

'Mr Donner told me to call you if I needed anything,' I said.

'I have Mr Dormer's briefing.'

'I need to look over the Park Avenue apartment,' I said.

There was a pause. 'Why do you want to do that, Mr Hogget?' she asked.

I used a phrase I'd always wanted to use.

'In pursuit of my enquiries,' I said. 'Have you got a key?'

'I'll bring it over right away,' she said. 'And Mr Hogget?'

27

'Yes?'

'Mr Donner phoned me before he left. He'd like you to return his jacket. To me.'

'Just as soon as I get it back from the cleaners,' I said. 'I'm afraid I spilled some tuna fish on it.'

'I'll be with you in half an hour,' she said, and hung up. She sounded disappointed. Maybe it was because of the jacket, I thought. Maybe she'd been looking forward to dragging it off my back.

She wasn't a bad looking bird. Nothing like Jane. Nothing like Melanie even. But not bad. Not at all bad. Redheaded Irish with a few freckles, though not enough to cause her dismay – and a very nice bone structure. But she didn't like me, and that was that. She didn't like me in the Plaza and she didn't like me in the Mercedes coupé she used to drive me to the apartment, and in the apartment she liked me least of all and it bothered me. I'm not *that* bad. Honestly.

We went inside and the accumulated heat there hit us like a blow from a hot towel, and she buzzed from room to room switching on air-conditioning, and I took my time and looked around. There seemed to be five reception rooms and six bedrooms, all en suite, and a lot of them overlooked the Park. Nice apartment. Nice view. I went to the master bedroom which was mostly an enormous water bed. Off to one side was Martin Donner's bathroom and dressing room. Everything in it was locked. The other side belonged to Jane. Bathroom and shower in a colour that was more glowing rose than pink, and beyond it *her* dressing room. Fitted cupboards, fitted wardrobe,

28

a vast yet elegant mirror and enough light for a chorus line. And a desk, and bookshelves, and a filing cabinet. And all of them crammed full, and none of them locked. A snoop's idea of bliss, and then Cassandra Milligan came in. I had just opened the top left hand drawer of the desk.

'What the hell do you think you're doing?' she said.

'What Mr Donner's paying me to do,' I said. 'Snooping.'

The top left hand drawer contained reviews of plays. San Francisco, Los Angeles, New York, London and provincial England. Plays she'd considered putting money into, I thought, and tried the next drawer down. She'd hardly have been murdered by an indignant playwright. The next drawer was stuffed with letters, and I put them on the desk, using an ebony ruler as a paperweight, and began to read. The first was from a poet whose work she'd printed. He didn't like her typography.

'You mustn't do that,' Cassandra Milligan said.

'I have to,' I said.

'Surely you don't have to pry like that,' she said. 'Just tell me what you want and I'll get it for you.'

I opened another letter. A wholesaler assured Jane that the price of quality paper had never been higher.

'I'm sorry,' I said, 'but I do have to pry. I don't know what I'm looking for.'

'You're going to go through all her things?'

'That's right.'

'No matter how private – how intimate?'

'She's dead, Ms Milligan,' I said. 'The dead

neither know nor care about privacy.' I opened another letter. A writer even I had heard of had sent Jane an outline for a short story. In a PS he outlined his ideas on how they could spend a weekend together.

'I think you're disgusting,' Cassandra Milligan said.

'I make a living.'

'It's *how* you make it that disgusts me.'

I sat back and looked at her.

'Ms Milligan,' I said. 'Did you like Mrs Donner?'

'Very much,' she said, and I didn't doubt her.

'She was kidnapped ... murdered... Don't you want whoever did it to be punished?'

'Well of course I do.' Somehow that didn't carry nearly so much conviction.

'Whoever did it has to be found. It's my job to find them – and snooping's the only way I know. Do you think Mrs Donner would object?'

'Don't call her that.'

'It's her name,' I said.

'No,' she said. 'Mrs Donner's the name of a chattel. Donner's woman. Jane wasn't that. She was herself... Jane.'

'All right,' I said. 'Would Jane have objected?'

'She wasn't – soft,' said Ms Milligan. 'She wasn't always looking for a big strong man to protect her. If she was attacked she'd defend herself. She believed in justice.'

'That's all I want for her.'

'But she wouldn't want to hurt people unless they hurt her.'

'The ones who hurt her are all I'm after,' I said.

'She was a busy woman, an important woman,' Ms Milligan said. 'She produced plays, published magazines. People told her things. Private things.' I waited, but that was all I got.

'I don't tout for gossip columnists,' I said, and went back to my reading.

'You mean you won't talk if you come across any scandal?'

'Well of course I won't.'

'I don't believe you,' she said, and slammed out of the room.

It was peaceful without her: tranquil: the air-conditioning's hum like a swarm of distant bees. I left the desk and went over to the fitted wardrobe, pulled it open. Dresses. More dresses than I'd ever seen together at one time outside a dress-shop. And pants. Suits. Coats. If Melanie had opened that cupboard she'd have thought she'd died and gone to heaven. Another cupboard was shoes. Rack on rack. Everything from Gucci to espadrilles. Then stockings and tights. Slips, panties, bras. A lot of them the same glowing rose colour as her bathroom. She must have been fond of that colour...

I went back to the letters. Like her clothes they were neatly stacked, almost fussily so. She had preferred her life to be orderly. Her death had not been like that... Every letter had a comment scribbled on it. Even the writer's propositioning PS had earned the words. 'Told him No'. But she had bought the story. A remarkable woman. It's an overworked word, but Jane really had been remarkable. To begin with she'd been accessible to an awful lot of people. I don't mean sexually – she chose her lovers with care – you could almost say with love – and there had been only two that I could discover... What I mean is accessible to people who needed her: for favours, for money, for just the strength they sensed she had and they had not. From what I could see, if they were genuine, she never turned them down...

I tried another drawer. This one was full of photographs, packed in so tight I had to use two hands to get the drawer open. No suggestion of order there: not this time. And there were all kinds. Instamatic, Polaroid, snapshots, glossies, newspaper clippings. All shapes and sizes. You could say they were divided into work and play: work being mostly the theatre, and promotional stuff for the magazines. Play was just that – swimming, tennis, boating, discos, parties. She'd been all over the place – Rome, Paris, Palm Springs, Venice, London – and always in the best hotels, always with the best people. And why not? She was married to sixty million dollars. And yet it wasn't just that ... I was sure it wasn't. There was something in the way people looked at her. They didn't look like that when they were with other people.

That isn't the way, I told myself sternly. You're getting involved again and you mustn't. I began to sort out the photographs into piles: work and play. Then I subdivided the piles: theatre and publishing; the USA and elsewhere. Then I subdivided the subdivisions: stage sets, action shots, promotions. Indoors, outdoors, sports, relaxation, clubs. The little piles multiplied, and in the end the desk was covered with them. And they didn't tell me a damn thing – except that her life had been very busy and that she had friends, a lot of friends. There were men and women – Cassandra not least. And mostly they were smiling and mostly they were glad to be with her – and that isn't me getting involved. That is a fact.

I abandoned the photographs and tried the filing cabinet. Accounts and contracts, letters from writers, letters from agents. All orderly, all methodical, all neat. If I'd been an accountant I could have worked out how much money she'd made – and lost – since she started. But murderers and kidnappers don't sign contracts ... I went back to the desk. Another drawer. More letters. But these were love-letters. I didn't fancy that much, but they had to be read. Then Cassandra Milligan came back in. She didn't fancy it much either.

'How much longer are you going to be snooping?' she said.

I shrugged. 'As long as it takes. Look – don't let me keep you – I mean if you want to go I'll let myself out.'

'Oh no,' she said.

I got mad. 'What the hell do you mean, oh no?' I said. 'I'm not going to steal anything.'

She considered the statement on its merits, and conceded, reluctantly, that I might be telling the truth.

'It isn't that,' she said.

'What then?'

'Mr Donner's made a rule. Nobody's to be here unless I'm present.'

'That's a weird sort of rule... Why?'

'Mr Donner didn't say. Mr Donner rarely does say.'

I gathered she wasn't too crazy about Mr Donner, either.

'You work for him, now?'

'I work for Jane's estate,' she said. 'But a lot of
that went to Mr Donner.'

So what Martin Donner said, went.

'What you're telling me is that you're keeping
an eye on me on Mr Donner's behalf?'

'That's right.'

'OK.' I said. 'I'm a snooper. Tell him I snooped.'

'Be a pleasure,' she said, and looked at her
watch. 'It's late.'

'I'm not a clock-watcher,' I said. 'Tell Mr Donner that, too. Do you have a date?' She nodded.

'Then we'll have to come back tomorrow.'

'I figured we might.'

'Before we go,' I said, 'let me ask you a few
things.'

'If you're quick.' It was a little better than no.

'Why doesn't Donner sell this place?'

She shrugged. 'Do you honestly think he'd tell
me?'

'No,' I said. 'But I think you might know.'

'He's waiting till he gets his price.'

'I believe you,' I said. 'Tell me who these people
are.'

I pointed out the people who occurred most
often in the piles of photographs I'd made, and
she named them all. I put them back, neatly, into
the drawer.

'Why was this drawer in such a mess? All the
others were so tidy.'

'Somebody must have been through it,' she said.

'Who?'

'Mr Hogget – I only work here,' she said. And that was a good enough answer.

We went down to the lobby, and she looked at her watch again.

'That's OK,' I said. 'I'll get a cab.'

'If you're sure you wouldn't mind.'

'I don't mind.'

She asked the duty porter to get me one, and we walked to the Mercedes coupé. It had been Jane's – down on the books as a company car.

'I'd like to start work again tomorrow – say nine o'clock,' I said.

'I can work just as well from here as the office,' she said. 'I'll pick you up at 8.45.' Then the doorman came to tell me my cab was waiting.

The driver was young, apparently friendly, and not unlike the photograph on his dashboard.

'Where to?' he said.

'You're not going to believe this,' I said.

'Do I get paid?'

'Sure.'

'Then I believe you. Where to?'

'There's a redhead in a Merc coupé going to appear in a minute,' I said. 'I want you to follow her.'

'I'd follow a redhead in a Merc any time,' he said. Then 'Who are you, mister? Sherlock Holmes?'

'I'm her husband,' I said.

The driver looked disappointed.

'I guess that says it all,' he said. 'You get the same problem in Britain, humh?'

'We do indeed,' I said, and we followed Ms Milligan to the Algonquin hotel on 44th Street, and

I paid off the driver and waited till Ms Milligan parked and followed her into the Algonquin cocktail bar, which is old and leathery and lived in and a very nice place to be, but not for me, because Ms Milligan had met her date. They didn't see me because I'm good at that sort of thing, besides being trained for it. But I saw them. And I knew who her date was. Twenty minutes ago I'd been putting a selection of his photographs away in Jane's desk.

Back in the Plaza I switched on the TV and thought about it – in New York I found that to have the television running was much less distracting than silence... The man's name, so Ms Milligan had said, was Sokolny – Frank Sokolny. From where I'd stood I'd seen a tall, slender, but by no means skinny geezer with dark, curly, close-cropped hair, a neat moustache, grey eyes set a little aslant, like a cat's. A set-designer, Ms Milligan had said, and a hot one. In demand all over New York. And a geezer who craved affection, from what I remembered of the photographs. In almost all of them he'd had his arm round somebody. Quite often it was Jane, a couple of times it was Ms Milligan, a lot of the time it was fellers. I thought I didn't like him, and asked myself why? Because I didn't like poofters? But that was stupid. Some I like and some I don't... And anyway neither Jane nor Ms Milligan was leaning into him like he was a poofter. Maybe I just don't like geezers who can't make up their minds... I dialled room service and ordered some fish called snapper and washed it down with what was left of the Riesling, took in the late show for dessert, then slept. I thought I'd had a hard day. Little did I know, as they say.

Ms Milligan picked me up on time in the Merc. It was a nice day in the high 70s, low humidity, but she didn't look as if she was enjoying it much. When we got to the apartment she asked if I wanted coffee and I said fine, cream, no sugar, and she went to the kitchen and I went to the office, and opened the desk and looked at the love letters. When she brought in the coffee I was ready for her. The coffee was in a silver pot, the cream in a silver jug. I told her how clever she'd been to send out for cream, and she said she never drank coffee without it and I told her to fetch another cup and she did. I was being matey, you see. Appreciative of favours given. So I asked her for another. She looked wary, but nothing like as bad as the day before.

'If I can,' she said.

'I'll live if you can't,' I said. 'Just a loose end.'

That surprised her. Annoyed her too. She didn't like the fact that she mightn't be important. Not where Jane was concerned. 'In the last year you had four shows you invested in,' I said.

'Jane had.'

'I've no doubt you advised her.'

That she liked. First the stick, then the carrot.

'There were two in New York, one in Paris, and one in London. The ones in Paris and London were disasters. In New York one lost a bit, the other made a fortune.'

'I know all that.'

'Of course you do,' I said. 'Do you also know why you and Jane spent all your time in London after the London show folded?'

'We had other properties to talk about,' she said.

'While back in New York you had two other shows that needed nursing ... maybe one even died for lack of it.'

'That's what I told Jane,' said Ms Milligan, and this time I believed her. 'But it was Jane's money and Jane's decision.'

Frank Sokolny had designed the set for the London flop, then like Jane he'd stayed on – according to her letters. Maybe he was looking for another property too.

'It was nice of you to pick me up this morning,' I said.

'All part of the service.'

'You didn't come in here earlier by any chance?'

'Does anyone say I did?'

Never let them ask the questions. That way an inquisition can degenerate into a debate.

'Ms Milligan,' I said. 'Last night I opened this drawer.' I tapped the one with the love-letters.

'I know you did.'

'It was obvious to me that the letters in it were personal. Extremely personal.' She said nothing. 'And yet the drawer was unlocked.'

'Mr Donner sent Mr Black over,' she said. 'I didn't realize he'd unlocked *every* drawer.'

'Or you'd have locked it again?' No answer.

'Ms Milligan,' I said. 'Last night I made a note of the letters in this drawer and the people who wrote them. Today I find there's one missing.' Still no answer. 'Would you care to comment?'

'What could I possibly say?'

'That you took it,' I said.

'Now wait a minute,' she said.

'I'm afraid I can't. What I can do is call a number for Mr Donner in Perth, Australia, and ask him for further instructions. Who do you suppose he'll blame, Ms Milligan? Who else is there?' I swallowed coffee. It was good coffee. 'The letter was written by a Mr Frank Sokolny. He was staying in the Carlton Towers in London. Jane was in Paris – at the Bristol would it be?'

'The Georges V,' said Ms Milligan. 'The apartment was being decorated so we stayed at the Georges V.'

I tried to look like a man who had become inspired.

'Your date last night,' I said. 'Was it with Frank Sokolny?'

'Of course not,' she said.

'So you deny any knowledge of the letter?'

'I didn't say that,' she said.

'What do you say, Ms Milligan?'

She sipped at her coffee. Like me, she didn't smoke, and coffee-sipping was the best pause she could manage.

'This is a terrible business,' she said. 'Oh I know that sounds banal and all that. But it really is terrible.' More coffee sipping. 'Jane and I were at college together. Did you know that?'

I shook my head. It's a terrible, banal business to tell investigators facts that may come in useful.

'I was very attached to Jane. I don't mean in a dykey way – nothing like that. I just liked her. Very much.'

'A lot of people did.'

'She was a good person. A *really* good person. But she was like everybody else. There were areas that weren't so good.'

'Frank Sokolny? She was cheating on Donner with him?'

'Donner?... He wouldn't have cared. Not unless it stopped him making money. But it was bad for *her*. She and Frank – together – it was bad. But it only concerned the two of them. And now she's dead.'

'So you took the letter to protect her good name? Give it back please.'

'I destroyed it,' she said.

'No,' I said. 'No you didn't. You're far too insecure to destroy something so important.'

'Insecure?'

'Well of course you are,' I said. 'Look at the way you feel about Donner – yet you go on working for him... Do I really have to phone him in Perth, Australia, Ms Milligan?'

She opened her handbag then, took out the letter, skimmed it to me over the desk. 'You're a lot nastier than you look,' she said.

Somewhere in that there might be the remains of a compliment, but that was not the time to work it out.

'Are you going to tell Donner?' she asked.

'No.'

'Why not?'

'Because what I'm after is facts, not blood feuds among the hired help. Thank you for the coffee, Ms Milligan.'

She left then and slammed the door – it was getting to be a custom between us – and I read

Frank Sokolny's letter. He loved Jane madly – he said so many times. What he loved about her was more than just the beauty of the body – though she had that abundantly and he adored that too – it was the beauty of the spirit, eternal and enduring that will remain forever virgin whatever the beauty of the body's demands...

There was a lot of that sort of stuff, the kind that's so easy to make fun of if you're not one of the parties involved. Then the letter changed. He would never cease to be grateful to her for helping him out of the terrible jam he'd got himself into... That meant money by the look of it. Then there was a bit about how sorry he was that Mickey had turned up like that, and made that awful scene. Mickey was a dear boy really. He just couldn't help it. It was all just insecurity. Of course he was finished with Mickey now, that went without saying – but he couldn't just abandon him, now could he? Not in the state he was in. And so on. And on. I read it all through again and when I'd finished I knew one thing for certain. When he told her he loved her he meant it. He meant every bloody word – which was more than he did when he said he'd finished with Mickey.

I got out the photographs again, found the ones of Frank Sokolny. There were twenty-nine of them, some just of him, some with other people, some of him and Jane together. One solo shot had been trimmed with a pair of scissors. A man's hand, disembodied, rested on Sokolny's shoulder. I wondered if the hand belonged to Mickey...

What I needed was gossip. It seemed to me that the place for that was the theatre, and *Honeyfall*, the play that Jane had financed, was still running, even if it was in its last week. No gossip till after the curtain – but I was in a hurry. So that meant lunch. The question was who? I looked at the photographs again, and so far as I was concerned there was only one choice, and that was Lenora Buell. According to the file Jane had on her she'd made two or three TV movies in Hollywood but her spiritual home was the theatre, preferably Broadway or just off it. The critics liked her, audiences loved her. The only fault she had according to Jane was three words scribbled on the bottom of her curriculum vitae: 'Talks too much'. But not for me. She couldn't talk too much for me. Also she was beautiful. Black but comely as the Bible puts it. It's the Song of Solomon. He could have had her in mind... I dialled the number on her CV, and she answered at the seventh ring.

'Miss Buell?' I said.

'Who is this?'

'My name's T.R. Hogget,' I said. 'You don't know me.'

'Jesus,' she said. 'Do you know what time it is?'

'It's 10.43,' I said.

'In the *morning*? Do you know what time I got to bed last night?'

'How could I, Miss Buell?'

'Three o'clock, that's when,' she said. 'In the morning. This morning.'

'I'm terribly sorry,' I said.

'Hey,' she said. 'You're British.'

'That's right,' I said. 'I work for the Syndicated Press Corporation of London, England. There's a chance that we might do a profile on you some day. Is it possible for me to buy you lunch today and talk about it?'

'Why sure,' she said at once.

'Where would you like to go?'

'The Four Seasons,' she said. 'Twelve thirty. I better tell you what I look like.'

'Miss Buell,' I said, 'I know exactly what you look like.'

'You're cute,' she said and hung up. Despite the air-conditioning I found that I was mopping my brow. I phoned the Four Seasons to make a reservation, then went back to the love letters.

Sokolny had written to Jane almost compulsively from London, from Boston and Chicago and Philadelphia and all over middle-America when *Honeyfall* toured. Even from New York when they were both there. The letters had been addressed to her office on 47th Street, but even so Donner could have known, I thought. Certainly he knew now. And yet he'd left his wife's letters from her lover for me to read, as if they were no more important than the shoes in the cupboard... No. Not lover. Lovers. Plural. Not in the sense that there was love returned. The way the letters read she'd turned them all down... Except for one other – and he was in England.

I looked at my watch. Time to take lunch with Miss Buell, so I tracked Ms Milligan down to a room that was part library and part office. She was doing accounts with a dedicated efficiency that was frightening to watch.

'I'm going to lunch,' I said.

'I could send out for something if you like.'

'No thanks,' I said. 'I'll be back around two-thirty.'

'That's a long lunch hour,' she said, and then, 'I'm sorry. It's none of my business.' But it might be, I thought, and maybe she knew it might be. The master telephone was right by her elbow. All the others were just extensions, including mine.


# 3


The Four Seasons is a great place to eat when somebody else is paying, so Lenora Buell and I could really enjoy ourselves, thanks to Mr Donner. In its summer decor, the restaurant looked like the coolest, most beautiful thing in New York – apart from Miss Buell herself. She wore a pink linen dress that made her skin look even blacker than it really was, and I doubt if there was a man in the room who didn't wish he were sitting in my chair, including the poofs. She was sensational. Not just the face and figure, though she had them of course – they were stock in trade – but the vitality, the magnetism – whatever you call it. It surged out of her like a charge of electricity powered by Niagara, switched on never to stop. The maître brought her to my table and as we shook hands the sommelier trotted up with a glass of champagne. At the Four Seasons, it seemed, Miss Buell's immediate needs were known. She looked at me, appraisingly. It seemed I passed inspection.

'Nice of you to ask me, Mr Hogget,' she said.

'I've never been bought lunch by the Syndicated Press Association before.'

'It's Corporation actually,' I said, 'and we're honoured you could join us.'

'That accent. It really gets me,' she said. 'But why should London, England, want to know about Lenora Buell?'

'There *are* the TV films—'

'Oh *God*,' she said.

'And there's also a rumour that *Honeyfall* may come over to London.' There was rather more than a rumour about *Honeyfall* going to London – I'd read Jane's correspondence. The trouble was getting British Actors' Equity to accept Lenora. 'Would you like that to happen?' I asked.

'I guess so.'

'You don't seem certain.'

Then food started to arrive. Miss Buell ate everything that was put in front of her, including a lobster flamed in Pernod, but it didn't stop her talking. Nothing could. And she had the actress's trick of apparently eating and talking at the same time.

'Look,' she said, when the waiter had gone. 'You know who produced *Honeyfall?*'

It was something every journalist would know.

'Of course,' I said. 'Jane Donner.'

The late Jane Donner.

'She got me the part,' Lenora said. 'Everybody else said it should be a white girl. Jane said it should be me... Not a black girl, Mr Hogget... Me ... Lenora Buell. Do you see the difference?'

'Not having seen the play it isn't easy,' I said. 'But I'll try. Because it didn't matter what colour the girl was – it was just who could play her?'

'Very good,' Lenora said. 'Perfect even.'

'She had a lot of faith in you.'

'Sure,' she said. 'Jane knew I could do it... I knew I could do it... We were the only ones.'

'You must have been very fond of her.'

'No,' she said, 'I wasn't. I admired her, Mr Hogget. I worked my ass off for her. But I wasn't fond of her.'

'May I ask why not?'

'She expected too much. From herself. From me. From everybody she worked with. It scared me. My part in *Honeyfall* is a killer, Mr Hogget. I can't wait for it to close. That's why I don't want to go with it to London or anywhere else. But I somehow get the idea Jane would want me to go, so maybe I'll have to – I don't know – but I sure as hell don't want to. It exhausts me.'

It was hard to imagine Lenora Buell exhausted.

'You get on well with the company?'

'No problems,' she said. 'A few bruised egos maybe – but how can you have actors without egos?'

'Good director?'

'The best. He tells you what he wants you to do and as soon as you do it he leaves you alone. I haven't seen him in months. He's a sweetheart.'

'And the set?'

'It's nice,' she said. 'Not an assault course like some you get.'

'And the designer?'

'A fag is a fag is a fag,' she said. 'Frank got the idea he was straight once. Comedy of the year. You could have charged admission.'

'Frank?'

'Frank Sokolny,' she said. 'The designer. He had a big thing about Jane ... I don't mean in a coarse sense. I mean he really did love her.'

'He told you this?'

'He told everybody ... Hey – aren't you going to write any of this down?' She had to be kidding: all I'd got so far was libel actions. I tapped the side of my head.

'Good memory,' I said.

'It must be. Of course who Frank really loves is Mickey Wood. He's a dancer.'

'What show's he in?'

'He's resting. Mickey rests a lot. He didn't like Frank being fond of Jane. It upset him. There was a scene.'

'What happened?'

'I wasn't there,' she said regretfully. 'Nobody was – just the three of them. It was at Frank's place. He threw Mickey out. Can you imagine?... On account of a woman. So Mickey took an overdose.'

'And?'

'And that's all. He and Frank are back together, and Jane's dead – and you're asking me all about it on behalf of the Syndicated Press Denomination.'

'It's Corporation actually,' I said.

'Actually it's nothing,' she said. 'Not a damn thing. You're asking questions on behalf of Martin Donner, Mr Hogget.'

'Who told you that?'

She ignored it. 'Martin Donner,' she said. 'I'd never have believed it. What does he want? The guys who killed Jane, or his million dollars back?'

'I really don't know what you mean,' I said.

'Well of course not. But I hope it's the killers. They deserve everything they get. Even Donner. But why would Frank Sokolny be mixed up with Italian hoodlums?'

'I honestly don't understand you,' I said.

'Of course you don't. I'm just thinking out loud, that's all. Free associating. Frank says he knows nothing about Italians. And anyway he *loved* Jane.'

It sounded like a cue. 'Mickey Wood didn't,' I said.

'Wood isn't an Italian name,' said Lenora. 'What's the Italian word for wood, Mr Hogget? You know – like a forest?'

'Bosco,' I said.

'Bosco.' She stretched it out. 'Sort of has overtones, doesn't it? A kind of menace.'

'It does the way you say it.'

'You're sweet,' she said. 'Really you're sweet. Did you meet a Mr White by any chance?'

'Briefly,' I said.

'We had a thing going for a while,' she said. 'It was a physical thing and that's all. But it was physical all right. I tell you this in case you should find out for yourself and maybe draw the wrong conclusions on account of Mr White having handled the ransom money. Mr White wouldn't steal a car-fare from Donner.'

'Why wouldn't he?'

'Because Donner scares the shit out of him, Mr Hogget – if you'll pardon the expression. Believe me I know.'

She swigged down the last of her coffee.

'I better go,' she said. 'I've got some shopping to do before the theatre. I bet your wife's nice.'

'Who told you I was married?'

'Nobody,' she said. 'Nobody had to. You're the most married-looking man I've seen in years.' She looked at me. 'Don't let it worry you. It's a compliment.'

'It doesn't worry me.' I tried her own trick and added in the same breath, 'Was it Cass Milligan who told you I worked for Martin Donner?'

'Why would Cass do that?'

'Because you asked her. Because for some reason you were suspicious of the Syndicated Press Corporation of London, England, and checked it out and found it doesn't exist so you phoned Cass Milligan and she told you.'

'That makes me a pretty smart lady,' she said.

'You are a pretty smart lady. All three. A lady, pretty and smart. But why did you tell me all this?'

'I hope you catch them,' she said. 'Like I told you – I admired her. There must have been saints like that. All ice and fire. No earth in them at all ... I really must go.'

I signalled for the bill.

'I take it Cass Milligan told you about me in confidence?' I said.

'Oh sure,' Lenora said. 'But you don't have to worry about me, Mr Hogget. Cass knows I don't talk.'

Back in the apartment Ms Milligan was still remorselessly attacking her accounts. When I came in she didn't even look up, but I spoke out anyway.

'I'm late back from lunch,' I said, 'but I make no apologies. As you know, it was a working lunch. I can't recall when I worked harder.'

Then back to the letters and the photographs and the Manhattan telephone directory. There were seventy four Boscos – nine of them with Michael or Michele as a christian name, but no indication of which if any might be an out of work dancer. With the Woods I didn't even try. There were hundreds. So rather late in the day I used my brains and looked up Michael Wood in the Actor's Directory. An agency called Maisky and Green handled him, and the phone was picked up on the third ring. Business didn't seem too brisk at Maisky and Green.

I used my imitation of Humphrey Bogart's voice. It isn't the least like him but at least I don't sound British when I use it. 'Have you got a Michele Bosco on your books?' I said.

'He calls himself Mickey Wood now,' said Maisky or Green.

'*Michele Bosco?* You sure?' I sounded incredulous.

'Sure I'm sure,' Maisky or Green said. 'Look, who is this?'

'He lives at 185, 75th Street, right?'

'Wrong,' said whoever it was. 'He lives at 19, Chestnut Street. In the Village. *Who is this?*'

'Ah,' I said. That explains things.' I hung up and got the number for the Bosco in Chestnut Street from the book, dialled, let it ring twenty-one times. While it rang I looked him up in the directory as Wood – and sure enough there he was. Only there he wasn't. He was out. I hung up and pressed a button in the telephone marked Library. There was a click, then the voice said, 'Cass Milligan.'

'Did you hear all that, Ms Milligan?' I asked.

There was a long, long silence, then: 'Yes,' she said. 'I heard it.'

'You'd better come in here,' I said.

At least she didn't try putting it off. She came in almost at the double.

'Lenora told you she phoned me?' she said.

'You didn't give her much option,' I said.

'Maybe not.' She sat and thought about it, and said at last, 'Lenora talks a lot, but she never tells you anything she doesn't want you to know.'

'So I gathered,' I said.

'Will you tell Donner?'

'If I have to. Not otherwise. Have you met Mickey Wood?'

'Yes.'

'Then you know who he is?'

'Frank Sokolny's boy-friend.'

'That's right,' I said. 'Mickey Wood. Literal translation of Michele Bosco. A dancer who rests a lot. See if he's resting at Sokolny's place.'

'How can I do that?'

'You could start by phoning Sokolny. Sort of suss out if he's there.'

'No,' she said. 'I couldn't. And anyway why should I?'

'Because Mr Donner told you to give me any help I needed,' I said. 'I need this.'

'But why Mickey Wood?'

'You're a smart lady, Ms Milligan,' I said. 'You work it out.'

'Are you saying he was jealous of Jane – because of Frank?'

'I'm not saying anything,' I said. 'Was he?'

She got up then, came to the desk.

'This isn't the way,' she said. 'Believe me. Keyhole peeping, backstage gossip. This isn't the way.'

'Bosco's an Italian name,' I said. 'He could have Italian connections.'

'Do you honestly suppose he's the type who could kidnap for a million?'

'I don't know,' I said. 'I haven't met him.'

She picked up the casting directory from my desk, flicked through it, then thrust it at me. A pretty enough boy. But the wrists were limp. The real fairy type.

'Well?' she said.

'It takes all sorts,' I said. 'Maybe even him. He has his uses. Ask Sokolny.'

'Are you saying Frank would be mixed up in this?'

'You keep asking me if I'm saying things,' I said. 'I'm saying nothing. You're the one who's saying things – things you don't like. That's the way it is in my business, Ms Milligan. There are far too many things we don't like. But we keep looking. And if we look we have to start somewhere – and Bosco's the only place to start.'

She wasn't listening. Her worries had closed her ears.

'Frank wouldn't,' she said. 'I know he wouldn't.'

'Then you've got nothing to be scared of.'

But this was far from the truth. She was scared rigid.

'What's the matter, Ms Milligan? Are you in love with Sokolny too?'

'No,' she said. Just that. As if it was enough.

'Then why did you tell him I'd been reading his letters?'

'I didn't tell him.'

'Certainly you did. Last night.'

Her eyes told me she didn't like me at all.

'I told you before – he wasn't my date.'

'But he was,' I said. 'You had a drink with him at the Algonquin.'

'You followed me there?'

I nodded.

'But – but why?'

'It was just an idea I had,' I said. 'It turned out to be a good idea... Why did you tell him, Ms Milligan?'

'Jane and he had this affair,' she said. 'I told you... It turned out to be pretty messy.'

'You mean dirty?'

For a moment she looked mad again, then she got it under control.

'All right. Dirty,' she said.

'How do you know?'

She sighed. 'Mickey Wood told me,' she said. 'He used to spy on them – Jane wasn't like that. I give you my word she wasn't.'

'All fire and ice,' Lenora Buell had said. But she'd meant the fire that purges. There had been no earth in her to inflame. 'It doesn't bother her any more,' I said.

'I won't have her memory blackened.'

'It won't be,' I said. 'All I want is the blokes who killed her – isn't that what you want?'

'Yes,' she said. 'That's what I want. But not if it hurts Jane's memory. If you were to tell Donner about Frank...'

What would be the point?' I said. 'He already knows.'

'Donner knows?' she said. 'That's crazy.'

'No,' I said. 'It's not. Look, Ms Milligan, when people die, one of the tasks they leave the survivors is going through their private papers – to decide what to keep and what to burn. Lawyers and accountants take care of the business stuff, but the private papers – that's the next of kin's job, Ms Milligan. Of course Donner knows.'

'But – he never said a word,' she said.

'That's his privilege,' I said. 'You should learn to be like him... What did you tell Frank Sokolny?'

'To keep away from you.'

'And if I went to him?'

To tell you as little as possible.'

'He'll do that anyway,' I said. 'You're a right little time-waster, aren't you?' I pushed the phone over to her. 'Give him a ring. Find out if Bosco's there.'

She dialled a number and got lucky – if she regarded helping me as luck, which I doubt. 'Hello,' she said, and the phone yacked. 'Is that Mickey?... This is Cass... Is Frank there?... Oh I see... Will you wait for him?... Ask him to call me will you? Thanks, Mickey.' And she hung up.

'He's waiting for Frank,' she said. 'They're having an evening in. Mickey's cooking the dinner.'

'Nice,' I said. 'Apart from telling him to get Sokolny to call you.'

'I had to tell him something.'

'It's what you'll tell Frank that concerns me. Except I know what you'll tell him – Frank, I behaved like a fool last night, you'll say. I over-reacted. All that stuff about you and Jane just because a limey snoop went through her papers.'

'I don't use the word limey,' she said.

'I'm delighted to hear it. The snoop's not interested in her love-life at all. The only thing he cares about is money. Who owed her – who she owed. Who's going to benefit because she's dead. So please forgive me Frank, you'll say, and try to forget it ever happened and thanks for the drink.'

'Money?' she said. 'Why mon-?'

'You're starting again, Ms Milligan,' I said. 'Please don't start again. You cross me in this and I give Donner the lot,' I said.

'I won't cross you.'

She left me to study a map of New York I'd bought at the news-stand in the Plaza that morning. Chestnut Street was too far to walk, and the weather was too hot. But a taxi should take me there – or rather near there – in ten or fifteen minutes, I thought. I hadn't allowed for rush hour traffic. It was just as well that Mickey and Frank were having a night in.

But we got to the Village at last and I paid off the driver, and walked to Chestnut Street, stopping off at a drugstore on the way. Number 19 was a four-storey building with an entryphone system, the kind where you stand on the doorstep and say who you are into a mike and wait for somebody inside to press a buzzer and let you in. Difficult, but not unexpected, and certainly not impossible. I walked off again and found a florist's called, for some reason, 'Waiting For The Mahatma'- but this was Greenwich Village. Why it had to be that flower-shop I'll never know. Still, it was doing all right. Three people there to serve: a very thin, very pretty blonde, a sort of superior thug and a slim, elegant man in charge. I got the blonde to put a dozen red roses in fancy wrapping and wrote a card: 'The Impossible Dream Came True And I Loved It. Al'... Then I took the flowers and went back to 19, Chestnut Street, and selected my girl of the day. 'Tony and Sonia Strobe, Apartment 23.' I rang the bell.

'Yes?' said a voice that might have been female.

'Flowers for Mrs Strobe,' I said.

*'Flowers?'* The door clicked open before I could even say 'Yes'. And that's how easy it is when you don't learn to suspect people. Believe me I know...

She was out there in the hall waiting for me as I climbed the stairs, and slipped me a coin and disappeared inside without even looking at my face. Not a bad looking lady, either, Sonia Strobe. She just didn't seem to get enough flowers... I looked at the coin. A quarter. Mr Donner wasn't exactly into profit... I walked down two flights to the Bosco apartment and studied the locks on it. Bosco it seemed was a fatalist. If you were going to be robbed you were going to be robbed, so why fight it? Or more to the point, why waste money on safe, expensive locks when there are so many cheap and useless ones around? I rang the bell and got no answer, so now it was up to me to open the door. I had a selection of credit cards – you can go anywhere nowadays with a credit card – and my Swiss Army knife. Cost me two hundred quid, that Swiss Army knife, but then it had been taken apart and reassembled by a bent locksmith I knew in Bermondsey. Neatest little kit of burglar's tools I've ever carried. Bosco's door took me four minutes, and I pushed it open with my knuckle and went inside, kicked the door shut with the back of my heel, and pulled on the plastic gloves I'd bought at the drugstore.

Not exactly palatial, the Bosco pad. Living-room and dining-room combined, bedroom the size of a large cupboard, kitchen and bathroom the size of small cupboards, and that was about it. And the place was a shambles, not like Jane's office at all. Unmade bed, uncleared table, unwashed crockery. Still, I wasn't there to criticize. My business was to find things, so I started looking. Mind you it helps to know what you're looking for.

In his wardrobe Mr Bosco had two suits, three pairs of slacks, five pairs of jeans, shirts and sweaters none too clean. He had the sort of gear that male dancers wear to rehearse in, and that was none too clean either. Also it smelt of sweat. Very stale sweat... In the living-room was a coffee-table with glossy magazines on it – all homosexual soft porn. He had a portable telly and a music centre, the records mostly ballet and opera, and most of the opera Verdi. But he was Italian after all. How could he not have Verdi? In the kitchen there was canned food – though not a lot – and a rubbish bin. There was also a copy of last week's Sunday edition of the *New York Times*. I took a couple of pages from the middle of the Financial Section on the theory that Bosco would never read the Financial Section, spread them on the floor, and emptied the rubbish bin out on to them. Sometimes you can learn a lot about a person from what they throw away. You can find things, too. Useful things...

Coffee grounds. A lot. Signor Bosco drank a lot of coffee, and being Italian, he drank it strong. Boxes from a bakery. Inside the remains of some very sweet, very gooey cakes. Not the ideal diet for a dancer, surely?... A paperback edition of *Last Exit To Brooklyn*. In the blurb someone had described it as a homosexual classic, but Bosco must have run out of steam. The bookmark was inserted in page seventy four. The bookmark was a book of matches advertising the Ristorante Cesare, Riva del Garda, Italia: a place I'd eaten in the year before, when I went to visit my cousin Lucio who lived not twenty miles away... There were bills, paid and unpaid, but all torn across before they were thrown away and a letter post-marked Seattle that began Dear darling Mickey, how can I possibly tell you how much I miss you? then proceeded to tell him. There were milk cartons and stale bread and yoghurt tubs and cola cans, and a couple of small transparent envelopes, the kind I used to buy stamps in when I was a kid and collected stamps. No booze. Not even a beer can. And no cigarettes. Just an empty book of matches.

I dumped the rubbish back in the bin and folded up the sheets of the *Times*, put them in a paper sack to be dumped later, outside. Then I went back to the bedroom. Under the bed there was a metal box with another lock the Swiss knife found amusing – and inside a hundred dollars in bills, a bunch of letters in pink ribbon – (from Frank Sokolny – he too had missed his little Bosco, and explained in detail how much) – and a passport. Bosco hadn't left the USA in two years, and even then it had been to go to Mexico. Jane had been dead just six weeks...

I locked up the treasure-chest and pushed it back where it belonged. There was something else, there had to be, and I wanted to find it and go out. I didn't like the place, and I didn't like what it told me about Bosco ... And there was always the chance he and Sokolny might have a row and he'd come home in a huff. All the same I had to be sure... It wasn't inside the toilet tank – that would have been too easy – and the music-centre was too tricky for him to open. That left the telly – and there it was. Typically, he hadn't even bothered to put the back on properly... Stowed inside were a hypodermic, a blackened spoon, and four little transparent envelopes, each with their carefully measured dose of dream powder. No wonder Mickey rested a lot... I reached inside the telly once more and came up with another prize: a notebook with lists of names, a row of figures after each name. One name was Sokolny's, another was Jane's. Hers was the only female's. There were twenty-seven in all. I copied them into my own book, and put it all back, the book, the hypo, the spoon, the filth he stuck into himself – exactly the way I'd found it. I even remembered to do a lousy job of screwing the back of the television on. Then I took off the gloves, stuck them in the paper sack with the pages of the *Times* and got out quick, dumped the paper sack three blocks from Bosco's house and flagged a cab. It was time to go home and watch television. I had a lot to think about.

# 4

A strong woman had fallen for a weak man. Start there. And the weak man divided his love between her and an even weaker man, who happened to be a junkie as well, and who had once supported his habit by a little discreet prostitution, and/or blackmail, if the figures in the notebook meant what I thought they meant, and it didn't seem to me they could mean anything else. At the front of the book there were lists of names – followed by figures – usually fifty dollars. At the back of the book there was just one name, Goody, and it too was followed by figures. Sometimes ten dollars, sometimes twenty, once as high as fifty. I figured the numbers affected how much heroin he bought and how scarce it was at the time. There were no dates in the book, but while Goody had been his supplier Bosco had handed over more than five thousand dollars... I went back to the list of names. Next to Sokolny's, Bosco had written 'Not from you. Dearest Frank, I could never take money from you.' Except he almost certainly had. Goody wouldn't be handing out free samples. And then there was Jane's name. Just that. Jane. In red. The only one in red. Because he hated her, maybe? Hated her – and needed the money

60

dearest Frank would get from her?

The telephone rang. I turned down the TV set, where a fat woman was trying and failing to name three American cities that began with the letter A, picked the phone up and said 'Hello.'

'Mr Hogget?' a man's voice said.

'Speaking.'

'You don't know me,' the voice said. 'My name is Richard Gregory. Jane's father. My son-in-law has told me about you.'

Somebody was throwing custard pies at the fat woman.

'What can I do for you, Dr Gregory?' I said.

'I'd like to talk.'

'Certainly.' No point in asking what about. Dr Gregory knew.

'Not now,' Gregory said. 'Not on the phone. Could you come to my place tomorrow evening?'

He gave me an address on 79th Street and I said it would be a pleasure.

'I don't think you mean that,' said Dr Gregory. 'There can be no pleasure in what either of us is doing. But I think we ought to talk.'

Then he hung up and I looked at the fat woman, now being sprayed with soda from a siphon. I turned off the set. She had suffered enough. So had I.

Bosco and Sokolny were having a night in. I could go over to their place and ask questions, I supposed, and they might answer me. On the other hand they might not. They might even throw me out. Two people who love each other, who seek above all things to protect each other, can be very tough when they're together. Much better to wait until they're apart, use the absence of the loved one as a weapon. And the one on drugs was obviously the softer touch. I'd have to see him soon, I thought, and phoned down for food, clam chowder and a corned-beef sandwich, and a beer, and fiddled around with my copy of Bosco's notebook. But all it was names and money and heroin, and why he'd even bothered I had no idea.

Next morning Cass Milligan was late, and that should have given me something of an edge, but it didn't. When she came into the lobby she looked so disorientated I doubt if she knew why she was there when I went up to her.

'Good morning,' I said. 'Are you all right?'

Slowly she became aware of who I was.

'They killed Mickey Wood,' she said. 'Over in the Village.'

'You're sure?' I said.

Maybe it was a stupid thing to say, but she had that look in her eye. It could have been her way of reacting to shock: it could equally well have been speed.

'For Christ's sake,' she said. 'Of course I'm sure. Do you think I'd make it up?'

Her voice was too loud: people were looking, prepared to take an interest.

'Did Sokolny tell you?'

'Frank?...Why would he tell me? It was on the radio.'

'You said "they" killed him,' I said.

'That's right.'

'Who's they?'

She got the vague look again.

'The ones who kill people,' she said. 'Muggers I guess.'

'Did you come here by car?'

'Not today,' she said. 'Not after that news. I couldn't face driving. I took a cab.'

That meant no parking problems: a little time to spare.

'I want you to call Sokolny,' I said.

'You want me to *tell* him?'

'I want you to find out if he knows,' I said. I could have added that if he did it was more than possible that the rozzers had told him, in which case he would not be available to people who find things, but she had enough on her plate. 'If he doesn't know,' I said, 'don't tell him. Just ask him to come to the Donner apartment.'

'Why?' she said.

'Because we won't be interrupted.'

'I mean why bring him there?'

'So we can talk,' I said. 'What else?'

'You'll tell him about Mickey?'

'One of us will.'

She shuddered. 'It'll hurt him terribly.'

'It won't stop him talking,' I said. 'It might even help.'

'You disgust me,' she said. Loud again. 'You really disgust me.'

'Keep your voice down,' I said, 'and stop trying to be everybody's guardian-angel. We have to find out who killed Jane and that's all. Go and make a phone call.'

She went. That was the bad time. I couldn't go with her into the booth – not in the state she was in – so I couldn't monitor what she was saying. All I could do was wait and feel awful. I did both... When she came back she still had the dazed look.

'He doesn't know,' she said. 'The poor darling. He doesn't know.'

'Did you ask him to come over?' She nodded. 'Didn't he want to know why?'

'I told him I wanted to talk about *Honeyfall* going to London.'

'Not very bright,' I said. 'When he finds out it's just a rumour–'

'As a matter of fact it's not. I got a letter from London Equity at the office two days ago. They might do a deal.' Loud again.

I shushed her. 'You didn't tell me,' I said.

'It's none of your fucking business.' That time she whispered, thank God.

We took a cab to the apartment and found we had nothing to say to each other. Not that it mattered. The cab-driver talked all the way, and I worried about whether Sokolny could have turned on the radio. In the library-office, I shared my fear with Cass Milligan.

'He always listens to music in the mornings,' she said.

No suggestion of how she knew, and it didn't seem like the time to ask. I asked her to turn on the radio instead, and she twiddled the knobs till she found a news-bulletin, and it was mostly death and taxes, like they always are. Mickey Wood was dead. That was official, or as official as Station WYXB could make it. Found by Patrolman Walfisch behind a stack of garbage cans in the village. Beaten, stabbed and robbed... The fourth violent

death of the week, and it was only Thursday...
Enquiries were proceeding... I switched off the set.

'Muggers,' she said.

'Looks like it.' If it wasn't muggers they'd lift his wallet anyway, just to make us investigators think it was.

'They beat him,' she said.

'Maybe he resisted. Maybe it was junkies. They don't like resistance. It makes them mad. They see it as getting between them and their fix.'

'Mickey Wood was a junkie,' she said.

'That wouldn't protect him,' I said. 'There's no junkies' trade union, Ms Milligan. Dog does eat dog.'

She got up and wandered to the window and I followed.

'Muggers,' she said. 'Poor Mickey. He wasn't the most marvellous man in my life – but he shouldn't have died like that. Poor Mickey... Poor Frank.'

Then she began to cry, just letting the tears flow; no turning to me for comfort, no search for a manly shoulder to cry on. If I'd touched her she'd have yelled rape. I passed her my handkerchief and she took it and that was all, till at last she said, 'I'm sorry.'

'Don't be,' I said. 'It's been rough for you.'

'It'll get rougher.'

The phone buzzed and she picked it up, and said 'The Donner Apartment', listened while the phone squawked, then said, 'Send him right up. He'll be met.' This time her voice was composed. She put the phone down.

'It's Frank,' she said. 'Do what you have to do – but please don't expect me to help you.'

She went into the corridor to meet him, but that was OK. I was just behind her in the hall of the apartment. No chance of her having a word in private. Instead she bustled him in to me at once as if she were afraid to be alone with him and maybe she was. After all, he might have talked about Mickey Wood.

'Frank,' she said. 'I'd like you to meet Mr Hogget. He's from London.'

'Hey,' Sokolny said. 'Hey this is great. You British certainly don't believe in wasting any time.'

He came up to me, his hand outstretched, and I took it. It was part of the job, and there was no suggestion of betrayal. Deviousness, yes; but not betrayal. Not by me.

'How do you do, Mr Sokolny?' I said.

'So you want to do *Honeyfall?*' said Sokolny.

'Let's go into my office and talk about it,' I said, and took him by the arm, steered him towards Jane's dressing room. Cass Milligan just stood in the hall and watched us go and that was fine with me. Sokolny and I would do better on our own. He looked around the dressing-room.

'This is your office?' he said.

'For the moment.'

This is Jane's room,' he said.

'Not any more,' I said. 'She's dead.'

He took a step towards me, and I became aware of something his photographs hadn't told me. He was a strong man. Lean, but strong; the muscles packed in tight. This wasn't exactly encouraging for the course of action I'd decided on, but we were talking about fifty, maybe a hundred thousand dollars, after all.

'Mr Sokolny,' I said. 'There are things I must tell you.'

'Go ahead.'

He stopped moving, but he got no smaller.

'I work for Martin Donner,' I said.

'So what have you got to do with *Honeyfall?*'

'That depends,' I said.

'On what?'

'On what kind of help I get to find out who killed his wife.'

At that he did begin to look smaller.

'Oh,' he said. 'Co-operate or you don't go to London – is that it?'

'I hope it doesn't have to be like that.'

I did indeed. No sense in upsetting him, the size he was. Sokolny said, 'You're the one Cass told me about.'

'That's right,' I said. 'I'm also the one who's going to find out who killed Jane Donner. Don't you want me to do that?... After all, you and she were friends.'

'We were lovers,' he said. 'You know that. You read the letters.'

'Doesn't that just intensify what I've said?'

He began to walk up and down. It was theatrical – but then he belonged to the theatre. It also drew attention to the physical energy of the man.

'Intensify,' he said. 'That's a good word. For me and Jane I mean. With us, everything was intensified... It burned us up. I mean it. It was like fire.'

'Right till the time she died?'

'Of course... For me anyway. She was gone a month before they – found her. What was left of her. She wrote to me the day before she disap-

peared. She was still burning then. Just like me.'
He moved to the door. 'That's all I have to tell you.'

'Nonsense,' I said. 'How can it be?'

He spun round on his toes, like a boxer.

'You better explain yourself,' he said.

'Of course.' I was trying to act like a man who has nothing to fear. I'm a terrible actor.

'You were with her here in New York. You were with her in London.'

'And Paris and Rome,' he said. 'OK. I was with her. I told you. We burned. You could say we were incandescent, Mr Hogget. I wouldn't argue.'

'Sometimes you burned in public,' I said. 'You were busy people, both of you. You couldn't be alone all the time.'

'Well of course not.'

'Who did you meet, Mr Sokolny?'

'You mean who did I meet who could have killed her? That's a very stupid question, Mr Hogget.'

I looked at his muscles, and refused to take offence. 'Not everybody burned for her, surely?' I said.

'Nobody hated her.'

'Nobody?'

'Of course not.' He looked at me, bewildered, then shook his head. 'You didn't know her. I should have realized. There was nothing about her you could hate.'

'What kind of people did you meet when you were with her?'

'Theatrical people, literary people,' he said. They make hopeless kidnappers and even worse murderers.'

'Did you meet a man called A. D. Carr?'

'The writer?... Sure... We met him.'

'In London?'

'That's where he lives.'

'How did he feel about Mrs Donner?' I asked.

He stopped walking, looked at me, then went on walking. 'Maybe I should knock your goddam block off,' he said.

'That wouldn't take *Honeyfall* to London.'

He smiled then, still moving.

'OK.' he said. 'Carr wanted her. I had her... Is that all?'

'No,' I said, and braced myself. There'd be no smile for this one.

'We have to talk about Mickey Wood,' I said.

He stopped again and faced me. This time he made no effort to resume the caged tiger act.

'You really have been digging in the dirt,' he said.

'You know I have.'

'Yeah ... Cass Milligan told me.' Suddenly he tugged at his moustache. It wasn't the self-satisfied yet randy gesture of the squire in a melodrama, but an act of cruelty, of pain self-inflicted.

'I'm bi-sexual,' he said. 'You know that.' I waited. 'That means I'm capable of being in love with a man and a woman at the same time. I'm not talking about threesomes – group sex. Any of that... Just being in love ... I loved Jane till she died. I'll love Mickey till *he* dies – or I do.'

I didn't like the way this was going at all.

'I believe that,' I said. 'I may not understand it – but I believe it.'

'Well good for you.'

'That means I accept it. Now what I really want

69

to know about is how Jane and Mickey got on together.'

'Can't you guess?'

'Guessing's not the way to find kidnappers, Mr Sokolny. I want you to tell me.'

'OK.' he said, and tugged at his moustache again. 'OK,' He tugged again, and I turned away to re-align the ebony ruler that was already in perfect alignment. 'Mickey hated her,' he said.

'You just said nobody hated her.'

'I know what I said... But he was the only one, can't you understand that? The only one and I love him.'

'And she?'

'She accepted him because she had to. She didn't like him – how could she? But she didn't hate him...'

'Did she know about his habit?'

For the first time I'd really surprised him.

'Who told you that?' he said.

Never let them ask the questions.

'Information received,' I said. 'Did she?'

'Yes,' he said. 'I told her. Mickey needed money and I was broke. 'She was the only one I knew who had the sort of money I needed... I had to tell her.'

'Money for a cure?'

'That's what I told her.'

'Was it true?'

'Mickey said it was. He lied to me... Junkies always do. You should know that.'

'Why did he change his name to Wood?'

'He thought there was a prejudice against Italians in the theatre.'

'And is there?'

'Of course not. He gets these weird ideas that's all... There's a prejudice against hopheads, Mr Hogget. Changing your name won't help you break a habit.'

'Did he ever try to hurt Jane?'

'Physically you mean?'

'In any way.'

'He came over to my apartment a couple of times. Made a scene. He does it very well.'

'Anything else?'

'He's an addict, Mr Hogget,' Sokolny said. 'He's not very big and he has no money and no clout. He's also what you would call a faggot. What harm could he possibly do to a million-aire's wife?'

'He might have had some Italian friends,' I said.

'Yeah,' he said. 'He might. As a matter of fact he does. But they all live in Manhattan except maybe two in the Bronx. Most of them are either dancers or hairdressers. None of them are kid-nappers. And even if they were, they'd never use Mickey. He's too weak to be trusted. Believe me, Mr Hogget, I know. Mickey is weak.'

Suddenly I just couldn't stand the use of the present tense any more. 'He was at your place last night,' I said.

'I guess Cass told you that.'

'What time did he leave?'

'Around three this morning.'

'Did you have a row?'

'He'd run out of dope. Needed a fix. What is this?'

'Mr Sokolny,' I said. 'I have bad news for you.'

71

'Mickey?' he said. 'Something's wrong with Mickey?'

'You'd better sit down,' I said.

'Don't give me that,' Sokolny said. What's happened?'

'I'm awfully sorry to have to tell you,' I said. 'He's dead.'

'Don't be stupid,' he said.

'It really is true,' I said. 'I'm sorry. It happened in Greenwich Village. Early this morning.'

'*What* happened?'

'I think he was mugged,' I said. 'I know he was stabbed. Mr Sokolny, I–'

He came at me over the desk in a standing dive, his hands grabbing for my throat. He had very accurate, very strong hands and he began to squeeze at once. 'You bastard,' he kept yelling. 'You bastard.'

I tried to grab for his wrists but he squeezed even harder. I could feel my eyes ballooning in their sockets and my hands fell away. I knocked over the telephone. Everything was out of focus now, the room was beginning to swim...

It was the ebony ruler that saved me. My right hand touched it – or maybe the ruler rolled into it – maybe I really was that lucky. However it happened I got hold of the thing. I only had the strength for one blow in me. If it wasn't my best shot I'd be dead ... It was a good one. Even in the state I was in I could hear it, and the wood jarred in my hand. What it did to his head I hate to think.

He went limp at once and his hands released my throat so that I could sit back and wheeze to my heart's content. Ms Milligan came loping in and looked first at Sokolny, then at me. For some reason I was still holding the ruler.

'My God,' she said. 'You've killed him.'

'It was nearly vice-versa,' I said. But it was Sokolny she went to.

'You hit him very hard,' she said.

'I panicked,' I told her. 'Maybe it was because he was strangling me at the time. What does he drink?'

She looked bewildered. 'Scotch on the rocks,' she said. 'Lots of ice.'

'Get it,' I said.

She went away and came back with a bottle of 'Black Label' and a bucketful of ice. I wrapped a handful of cubes in a towel, and held it to Sokolny's head.

'Pour him a drink,' I said.

'Won't it be bad for him?' she asked.

'Of course not,' I said. I lied. It certainly wouldn't be good for him, but it might help him to talk. After a while he groaned, tried to move, and I helped him into a sitting position. He opened his eyes.

'You said Mickey had been killed,' he said.

'I didn't lie to you,' I said, and turned to Ms Milligan. 'Did I?'

'It's true, Frank,' she said. 'It's been on the radio all day.'

'How was he killed?' Sokolny said.

She hesitated.

'Tell him,' I said.

'He was beaten,' Cass Milligan said. 'Then he was stabbed.'

'He was beaten and he was stabbed,' said

Sokolny. 'Did you maybe think that was too trivial a matter to mention when you phoned me?'

She looked at me. 'I was told not to,' she said.

It was Sokolny's turn to look at me. 'You bastard,' he said, and tried to get up. It was just my good luck he couldn't.

I eased him back to the floor, then went to the desk and retrieved the ruler. 'You've made your disapproval clear,' I croaked at him. 'That's fair enough. It wasn't a very nice thing I did to you – but then it wasn't a very nice thing you did to me.'

'You bastard,' he said again. It seemed I no longer inspired him to eloquence.

I went over to Ms Milligan, took the Scotch on the rocks from her hand and gave it to Sokolny, who seemed to have no problem in drinking it.

'Thank you, Ms Milligan,' I said. 'That'll be all.'

She didn't want to leave, and I could think of no way of moving her. Just as well. Sokolny did it for me.

'He's right, Cass,' he said. 'You're in too deep as it is. You better go.'

She left without a word, and I helped myself to the Johnny Walker.

'How's she in deep?' I asked.

It seemed he didn't hear me.

'You don't look the kind of guy who would do it,' he said.

'Do what, Mr Sokolny?'

'Pull a gag like that. Tell me Mickey's dead just so-so–'

'So what?'

'So you could earn a fee from Donner.'

He tried again to get up, and this time, with my help, he made it to a chair. He didn't look good, but I kept the ruler handy even so.

'I only earn my fee if I find who killed Jane,' I said. It was a half-truth at best, but then how much truth would he tell me? 'That's why I did this to you... I'm sorry – but it's Jane's death I want to know about. Not that it mightn't tie in with your friend's.'

'He was mugged, you said. Mugged and knifed.'

'That's what it sounds like. That doesn't mean that's what it was.'

'I told you,' he said. 'Mickey knew hairdressers, not killers.'

'Tell me about Goody,' I said.

'Goody?'

'Oh come *on*,' I said. 'He had a habit. Before he met you he had to hustle for it.'

'We don't need to go into that,' he said, and drank.

'OK – he could give up hustling, once he met you, but he couldn't give up Goody. Goody was his supplier. Would you care to comment, Mr Sokolny?'

'That bitch,' he said.

I waited for more. Among gays, bitch could just as well be a man as a woman.

'She took him for thousands,' he said. 'Thousands. And all the time she was killing him. Even if he hadn't been – murdered – she would have done it. Mickey knew that.'

'Yet he called her Goody?'

'It's her name,' he said. 'Gudrun Müller.'

'German?'

'Smartass,' he said. 'Except you're wrong. She told Mickey her family came from Austria.'

'A nice, friendly pusher. What's she like?'

'To look at?' He sipped his Scotch. 'I've only ever seen her from a distance... A blonde. On the skinny side.'

'Is she on the stuff, too?'

'I hope so,' he said.

'What sort of cover does she use?'

'There's a flower shop near where Mickey lives ... "Waiting For The Mahatma"...'

Indeed there is, I thought. Complete with skinny blonde.

'Does she ever go to Italy?'

'No,' said Sokolny. 'Austria is where she goes to.'

'Any idea where?'

'For Christ's sake,' he said. 'Mickey's dead. What do I care where she goes?' He began to cry.

Again there was no comfort I could offer. All I could do was wait; so I waited, and he got himself together at last.

'You through with me?' he asked.

'Nearly,' I said. 'Just tell me how Cass Milligan's in deep and we're finished.'

'She tipped me off about you,' he said. 'You know that.'

'Is that all she did?'

'What else could she do?'

This was a question that not only dodged the truth, it implied a lie, but though Mr Sokolny wept pretty freely, he still had muscles. I let it go.

'That's it,' I said, and he rose, went to a mirror and looked into it. Even at that moment there was a sort of critical appraisal in his look, like that of a woman who had just freshened her makeup before she joins the party.

'Jesus,' he said. 'I better wash up.'

He found his way to the bathroom without my help, and I sat and wondered what to do about Goody – or rather how to do what I had to do without getting hurt... I wished Dave was with me.

Sokolny came out of the bathroom. He looked clean and spruce. Even his moustache had been combed. He looked worried, too.

'You say Mickey was killed in the Village?' he said and I nodded. 'Nothing was said about me – right?'

'Not a thing,' I said. 'Of course the police will get to you eventually—'

'How will they?' he said. 'I kept nothing at Mickey's place. He always came to me.'

'They'll ask around,' I said. 'Talk to people. That way they'll find out about other people. Eventually they'll get to you.'

'You're really enjoying this, aren't you?'

'No,' I said. 'Just warning you what you're in for. I'm doing you a favour really.'

'Thanks a bunch.'

'I mean it,' I said. 'You'll have to prepare yourself. Get your story ready.'

'I've got to talk to Cass,' he said, and left me without farewell. Somehow I got the feeling that he hadn't been entirely open and above board with me, as they say, especially about Gudrun Müller. I went to the window and watched the street and thought about her. I was very frightened, but not enough to pass up a hundred thousand dollars. Not yet. Ten minutes later Sokolny came out at a run and waved for a cab, a man in a hurry. It was time to go to see Ms Milligan, who was insecure, and not nearly as muscular as Frank Sokolny.

She was still seated in front of her accounts, but she wasn't seeing them, wasn't even looking at them, wasn't looking at anything that belonged in the outward and visible world.

'What did you and Sokolny talk about?' I said.

She became aware of me then. It took a little time.

'Frank?' she said at last. 'We had business to discuss.'

'What business?'

'Not yours,' she said.

I could have threatened her with Donner again, but it bored me. It was a trick that worked, but it was always the same trick. I tried another one.

'You talked about taking *Honeyfall* to London,' I said. 'Designing new sets. Sending him over straightaway to get things moving. Cash in advance.'

She looked appalled. 'You were listening,' she said.

'Coming from you that's bitter,' I said. 'And anyway I didn't have to. Your chum wanted to go away – so he came to you. It was obvious. How much did you give him?' She was silent. 'Please, Ms Milligan. Don't make me call in the accountants.'

'Five thousand dollars,' she said at last. 'It's a legitimate expense on the company.'

'I doubt it,' I said.

'He told me he couldn't face a police investigation,' she said.

'He had something to be afraid of, then?'

'Of course not,' she said. 'But the police can still be pretty rough on gays.'

'So when does he leave?'

'The first flight he can get.'

'What about his apartment?'

'I said I'd keep an eye on it,' she said, and waited for me to ask if she had the keys. I didn't ask her. She looked up at me.

'You're not going to stop him? I mean it isn't as if he could help the police–'

'It's me I want him to help,' I said.

'He's already done that,' she said. 'Please let him go.'

I thought: Of course I'll let him go, Ms Milligan. It was me put the idea of going into his head, because it's the only chance he's got, but I want a little openness first, a little above-boardness. Aloud I said, 'Thank you for saying please, Ms Milligan.'

Bleeker Street is cute the way the tourists like it: neat, brick houses, inappropriate wrought-iron work, yards with flowers and trees; cute people sitting on the stoops, cute shops with cute things to sell. Goody's shop for instance. I made myself go inside at once. If I hesitated I'd never have gone in.

It had the dark, musty smell that flower-shops always have. Loam is it? Peat-moss? Whatever it is it's a lot stronger than the scent of the flowers you get nowadays. I looked around the shop. No customers, one assistant. The slim, smooth one. All by himself.

'Yes sir?' he said. Polite, well mannered, anxious to help. Not the criminal type at all – unless he was the polite, well-mannered, helpful sort of criminal.

'I'd like to speak to Miss Müller,' I said.

The politeness stayed in place, but he also looked wary.

'I beg your pardon, sir?' he said.

'Oh excuse me,' I said. 'Please don't think that I'm here on a personal matter. No indeed. It's just that she sold me some roses the other day – they were for my wife – it's our anniversary – and she suggested the name of some other flowers I might buy for a friend of ours in hospital. Only I've forgotten the name of the flowers and I wondered if Miss Müller could help me.'

'Miss Müller's on vacation,' the man said, still polite. 'But roses are always popular, sir. Whatever the occasion for flowers. May I show you some?' But I wasn't to be bullied into a purchase like that. I bought carnations instead.

So that was it. I'd done a recce into enemy territory (if 'Waiting For The Mahatma' was the enemy) gathered my information, and made good my escape as they say. A triumph for our side, in fact, except that I was almost run down by a car on the corner of Bleeker Street and 7th Avenue. What saved me was the fact that I was a mass of nerves (cowards usually are) and that therefore my reflexes work quicker than most. The car screamed round the corner and came at me head on and I made a sideways leap Nureyev in his prime would have been proud of. I even landed standing up, still clutching the carnations, and I didn't waste any time loitering about, looking indignant. I just moved into the crowd and kept on moving, and the rest of New York moved with me.

Back to the Donner apartment. Cass Milligan let me in reluctantly, and who should blame her? I didn't waste time telling her that somebody had tried to hit me with a Chevrolet. It wasn't my business to give her good news. Now all I had to do was keep an eye on Ms Milligan's door and wait for her to be out of the way for a bit.

When she finally did go to the bathroom – or at least she wasn't in the office-library – she left her handbag behind, which showed what a trusting soul she was. Nothing much in it – a diary kept in shorthand I couldn't read; a wallet, a change-purse, make-up, car keys, and two lots of house keys. Interesting, that. Two lots. She didn't look the type who owned two houses – and the keys to the Donner apartment were on the desk, so that wasn't the answer. Then I looked at the two lots of keys. Attached to one of them was a flat metal disc with a Sagittarius Zodiac sign on it. The other one consisted only of keys – and a French franc with a hole in it attached to the key-ring. Ms Milligan was a Sagittarius. Her birthday was 29th November. It said so on her CV, which Jane Donner had kept in the third drawer on the left, so I lifted the other set, put it in my pocket, returned the other stuff to her bag, and left before Ms Milligan could come back and be upset at the sight of me going through her things.

What I needed was time to relax, and the only way I can do that properly is in a hot bath. A shower just doesn't work. Besides, every muscle in my body seemed to ache, what with all the jumping and trembling I'd done. So I went back home to the Plaza and ran a bath as hot as I could bear it, and got in carefully, and let it do me good, and began to think about the Chevrolet. The reason I knew it was a Chevrolet was I'd hired one just like it when I'd been on that child-snatching lark in Canada. Big, burly, comfortable sort of a car. I'd liked it. So I'd recognized the one that had nearly killed me. I hadn't recognized the driver. I hadn't had time. Anyway what was there to recognize? Dark glasses, golf cap with a long visor. That was about all I'd seen. My guess was he was Caucasian, but I wouldn't even have been prepared to swear to it, not if it was a matter of life or death, and the life or death were mine ... I wouldn't even have been prepared to swear it wasn't an accident. After all, the polite man had got things moving pretty quickly if he'd suspected me. Seven minutes after I'd left his shop he'd run a Chevvy at me. Even pushers, who don't take at all kindly to having their cover blown, rarely move at quite that speed. But somebody had.

Time to get out of the bath, turn up the air-conditioning and let myself become dry, then dress to go and visit Dr and Mrs Gregory. The older generation, conservative, but good-looking still, according to their photographs, so I put on a pair of slacks and the lightweight jacket I'd had made in Hong Kong. Shirt *and* tie. I wanted them to talk to me. I wanted them to be at ease... As I left my room the phone rang, but I kept on going, took the lift down to the lobby and went to the cocktail bar for one slow, cautious bourbon. Somebody had left a paper and I picked it up, flicked through it. There was a picture of

82

Mickey Wood's body on page three. I had never seen a dead body as a result of the way I earn my living – or as a result of anything else for that matter. Even my mother – they hadn't let me see my mother's body, and I was glad of it... Mickey Wood looked terrible. But even so I felt pretty sure they'd touched up the picture because of the delicate stomachs of their readers. The original would look even worse...

I went to the desk-clerk and asked if anybody had left any messages for me. There'd been three, I gathered; all from a Ms Cass Milligan: she wanted me to call her. I had better things to do, like go to see Dr and Mrs Gregory, who had an apartment on 79th Street, not too far from where their son-in-law lived. A very nice apartment, but then Dr Gregory was a very successful doctor, and according to Cass Milligan his wife had money. That the apartment should be charming was not in the least surprising: after all their daughter had been charming too. What did surprise me was that they should be giving a party.

# 5

According to Dave it was more of a *soirée musicale*, technically speaking, meaning there were a lot of people sitting on chairs listening, and two girls and two blokes sawing away on stringed instruments. I know what I like, a state of mind I'm not ashamed of, and I didn't like what I was hearing, not from the very beginning, when the butler, who looked like a Cuban or a Puerto Rican or something, showed me in. By the look on his face he didn't like it either.

When it comes to the classics almost all of what I like is by dead people, and the geezer who had written this was very much alive. It sounded like cats fighting in a hailstorm, but there wasn't anything I could do about it. There I was and there I stayed till the cats sorted out who was the winner ... I was still applauding – because I'm polite as well as cowardly – when Dr Gregory came over to me. He looked like and ad-man's vision of what a doctor should be: tall, distinguished, handsome, grey-haired. He even had eyes that twinkled. Shrewdly.

'Mr Hogget?' he said. 'Nice of you to come. Let's go to my study and talk.' He led the way and I followed him. His study was another handsome room, but it looked used, and it had a lot of pictures of his daughter at almost every age from birth to death.

'You didn't seem to be enjoying the music,' he said.

'Not much, I'm afraid.'

'I don't hear it any more,' he said. 'It's a hobby of my wife's you see.' He produced a pipe. It was all that was needed to make him perfect.

'You wife's hobby is music?'

'My wife's hobby is musicians. And painters. And writers. The ones at the start of their careers. She enjoys it and it doesn't bother me. Just lately it's been a godsend. Kept her occupied.'

'I see,' I said. He nodded.

'Of course you do,' he said. 'You're investigating my daughter's death.' As a definition it was near enough.

'Did Mr Donner tell you that?' I asked.

'After I asked him, yes.'

'Asked him what, Dr Gregory?'

'What he was doing about Jane – about her—' His voice faded, died. He relit his pipe. 'Do you understand what kind of person my daughter was?' he asked.

'I'm beginning to,' I said.

'I'd like you to tell me.'

'She was beautiful and she was intelligent,' I said. 'She must also have been very likeable – loveable even.'

'You're a very perceptive man, Mr Hogget,' he said. 'She was indeed. And yet she was murdered. Decapitated.' For a moment the ad-man's image faded, as his voice had done; he became ageing and sad; then the pipe went back into his mouth, the eyes twinkled again.

'The shock of it nearly killed my wife, too,' he said. 'Even now she won't talk about it. It was only her interest in people like those clowns in the drawing-room that kept her going. Their caterwauling's a small price to pay for that. Incidentally I must apologize for inviting you in the middle of all the uproar – she doesn't know why you're here. She thinks you're just another music lover.'

'Then what am I doing here?'

'You're a music lover with a heart murmur. You don't mind?'

'Of course not. But I take it you don't feel the same as she does about your daughter?'

'No,' he said. 'I don't object to talking about Jane – quite the contrary. I'm well-known as a bore on the subject. And I want you to catch the bastards who did it.'

'Do you have any idea who it was?'

'Of course not,' he said.

'Do you suspect anyone?'

'She died in Italy, Mr Hogget,' he said. 'A country I've never visited.' It seemed my perceptiveness was slipping.

'Somebody could have set it up,' I said. 'Somebody close to her.' There was a long silence. 'No,' he said at last. 'I can't believe that.'

'Was Jane like her mother?'

'Physically you mean? Quite a lot.'

'As a person,' I said.

'Not in the least.'

'They shared the same hobby,' I said. 'Promoting talent.'

'My wife likes to hear the babbling of the intellectual young,' he said. 'She likes to hear words like integrity and sensitivity and commitment. In order to pay for this pleasure she hands out money from time to time. I make sure she doesn't hand out too much. But Jane wasn't like that – she became a promoter because she was good at it. She didn't give handouts. Maybe she did like pretentious bores too, but she knew how to control them. She made money. Her mother could never understand that.'

'How did she meet Martin Donner?'

'Millionaires meet each other all the time,' Gregory said. 'There are places for millionaires to go to – Palm Springs, Bermuda – places like that – and they go there. My wife and I are millionaires – and so is Donner. The difference is that we are poor millionaires and he's a rich one. But he never condescends.'

'You don't get on?'

I doubt if he even heard me.

'You sense a difference between Jane and her husband?' he said. 'I did, too. But he can be very attractive you know, and Jane is – was – human.'

And that was all he was prepared to say.

'Did you ever meet Frank Sokolny?' I asked.

'Once. At the theatre,' he said. 'My wife liked him.'

A bit cryptic, but I saw what he meant. I kept on pegging away. He'd sent for me, he'd told me in so many words that he'd wanted his daughter's killers caught, and yet when it came to the crunch he found it difficult, at times almost impossible, to tell me what I wanted to know. It was like pulling teeth. When I finally gave it up we were both exhausted.

'I'm sorry,' he said, 'but I loved her, you see. I still do.'

Then he showed me to the door. The musicians were at it again. From the hallway I caught a glimpse of Mrs Gregory. She looked like a shorter, older Jane.

Time to move on. First a drugstore, then a restaurant for a hamburger and a beer, and then the last call of the night. Frank Sokolny's place. He lived in a residential block in the fifties. Entry-phone, self-service lift: but with a hell of a lot more style than his boyfriend's had had. A hell of a lot better locks, too. My Swiss Army knife wouldn't have a chance – but the keys I'd lifted from Ms Milligan worked a treat. So for the second time I broke into and entered a New York apartment, put on a pair of drugstore plastic gloves... He was a designer, and everything in the apartment had been designed. What I mean was every room looked like a stage set. They were all good stage sets, but they weren't real, somehow. Except for the bedroom. There was reality there, all right.

Frank Sokolny hadn't caught his plane. His bags were packed, stacked neatly by the door, and on the dressing-table were tickets, passport, traveller's cheques, but Frank Sokolny was on the floor, staring up at the ceiling. There was a switch knife just below his ribs. Beside him, face down, lay a young man, supine yet tough, who, to judge by the angle at which his head lolled from his body, would never wrap up carnations again. 'Waiting For The Mahatma', I thought, was definitely getting to be short of assistants.

I went through the things on the dressing-table, but there was nothing there for me; just the means of leaving New York, getting to London. I wiped his door keys, added them to the collection, then tried my friendly neighbourhood flower and drug seller instead. Nothing in the pockets that I could reach, so I tucked the toe of my shoe below his ribs and levered him over. He turned with a quite audible bump, and his head lolled at a crazier angle than ever. Sokolny had been at least as strong as he looked, to break his neck like that. I thought I was going to be sick, and I still can't understand why I wasn't.

I went through his remaining pockets but he

was a careful man. He carried nothing except a few dollars in change. The only thing he had that was worth having was a piece of stiff and shiny paper in his left hand. I squatted down beside him and worked the paper loose. Even in death he didn't want to let go... It was a photograph of a girl, posing in what looked like Central Park. Just the day before the girl had sold me flowers. It was Gudrun Müller.

Behind me there came a sound that was like a sigh, and this time I didn't want to throw up, I wanted to faint. But instead I turned, looked behind me. There was nobody else in the room. I looked down. Sokolny's eyes were open. He spoke, but his voice was so soft that I couldn't hear him. I squatted beside him.

'You went to look for Goody,' he whispered.

'That's right.'

'You won't find her now.'

Then his eyes closed again. Whether he had died or not I didn't know, had no wish to know. There wasn't time. I had to leave.

I found a phone booth that worked, read the notice that told me what to do in an emergency and did it. I got the police and used my Bogart accent again.

'Frank Sokolny lives in Apartment 9, Warwick Arms, 53rd Street,' I said.

'Well I'm very glad for him,' said the desk sergeant. 'That's a nice neighbourhood. But why tell me?'

'Because he could be still alive,' I said. 'But the guy with him isn't.' Then I hung up, walked a while, ditched the plastic gloves and took a cab back to the Plaza. It came as no surprise to find Ms Milligan was waiting for me.

'Where the hell have you been?' she said.

'You're impatient,' I said. 'That's nice.'

'You've been to Frank's place, haven't you?'

She wasn't screaming. Not yet. But screams weren't all that far away. I took her arm, steered her to the lift, requested silence until we reached my room – and got to it.

'What can I get you to drink?' I asked, when the door was closed.

'I don't want a drink.'

'Oh yes you do,' I said.

In the end she had six, and finished the evening pretty near legless. It was the only way she could fight off hysterics once I'd told her what had happened. She had loved him, that was obvious, from the moment Jane had first produced him. It was equally obvious that he hadn't loved her, neither before nor after Jane's death. It was also obvious to me that she hadn't enough money ever to even hope of qualifying. Not that Sokolny hadn't loved Jane – I accepted that by then – but if she couldn't produce the money to support Mickey Wood and his habit he couldn't *afford* to love her. His had been a very complicated love-life... She knew nothing about Gudrun Müller, she said, and nothing about an Italian town called Riva del Garda. She only knew that Frank might be dead and she couldn't bear it. At last she said: 'What happens now?'

'About what?'

'About *me* for God's sake.' The words were almost a scream. Whatever she was suffering, Ms

Milligan wasn't ready for suicide. Her concern for herself was real.

'The police will maybe look at his bank account. If they do they'll find the cheque you signed. They'll come calling.'

'And what do I do?'

'Tell them you were going to send him to London to set up *Honeyfall.*' She drank Scotch from the mini-bar. Ice. No soda.

'Is that all?' she asked.

'That's all there is,' I said. 'All that concerns you anyway.'

I swear I didn't mean it to hurt her. But it did. Once again she began to cry, and once again I had to stand and watch her do it. In the end I had to get a cab to take her home. It wasn't an easy journey. Getting her into the cab, that was all right, she still seemed to have some reserves of sobriety to draw on – but getting her out of it – was something else. And the cabbie didn't wish to get involved, and I can't say I blamed him.

But I got her out at last and into her apartment. It was a walkup and she was on the second floor and she flowed around as if she was made of mercury but I got her up to where she belonged, took the keys from her bag and eased her inside.

'I don't like you,' she said, 'but you have the instincts of a gentleman. I admit that.'

'You want coffee?' I asked her.

'The room's going round,' she said. 'Help me, you fool.'

There didn't seem much I could do except hold on to her, so I did that, and she held on to me. She was nice to hold. 'You ought to lie down,' I said.

'Are you propositioning me?' she said.

'No,' I said.

'You really are a bastard,' said Cass Milligan. 'A bastard and a gentleman both.' Then she passed out cold.

So I picked her up, which wasn't easy, and carried her into her bedroom, laid her on her bed, loosened her dress. There was nothing lustful about it. I wanted her to be comfortable, to sleep, while I took a look at her apartment.

She had two rooms, kitchen and bath, and it was nice. Nothing fantastic, but nice; just right for a working girl of cultured tastes and modest means. A lot of books. Paper backs. The thick expensive kind Dave reads. That was OK. She was an intellectual – been to the same college as Jane. The books were fine. No problem. What worried me was the picture. And the carpet. The picture was an oil by Turner of what looked like a mountain pass; and it was beautiful. All colour and light. It was also expensive. A couple of years back one just like it had made over sixty thousand quid at auction. I know because a client of mine had fancied one and asked me to see if I could find one for him, only he went into liquidation before I could really get going. As for the carpet, the Swiss are into them in a big way nowadays, and I found one for this geezer in Zurich. Persian it was. Silk. What they call a Heriz. I happen to know he has it insured for eighty thousand Swiss francs – more than twenty thousand quid. It was a little smaller than the one Ms Milligan owned. Picture and carpet together worth around say eighty thousand pounds.

I went back to the bedroom and looked at her. Still out cold. Not the time to start talking about art appreciation. But at least I knew I'd been wrong about one thing. She had enough money to support Frank Sokolny after all. I went back to the living room, used the Swiss knife on her desk and went through its contents. No sign in her bank statements of a massive cheque for rugs and pictures. Salary in. Expenses out. Month after month. No diary. No drugs. Bills all in order. Receipts too. But not for a Turner oil, a Persian Heriz rug ... One other item of interest though. Or rather a stack of them. Brochures from real estate agents, with certain properties marked. Not in the United States, and not in the UK either. Snug, smart little places on the Mediterranean coast: France, Italy or Spain. Nothing grand, but nothing humble either. The sort of place where a girl on her own could be very comfortable, if she had the eighty to a hundred thousand dollars the villas cost. I put it all back, left everything as I found it, and took one final look at Ms Milligan. I doubt if she'd moved six inches. She was snoring, and by morning she'd have a hangover I'd be glad wasn't mine, but at least she was out of things for the moment, and it was just as well. There'd been more reasons for her insecurity than I'd realized.

Time to go home... The city that never sleeps, as the song says, though by half past one in the morning it can be dozing a little. Still, just for luck, I took a peep out of the window. There were two men in the street below. Now it could have been nothing. They were sitting on the stoop of the house opposite, and they were talking, and it was a hot night, and on hot nights in New York people do sit on the stoop and chat. But they were watching the street as they talked, and they looked young and hard: I wanted no part of them.

I left Ms Milligan's drawing room light on, and went into the kitchen, where the fire escape was, and in the darkness let myself out and began an upward, not downward climb. If the fellers below wished me harm, they could well have an ally at the foot of the fire-escape. I doubted if they'd have anybody on the roof, and I was right. The darkness was the only friend I had, except when I had to jump from one flat roof to the next, but it was the only way I could go, weaving my way along clothes-lines and flowerpots and sun-loungers, one of them occupied by a frantically grappling couple who didn't even know I'd passed them by, till I had almost reached the corner of street and avenue. I climbed down into a pool of shadow and walked briskly to the avenue without getting mugged, called my fifth cab of the day and went back to the Plaza once more.

As I went into the lift I was shaking. When I opened my room door I had to dash to the bathroom to throw up and only just made it in time. Until that day I had never seen a dead man; by now, the way Sokolny had looked, I had probably seen two, and if I hadn't been so good at jumping I might have become a third, or rather fourth. I was forgetting Mickey Wood. When my stomach relented a little I took a cautious sip of water, cleaned up the bathroom, undressed, lay on my bed – and couldn't sleep. I wanted out. People were dying, and I might be one of them. This wasn't my game. No way.

The sensible thing would be to go home, but that would mean passing up on a hundred thousand dollars... Or would it? Maybe the time had come to pursue my enquiries somewhere else. Somewhere quieter, more peaceful, more like home. And then if I still didn't manage to come up with the goods at least Donner had paid me half my fee. I got up, checked that my door was locked and the chain bolt on, and went back to bed. This time I slept.

Next morning over breakfast I considered the idea again – which is the only sensible thing to do when you've been inspired in the middle of the night – and it still made sense. I'd got all I could from Sokolny, Ms Milligan, Dr Gregory, even Mickey Wood – and there weren't any other leads in New York. In London, there just might be. It was time to go and find out. And in any case, it was impossible for me to stay where I was. I was too scared. So I phoned the airline and got lucky. They had a Business Class cancellation for that afternoon. I took it and called Bergdorf-Goodman about a dark red dress I'd seen advertised, and asked if they had a size twelve and they had. It cost two hundred and eighty five dollars, which caused a pang, but Melanie looks fabulous in dark red, so I asked if they could deliver it to the Plaza in exchange for cash, and they could, so that was OK. Then I phoned Ms Milligan. All I got at the Donner apartment was the answering machine, so I tried her number instead. What I got there was a groan.

'Ms Milligan? Are you all right?' I asked.

'Ask me again in a couple of months,' she said. 'Did you bring me home?'

'I did.'

'Thank you for that anyway. Do you want to go to Jane's place? I honestly don't think I could make it this morning—'

'That's all right,' I said. 'As it happens I'm going back to London.'

'London?' she said, then groaned again. I assumed she'd sat up too quickly.

'There's a lead I want to follow,' I said. 'Don't worry about letting Mr Donner know. I'll send him a cable. You stay in bed and rest.' She still didn't like it.

'But listen,' she said. 'Won't you need to pick up photographs and stuff from Jane's?'

'I did that the first day I went to the apartment,' I said.

She got mad. 'Who said you could do that?' she said.

'Martin Donner,' I told her. 'Don't lose your temper, Ms Milligan. 'You're not nearly strong enough yet. You've got my London address if you need me.' Then I hung up.

I went to Kennedy in style in a chauffeur-driven limousine that picked me up at the Plaza and delivered me right to the terminal, not because I felt stylish but because I was afraid. But the airline officials were nice and the immigration officials were nasty and at the end of it all I was in the private lounge drinking bourbon and beginning to believe I was safe. Safe enough anyway to go over what I'd got in my mind, until the flight was called, then again on the Jumbo while the Japanese beside me worked out interminable sums on a calculator...

Gudrun Müller now. A link with Mickey Wood and Sokolny and therefore perhaps with Jane, too. Maybe even Donner himself. A link with Austria, and therefore perhaps with Italy. Find her and the case was solved. But how could I find her? She'd gone and disappeared, and people foolish enough to know her became dead, and people foolish enough to look for her maybe became targets for Chevrolets and possibly hit men on foot as well. All the same, there was a chance I'd still have to look for her, but next time I'd take a bit of company with me...

The stewardess brought round late editions of the paper. The Japanese went on with his calculating, but I took one. It was on page seven. 'Double Kill on 53rd Street', it said. And again there was a picture, but this time there weren't any corpses. Just the scene of the crime. The Murder Bedroom, the paper called it. I read the account. Detective Pardoe was in charge of the investigation. The deceased who owned the property was a man of great talent in the theatre, Detective Pardoe said. The other deceased, one Arthur Hoyt, had a criminal record. The reason he was in Sokolny's place appeared to be robbery. The two men must have killed each other almost simultaneously. It was a sad loss to the theatre, Detective Pardoe said. And to the heroin business too, I thought. But the way I read it the case was closed. The NYPD had enough to do investigating the living...

The stewardess brought me another bourbon and I considered Dr Gregory. He hadn't told me a lot, except that he was proud of his daughter, because of her success, and ashamed of her because she'd had a lover – or maybe two – and that she had succeeded where her mother had failed. And that he didn't like her husband. Of course he mightn't have liked her husband whoever he had been – straightforward daddy's girl stuff – but I didn't think it was that. He didn't like Donner and he didn't think anybody else liked him either, and yet his beloved daughter had married him... And one other thing. Like her mother, Jane enjoyed the company of what he called pretentious bores, which seemed to mean intellectuals... He'd wanted his daughter's murderers caught, he said, but he'd said it the way Melanie says she'd like to win the pools. And yet he'd invited me over to see him. The only reason I could think of for his lack of cooperation was that he'd taken one look at me and decided I hadn't a hope in hell of succeeding, which wasn't very flattering. I was glad when they brought the food round – and after that it was the movie and it was Streisand and Redford again, so I had a bit of a kip.

At Heathrow it was raining, no novelty, and anyway I had a collapsible umbrella in my zip contraption. I also had a two-suiter and a suitcase to cope with so I hired a porter and went through the green and phoned Melanie. It was only in the taxi on the way home that I remembered her dress from Bergdorf-Goodman. Preoccupied, you see. I'd been preoccupied. By deaths and kidnapping and things. All the same – I didn't like taking chances in what you might call an amateur sort of way. Presents for the wife and that. It interfered with my professional life – might even cut my luck a bit. It wouldn't have done any good to start a fuss, have my name taken.

But Melanie would look good in that dress, no question. She'd been excited when I'd called, too. I could tell by her voice. 'Why didn't you let me know sooner? I could have had my hair done. How long'll it take you to get here?' All that... It doesn't take long to get to Fulham. Not really. Down the Cromwell Road then over to World's End and keep going because that's where Fulham is – just beyond World's End. Still there's worse places. I mean I know it's full of villains but you get villains everywhere nowadays. And it's not all like that. My place for instance, Melanie's and mine. Nice little house. Two up two down but cosy if you see what I mean. Bathroom and shower. Bit of garden front and back. Mine was all roses in the front. In the back was lettuce, tomatoes, spring onions, radish. Melanie's very fond of a bit of salad on account of her figure.

I paid off the cab and she was out of the door and coming to meet me and grabbing at the two-suiter, rain or no rain, then she took my hand and raced me down the path and into the house and she kissed me as if I'd been away a twelvemonth, and I knew I had to make that hundred grand, risks or no risks.

'Let me look at you,' she said.

I looked at her. Very dark hair, very pale skin, big brown eyes. I think she's beautiful. But then

I would, being in love with her...

'Have you been sleeping all right?' she said.

A lot of people have the idea Melanie's not too bright, but when it comes to knowing what I've been up to she's right every time.

'I've been busy,' I said. 'You wouldn't believe how busy I've been.'

'I hope it was worth it.'

'Cash on delivery,' I said. Actually it was a cheque, but the principle's the same.

'Oh lovely,' Melanie said. 'Now we can take a holiday.' She put her arms round me again. 'Wouldn't you like that, Ronnie?'

'You know I would,' I said. 'Only I've got this other job...'

*'Already?'*

'The same geezer,' I said. 'There's something else he wants me to look into.' She looked disappointed. I can't stand it when she looks disappointed. 'It's worth a lot of money, love.'

But I didn't tell her how much. I never did, and thank God she never asked. Sort of an agreement we'd arrived at.

'I got you a present,' I said, and opened the two-suiter.

The dress rang the bell all right. She loved it as soon as she saw it, and couldn't wait to try it on. Nipped straight upstairs to the bedroom. And I went with her. It was great to be back home.

# 6

It wasn't until the next day that I began to get back to work, and not all that early the next day either. Melanie kept saying I needed a rest, then she wouldn't let me have one. But in the end I had to make a start. A hundred grand. A hundred K, the computer men call it. When I'd got that in the bank, then we'd take a holiday. My God we would. Maybe even start a family. In the meantime we ate brunch – eggs and bacon, peaches, bottles of Sainsbury's sparkling – and I thought about A. D. Carr. Anthony Donald Carr. About my age by the look of him. Maybe a bit younger. Been on the telly a couple of times – arts programmes – but I hadn't seen him. Not all that keen on the telly, to tell the truth. He'd also written four novels people said were good. Lived over in Shepherd's Bush. That could mean anything: a Georgian house to a heap of rubble.

'You want the car today?' I said to Melanie.

'I said I'd go over to mum's,' she said. Her mum lives in Wood Green, miles away. They should run a helicopter service. 'But if you need it—'

'No,' I said. 'You have it.' Mr Donner was paying...

But all it cost him was a couple of bus rides. One to Kensington, then change for the Bush. That's what the locals call it. Sometimes they're not far wrong. Where A. D. Carr lived for instance. A long row of houses pleading to be condemned. What they call an ethnic mix of people. About half and half, from what I could see; but the blacks mostly a lot younger than the whites. Soon the whites would go. It was a bright clear day and the sun shone – not so hot as New York, but cleaner, clearer, and that only made it worse: the bright, pure light showing up the rotting brick, the tired, dried out woodwork.

Alongside me black kids and a few whites whizzed round on chopper bikes or roller skates; trannies blared. Mostly it was reggae; here and there hard rock. There were cars parked all the way up the street, nose to tail. But this wasn't the affluent society. The cars were the mobile equivalents of the houses, and my guess was there'd be two or three cars to a house. A family that owned more than two rooms in this disaster area would be reckoned to be plutocrats...

I looked out for number seventy-three, Carr's number. Over brunch it had seemed a good idea to turn up without warning, charge right in. I'd figured even if he was out I could do a recce, chat up the neighbours. Find out about him ... I wouldn't chat up these neighbours. Whatever approach I used they would know I was the filth, and that meant they wouldn't tell me a thing, on principle, not even if A. D. Carr had just raped their sister... All I could do was hope he was in.

Number seventy-three had two cars and a motor-bike outside it. The motor-bike looked worth about four times as much as both cars put together – and there were three dustbins on the narrow strip of ground between the railings and the window. So the house had three tenants. There was no point in calling the strip of ground a garden. Nothing grew. I went up the cracked steps and looked for doorbells. There weren't any, so I tried the door-knocker. I knocked hard enough to shake the door, and a young pretty black woman appeared and looked at me reproachfully.

'You got to be gentle,' the black woman said. 'These doors are old. Who d'you want?'

'Mr Carr,' I said.

'He's busy,' she said, in a voice that implied that I should know that.

'It's important,' I said. 'Please let me see him.'

'Not before five-thirty,' she said. 'That's the rule.'

'I came all the way from New York,' I said. 'Just yesterday.'

'From New York? To see A.D.?' She liked that very much. 'Maybe I better tell him.'

'I think you should,' I said. 'Tell him it's about Mrs Donner.'

She didn't like that at all – the idea of another woman's involvement – but she went upstairs and I stood in the hall that was very clean, and smelt only of soul-food and pot. After a couple of minutes she yelled down the stairs: 'A.D. says come up.'

I gathered that what A.D. said went, so I climbed the stairs and she nodded to a half-open door and left me to it.

A. D. Carr was another muscular egg-head, but in a different way from Sokolny. It had seemed to me that Sokolny had looked strong because he

103

went to a gym, lifted weights, did press-ups. A. D. Carr looked strong because he *was* strong. He was born that way and he would die that way. Not too tall, very broad, with a face that had seen a lot of hard wear in its time. He was standing beside a roll-top desk that looked the most expensive thing in the room. The rest – table, two chairs, fridge – might have been bought at a jumble sale – but the roll-top was solid and gleaming. On it there was an A4 size notebook covered in small, neat writing.

'I'm A. D. Carr,' he said. 'Violet didn't give me your name.'

'Ronnie Hogget,' I said. 'I came from New York–'

'About Jane Donner?'

'That's right.'

'What about her, Mr Hogget?'

'Her husband's hired me to find out who killed her.'

'Good Lord,' he said. 'Do I find myself in the presence of a private eye?'

'Well – yes,' I said. 'Do you mind if I ask you a few questions?'

'It'll be fascinating,' he said.

I didn't like that. I was looking for killers, not providing copy for a telly show. 'Your house-keeper seemed to think you wouldn't want to be disturbed,' I said.

'Housekeeper? Oh, Violet ... I suppose you could call her that. These are my working hours, Mr Hogget, usually they are sacred. But for a private investigator...' He made a gesture that seemed to bestow the freedom of the city. 'Go ahead.'

Then he motioned me to a chair and sat down

facing me as if he was in the front row of the stalls. I didn't like this one bit.

'You met Mrs Donner because of a magazine?' I said.

'We met at a publisher's party. A man I knew had just published a book on Gide. There was a chance I might review it. She was there.'

There was a sort of depth to those last three words – it could have been delight, it could have been despair – that I'd never heard before in a man's voice. 'You got on well?'

'From the beginning. She took me to dinner at Le Bressan.'

'She took you?'

'A dinner for two at Le Bressan costs about sixty quid if you order a decent wine. Do I look as if I've got sixty quid for dinner – or anything else?'

'No,' I said. 'You don't.'

He grinned.

'She must have liked you,' I said.

'Well of course she liked me. Sixty quid's a lot of money.'

'Your stuff gets published.'

'Occasionally.'

'And you go on the telly–'

'Every chance I get. There aren't all that many. I see what you're driving at, Mr Hogget. I get paid so why shouldn't I buy the food and wine? A perfectly tenable male-chauvinist view. The thing is, Mr Hogget, that I don't get paid enough. Showing off on the telly just about covers my rent here, and food, and the insurance on my bike. Writing – my kind of writing – wouldn't keep me in cigarettes. That's why I don't smoke.'

'Why d'you keep the bike?' I asked.

'You're bloody nosey,' he said.

'Well of course I am, I get paid for it,' I said. 'Anyway, it'll help me to know about you.'

'You'd better watch that,' he said, and relaxed again. 'It might turn you into a novelist. Good question, though. Why do I keep the bike?... I like to travel a lot, Mr Hogget. Camp out, sleep rough, all that. And the bike's the only way I can afford it. Next question?'

'What did you talk about? At dinner?'

'Me,' he said. 'It's my best subject.'

'What about you?'

'What a good writer I was. Then she reduced me to silence. She said she knew it, and she said it without irony. Then she asked me to write a couple of pieces for *Vistas* – that's the magazine she was starting here.'

'What kind of pieces?'

'The kind I usually write. Short, convoluted, incredibly difficult pieces of narrative. She offered me two hundred and fifty a piece for them. Usually I'm lucky if I get twenty-five.'

'She must have liked you very much,' I said.

'Don't presume on my good nature,' he said, then after a bit: 'Yes. She did. She liked my work. She wanted to publish it – but she could have got it a hell of a lot cheaper than she did. Ergo she liked me.'

'Was Frank Sokolny with her at the party? Or at dinner?'

'No to both,' he said.

'Mrs Donner was a friend of Sokolny's.'

'So she told me.'

'He says he met you.'

'In that particular instance he did not lie.'

'You don't like him?'

'He was jealous of me,' said Carr. 'A situation somewhat complicated by the fact that he fancied me as well.'

'He made a pass?'

'Just the once,' Carr said, and I believed him.

'Were you ever a boxer?' I asked.

His hand went to his face.

'Briefly and ingloriously,' he said. 'But not any more. Now I'm merely a brawler – if I'm forced into violence. Sokolny didn't force me.'

'Sokolny's dead,' I said, and he froze.

'Very good,' he said at last. 'Excellent in fact. You had me off balance for a moment.'

'It's true,' I said. 'He was murdered in his apartment two days ago. Believe me.'

'I believe you,' he said, 'and it's still good. I'm bothered again.'

'Why? You didn't kill him.'

'You can't be a hundred per cent sure. But of course you're right. Two days ago I was here. Writing my convoluted prose, eating Violet's soul food.'

'Then why be bothered?'

'I hated him,' he said. 'I wanted him to die. Now you tell me I've got my wish. It bothers me.'

'You were jealous of him?'

'About Jane? No... He was jealous of me.'

It wasn't what Sokolny had said, but I let it pass.

'What then?'

'It was after Jane died. I think maybe Sokolny

107

helped kill her.' He paused, then looked at me. I didn't react.

'I'm listening,' I said. 'How did he help kill her?'

'It starts with a girl called Gudrun Müller.'

This time I did react.

'I see you've heard of her,' said Carr. 'You'll know about that little fairy that runs around with Sokolny?'

'Mickey Wood?'

'That's right. He's on the needle.'

'You met him over here?'

'New York,' he said. 'Jane took me to New York and Paris. She wanted me to meet people. Her kind of people.'

'What kind are they?'

'Publishers, producers, backers. Angels do they call them?'

'You didn't like them?'

'They like to tell you about how they're creative too. I don't mind if they pay me for it.' He scowled at me. 'You make me digress. I met Mickey Wood at Sokolny's place. He took us to a party. Goody Müller was there. Goody...'

'You knew she was Mickey's pusher?'

'They looked intimate, you know. Sort of cosy. It couldn't be sex. I think I knew straight away.'

'And Jane was there?'

'She and Goody got on from the word go.' He scowled. 'Mickey's pusher – and Jane.'

'Mickey's dead too,' I said.

His head moved then, chin tucked in, eyes wary, and I saw how he must have looked when he was a fighter.

'Near his place in the Village,' I said. 'Beaten and stabbed. The night before Sokolny died.'

'I hated Mickey, too,' he said. 'He introduced Goody to Jane. Was it muggers?'

'That's the theory.'

'Theory's a cautious word. What about Goody Müller? Don't tell me she's dead too?'

'Disappeared,' I said.

'Of course she did.' He got up, went to the roll-top desk and took out a bottle of white spirit, two chipped but gleaming glasses. 'Rum's all I've got,' he said. 'Will it do you?'

'Fine,' I said. I hate rum.

'Goody got very close to Jane,' he said, and sipped at his drink.

'It was like a Victorian melodrama or something. She even got Jane believing she'd repented of her wicked ways. Only—'

'Only what?'

'She said she was still on the stuff. Couldn't break the habit.'

'And Jane offered to help her?'

'I told her not to get involved. I often do that. Tell people not to get involved, I mean. But Jane was all for involvement. And now she's dead.'

'You think there's a connection with Goody?'

'There's a doctor Jane knew of. The only one who could bring off a cure, she said. And Jane was the only one who had the money. But she didn't mind spending it so that was OK. The trouble was her – occupation. Not minding the shop – peddling the dope. Her bosses weren't all that keen on accepting her resignation, she said. To the point where they would inflict pain on her if she tried it.'

'So it didn't work?'

'Please,' he said. 'Allow my narrative to develop. Jane was an organizer. She made things happen. One day Goody Müller walked out of her flower-shop and disappeared – I'm told – into Canada. Three days later she was sharing my austere bachelor quarters before setting off with Jane to visit her doctor.'

'Where?'

'She grew coy on the subject,' said Carr. 'She didn't say. And Jane had promised that she wouldn't either. You haven't touched your rum.'

I sipped to be sociable, and it took me by the throat and twisted and I gasped.

'I'm sorry,' said Carr. 'I should have warned you. Violet gets it from her brother.'

'From Jamaica?' I croaked.

'Wolverhampton,' he said.

When my voice came back I said, 'It's a nice story.'

'Glad you like it.'

'There's only one little thing wrong with it,' I said. 'Goody Müller disappeared the same day Mickey Wood was killed – three days ago.'

'That's really quite a problem,' he said, and grinned. 'I'm glad it isn't mine.'

'So that's it?' I said.

'Don't be greedy,' he said. 'I've given you quite a lot. And all of it true.'

'I wonder why?' I said.

'I want you to find the bastards. I want them destroyed.' He drank more rum. I did not.

'You know about the kidnap?' he said.

110

'I've read about it.'

'I was very nearly in on it.' He looked at my face, and laughed. 'Not as protagonist. As victim. I was in Paris with her when she said she was going to Riva. She wanted me to go with her. I couldn't. I'd just got a telly.' He made it sound like hives.

'Why did she decide to go?'

'She wouldn't tell me. What did the papers say?'

'She jetted to Milan. Drove on to Riva.'

'Jet-setters don't do that. They jet to Rome, or Venice, or Taormina maybe. Riva's for the bourgeoisie – the peasants even.'

'Then why do you think she went?'

He shrugged. 'I got the feeling somebody she knew had asked her. Somebody she knew well.'

'Sokolny?'

'She'd hardly have asked to me go too, would she?'

I found I was blushing: not because of sexual shame, but stupidity.

'Mind you I could have gone,' he said. 'I had the bike with me. Wouldn't even take a day.'

'You had a telly to do,' I said.

'Not till three days later,' said Carr.

'Why are you telling me all this?'

'You'll think it anyway,' he said. 'You're a detective... Who lifted her? Professionals?'

'They asked for a million,' I said. 'That sounds like professionals.'

'The Red Brigade's short of funds too,' he said.

'Are you into politics?'

'Politics would be bad for my prose style,' he

111

said. 'I just listen to the news on the radio.'

'If it had been the Red Brigade,' I said, 'they'd have issued statements, shown pictures, made tapes, maybe even videotapes. All that happened was that Donner was asked for a million and he paid and they – reneged on the deal.'

'Cut her head off,' he said, and drank. 'Why would pros do that?'

'Why do you think?'

'Maybe it wasn't her.'

'It's her,' I said.

'Who says so?'

'Donner,' I said.

He sighed and finished his rum and I offered him mine. He poured it into his glass. 'I shan't work any more today,' he said.

'I'm sorry.'

'Not your fault. As a matter of fact I enjoyed talking to you. You're a new sort of person for me. Tricky. I'll get you. But it'll be tricky... Like Jane. Did I tell you she paid me more money for a story than I'd ever made in my life?'

I left him to brood. Money, love and what he called convoluted prose would stand a lot of brooding...

Halfway down the street I heard the sound of running footsteps. In that neighbourhood it was not an agreeable sound, and I looked behind me. It was Violet. I waited till she caught me up. She looked mad.

'You been upsetting A.D.,' she said.

'I assure you,' I said, 'I–'

'Don't you give me no shit, man,' she said. 'He's locked his door.'

This, I gathered, was bad. Very bad.

'All we did was talk,' I said. 'He *wanted* to talk.'

'About wonderful Jane?'

'You don't think she's wonderful?'

'No,' she said. 'I don't. I think A.D.'s wonderful.'

Suddenly and without warning she began to cry. Three black youths wearing dreadlocks drifted towards us and I felt far from happy.

'You all right, Violet?' said one.

'I'm OK,' she said.

'Whitey bothering you?' said the second.

They waited for her answer and so did I. It was important to me.

'No,' she said. 'He's not bothering me. He just come to help A.D. with a problem.'

'Then what you crying for?' said the third.

'I can cry if I want to,' she said. 'They're my eyes.'

The three Rastafarians shook their dreadlocks in bewilderment and went off laughing.

'Thank you,' I said.

'I told the truth,' she said. 'You weren't bothering me. Was A.D. drinking?'

'We had some rum,' I said, and the tears welled again. 'It was because of Mrs Donner.'

'I know that,' she said.

Why didn't you like her?' I asked.

'She took A.D. away from me,' she said.

'But he's back now.'

'He's not the same A.D.,' she said.

She was looking restless. I pressed on while there was time. 'How did you like Gudrun Müller?' I said.

'I don't know anyone by that name.'

'Goody,' I said. 'A.D. put her up for a while.'

'Poor cow,' she said. 'Goody wouldn't hurt a fly. How could she? The habit she had...'

'How long have you known A.D.?' I asked.

'Four years.'

'Where did you meet him?'

She looked straight at me. There were no more tears in her eyes: only distaste. 'Now you're beginning to bother me,' she said, and I left her at once. She'd given me enough. And anyway I'd decided to call on my sister. Another impulse...

# 7

My sister lives in Putney, nice part, quiet, near the river. She'd married a bloke called Sydney Muspratt, which made her Anna Maria Muspratt, her being called after our mother. I took a cab to her place, but even so it gave me a bit of time to think. About A. D. Carr, mostly. In a weird kind of way I liked him. I didn't always understand him, but I liked him. I suppose, him being an intellectual, it was strange that I understood him as much as I did. I don't mean his answers to the questions – I understood them all right. It was the man himself I could understand sometimes. Because he could be so sensible. There's not too many eggheads I've met you could say that of – at least not the ones I met... The taxi put me off outside my sister's place. Nice little house – Sydney's an assistant bank manager, doing all right – and I walked up the path and rang the bell.

She was there in a flash – moves like greased lightning, my sister – but she didn't seem all that keen to see me. Just stood in the doorway and goggled.

'Tommaso,' she said. Of all the family, she's the only one who calls me by my first name. Very Italian, my sister.

'Got it in one,' I said. 'All right if I come in?'

She hesitated, then shrugged. The shrug was very Italian indeed, just like our mamma.

'Of course,' she said. 'If you want. Dad's here.'

'Oh,' I said. Dad and I don't get on. Dad and Anna Maria don't get on, come to that, but you'd need machine guns to keep him away, especially when he needs a few bob for the boozer.

'How is he?'

She made another very Italian gesture. Our surviving parent, I gathered, was pissed.

'You want me to go?' I asked.

'Of course not,' she said. 'It's just – you know what he's like.'

She stood to one side and I went in and she nodded towards the sitting-room. Our dad was sitting in the best chair, a cup of tea in one hand, a sandwich in the other, glaring at the telly. England were a hundred for three, Botham taking strike.

'Who was it?' he said.

'It was me,' I said.

He turned to glare at me.

'So we're back, are we?' he said. 'Flown back to connubial bliss, have we?'

'That's right, dad.'

If I let him get me mad, I'd lose, and we both

knew it.

'I had my share of connubial bliss,' dad said. 'You both stand there to prove it. Where's your proof, son?'

There was a sort of genteel roar from the crowd, and a spatter of applause. 'Hell,' said father. 'What happened?'

'Botham pushed Hadlee through the covers for four,' I said. 'One of the best strokes I've seen him make this season.'

My father grinned at me, not with affection.

'You know how to make people miserable,' he said. 'You get it from me. Now push off. We'll have a word at close of play.'

I followed Anna Maria out to her kitchen. Very Italian, Anna Maria's kitchen. Dried herbs, garlic, machine for making pasta. She's got the lot. But then mamma had taught her to cook. I wish she'd taught Melanie.

'Tea? Coffee? A drink,' she said. 'There's some white wine.'

'Wine, please,' I said, and she got a bottle of Soave out of the fridge. 'How's the kids?'

'Doing all right,' she said. 'They're at a birthday party. I'll have to fetch them at six.'

'I won't keep you,' I said.

She flushed. 'I didn't mean that,' she said. 'It's – you know.'

'He gets no better, does he?' I said.

'If I hadn't brought him in and given him a sandwich he'd have fallen over,' she said. 'I couldn't just turn him away.'

'What's he so mad at me for?'

'He wanted to borrow money from you and you

116

were in America.'

'Who told him?'

'Your mate Dave.'

'Oh, yeah... He lives in the next block to Dave – if they haven't thrown him out.'

'Not yet.'

'Why doesn't he get a job?'

'Have a heart,' Anna Maria said. 'Who would employ him?'

A good question. Until a few years ago my father had owned a corner shop, but after he killed my mother he decided the supermarkets were killing him, so he sold out to a bunch of Ugandan Asians. They're making a fortune, while dad keeps the brewers happy... Anna Maria handed me a glass.

'How was New York?' she asked.

'Hotter than here,' I said. 'Too hot.'

'I wouldn't mind being in Verona,' Anna Maria said.

Verona was mamma's home town. We've got about nine thousand relatives there.

'I may be going,' I said.

'If you do can you bring me some fresh basil back,' she said. 'And go and see Uncle Pietro, too. Last I heard he's very worried about cousin Adriana.'

It was cousin Adriana I wanted to know about.

'She still a student?' I asked.

'Yes ... Padua.'

'What's she study?'

Anna Maria shrugged once more. It was the shrug which had first enslaved Sydney Muspratt.

'Sociology would it be? I don't know. Adriana's a very clever girl.'

117

'Who says so?'

'Her mother.'

I don't know whether Anna Maria was serious or not. I often don't.

'Has she got a feller?'

'Of course not,' said Anna Maria. 'She's a *student.*' I still didn't know if she was serious.

'Why's Uncle Pietro worried?' I asked.

'She doesn't study enough. She wastes too much time on politics.'

'The Red Brigade?'

'Talk,' my sister said. 'Nothing but talk. Talk all the time. It's why she doesn't study. How's Melanie?'

'She's fine,' I said.

'Good.'

From an English sister that would have been OK, but my sister's Italian. You expect more than just one word if your sister's Italian. I wondered if they'd quarrelled. 'You seen her recently?' I asked.

'No,' she said. 'I phoned her a couple of times. Didn't she tell you?'

'Give her time,' I said. 'I just got back.'

From the sitting-room there came a television roar. Botham must have hit a six at least. I looked at my watch. Ten minutes till close of play.

'I'd better be off,' I said. 'I don't think I'm in the mood for a chat with dad.'

'You better slip him a few quid,' Anna Maria said. 'He'll be an awful nuisance if you don't.'

I passed her a tenner. 'You give it to him,' I said. 'I'll let myself out.'

But she wasn't having that, not Anna Maria. She took me to the back door, walked with me to

118

the gate.

'Where's your car?' she said.

'Melanie's got it,' I said. 'She went to see her mum.'

'I see,' she said. 'Tell her I was asking after her.'

Not like my sister at all.

I went to see Dave. Bit of a treat that, going to see my mate Dave. Things were always easy with Dave. No hassles. He didn't believe in them. The quiet life, that was what Dave believed in. We'd been at school together for a bit – only Dave went to the grammar school and I didn't. Still we saw each other in the evenings. Funny thing was I could lick him in those days. I was stronger than him. A bit older too... Then dad thought I'd got enough education – after all I could do joined up writing and say my twelve times – and let me come and help him and mum in the shop, which meant mum and me did the work and he went down the boozer; and Dave stayed on at the grammar. 'O' Levels, 'A' Levels, the works. He even went to university. Leeds it was. But we still saw each other in the vacations, which was what he called his holidays. Months and months he used to get, only he had to take on jobs of course, him being skint all the time. The birds he fancied cost a fortune... Then he graduated. David Baxter, BA, second class honours in English Literature, and it dawned on him he'd have to be a teacher. Like a thunderclap, he said it was: a shock of recognition. Good with words, is Dave. He helped me with all this stuff I'm writing down – when I let him. I said surely he must have known when he went to the university what he was in for and he said when he went to the university he didn't know a bloody thing except it was a marvellous opportunity to read all the books he wanted, and get a government grant for doing it. Then three years later his time was up and the teaching was waiting. Only he just didn't fancy it.

He joined the army instead. Paratroopers. By then he was a big, strong feller. Clean cut, as they say. The army were delighted to oblige. He didn't even join as an officer. Just signed on to learn how to jump out of aircraft and blow people's brains out. Or beat them out. Very strong on unarmed combat, the paratroopers

We used to spend all his leaves together. He was best man when I married Melanie... Then his time was up and he took his discharge, and I asked him what he was going to do next and he said as little as possible. So he became a mini-cab driver.

Don't think I'm knocking mini-cab drivers. It's just that in that particular line of business you can work as much – or as little – as you want. Dave didn't want much; just enough to pay his overheads and buy a few lagers. Once a year he'd really slog for a bit then disappear on holiday; weird places. Thailand, Norway. The Loire Valley. Then he'd come home and sit in the boozer and read a book. Always a book, never a newspaper.

He was there that evening I went in. Usual place, half a lager in front of him, big heavy book in one hand, fag in the other. I think it was *The Brothers Karamazov* that time. By Dostoyevsky. He put it down as soon as he saw me, went over to the bar and bought me a gin and tonic.

'Ron boy,' he said. 'Great to see you.'

'Great to be back,' I said. 'How you doing?'

'Mustn't grumble,' he said. The work's there if I need it. You busy?'

'Too true,' I said.

'It suits you,' he said. 'You were born to be busy, Ron. Not like me. What are you finding this time?'

'An American gentleman's lost his wife,' I told him, and that's all I told him. Best mates is one thing. Business is another. Tell him when he was in and not before.

'Careless of him,' he said. 'Does it pay well?'

'Handsomely,' I said. His sort of word, but I've been mates with Dave so long some of it's rubbed off on me. Anyway, I do try to improve myself. It's part of getting on... He took a pull at his lager.

'I somehow get the idea you've come to ask me something,' he said.

Don't ask me how he does it because I don't know, but he can always tell when I want him to do a job for me. Every time.

'I might be needing a driver,' I said. '*And* a minder.' As I say, I always ask Dave when I need muscle. I know plenty of that sort of talent round where I live, but Dave's the one you could trust.

'Usual rates?' he said.

'No,' I said. 'Hundred a day. Guaranteed five days' minimum if I use you at all. Plux exes of course.'

'It must be dangerous,' Dave said.

I tried to make my voice sound casual, like his. 'The client's rich,' I said.

'I could just do with five hundred,' Dave said. 'I fancy a trip to the Dordogne.'

I couldn't answer that: I didn't even know where the Dordogne was; so I bought another round instead.

'You'll let me know soon?' he said.

'Soon as I get back from Paris,' I said.

'You taking Melanie to Paris?'

'I wish I was,' I said. 'This is work.'

'You shouldn't leave her alone so much,' Dave said.

'Chance would be a fine thing,' I said. But I knew he was right. Melanie always could get lonely.

'How is she by the way?'

'She's fine,' I said.

'You're a lucky man, Ron.'

'I know it,' I said, and gulped at the gin and tonic.

'What's the rush?' said Dave.

I remembered my dad's word.

'Connubial bliss,' I said, and Dave nodded.

I emptied my glass.

'I'll be seeing you, Dave.'

'You know where to find me,' said Dave. 'Have a nice bliss.'

But it wouldn't be quite the way my old man had meant it. There wouldn't be any kids. I wanted them, but Melanie didn't. It used to sadden me. As a matter of fact it still does...

The bliss lasted two days, which isn't bad for bliss. In fact it's pretty good. After that I had to go to Paris. A lot of people think that's bliss too, oo-la-la and Gay Paree and all that, and maybe it is if your idea of bliss is the Crazy Horse Saloon, but not for me. For me Paris meant work, and work meant Jane Donner.

I flew first class and I drank champagne all the way on account of Mr Donner's image, then I took a cab to the Banque Vattier, which is just round the corner from the Bourse: dead handy if you want to check your stocks and shares. Banks like the Banque Vattier are the nearest the French get to our merchant banks: nothing vulgar, like cheque-books for the masses: just a quick twenty or thirty million if you want to build a new factory... It was Donner's bank, maybe quite literally. Maybe he'd bought it. Anyway when I walked inside and asked for M. Auriol I was there in minutes – and all because I'd phoned and told the banque who had sent me.

The banque was big, dark, old; not gloomy, just serious, because the French take their money seriously. Monsieur Auriol's room was also big and dark and old, but not M. Auriol. He was fortyish – which is young by bank standards, small and spry. But he had the eyes that go with the job: eyes that tell you nothing – unless you want money. Then they tell you no. He got up to greet me and shook hands and made a fuss, and said we must have lunch and I agreed. The room oozed wealth the way an orange oozes juice. The desk, the chairs, the paintings – it all meant money. Big money. If Auriol didn't belong to the Vattier family, he'd married one. I handed over Donner's letter of authorization, and Auriol read it, then read it again, handed it back.

'A tragic business,' he said. His voice had a very

slight American accent.

'Tragic,' I said.

'A young and beautiful woman. And charming,' he said.

'You met her?'

'Only once. At the Josselin ball. But it was sufficient for me to appreciate her very special quality.'

'Who was she with?' I said.

'I beg your pardon?'

'At the ball? Who was her partner?'

'You must forgive me,' he said. 'My memory is not very good.'

M. Auriol could remember how many francs he'd spent on bus fares twelve years ago, but bankers hate to give anything for nothing. They call it being discreet.

'Where will you stay?' he asked.

'At the flat,' I said.

'Mme Donner's flat?' Not M. Donner's, I thought. Not even when madame was dead.

'That's right.'

He didn't like it, letting the peasantry in, but there wasn't much he could do about it, except what I told him, which was to hand over the keys and phone the concierge and tell her I was coming. Then we went out to lunch.

I thought he'd take me to the Ritz or somewhere flash in the Bois du Boulogne or something. Not him. Bankers know better than that. We went to a little place round the corner, as dark and gloomy and old as the Banque Vattier, a place stuffed with bankers, where I ate some of the best food I've ever tasted, then M. Auriol took me back to the bank to collect my case, summoned a company car, shook me by the hand and wished me luck in the tone of voice that said I might need it.

She had lived in the 8th arrondissement. Naturally. It's the best place to live. Paris's equivalent of Mayfair – or Park Avenue. Handy for the Plaza-Athenée, or the Crillon, or the Archestrate restaurant if you felt peckish. Or the Invalides if you wanted a walk in a garden. Wide streets. Trees. Big houses, And gendarmes. Lots and lots of gendarmes. A place where the rich could feel secure... The car pulled up outside a house that looked like a sizeable chunk of the Paris Opera, and I got out and rang the bell marked 'Concierge'. It was a lady, as it so often is in France, but this wasn't the quaint, picturesque old girl you see in the movies. This one bought her clothes at Galeries Lafayette and had a diploma in hotel management. This one was the kind that only the 8th arrondissement can afford. She would also be colonel-in-chief of whatever security squad guarded the place. I was nice to her.

'My name's Hogget,' I said. 'I believe M. Auriol called you about me.'

'Yes of course,' she said. 'Please come in M Hogget. I am Madame Lenôtre.'

I went in and a geezer dressed like a porter in a five-star hotel took my suitcase. I couldn't see where he kept his gun, but it would be there somewhere. We walked on marble to a copper-lined lift and floated up like a leaf in the breeze. The Donners had the penthouse apartment, which didn't surprise me. Its front-door was of mahogany polished smoother than satin. The concierge waited till she was sure my keys fitted.

'I think you will find everything in order, M. Hogget,' Madame Lenôtre said. 'I made sure the refrigerator was filled after M. Auriol called. If there is anything you should need, please use the blue telephone.'

Then the man dressed like a porter put my suitcase inside the door and they left me to it.

More wealth, more luxury, but of a different kind from New York. This was more lived in, more *used*, but none the worse for that. Curtains of heavy silk, vast, comfortable furniture, heavy black tables inlaid with gold. That was the hall, and the drawing room. Dining room more of the same. Master bedroom light and airy; floating, even. A big white bed with a canopy like a tent, white and green carpet, green and white curtains. Dave said it sounded more like a bower than a bedroom. Dave was right.

I chose the biggest of the spare rooms. There were four of them, though two of them looked as if they might have been meant for servants. There was an office-studio, too; just the place for a snooper like me. But I took my time. I looked around. A kitchen big enough to cook a banquet in, bathrooms out of a Cecil B. de Mille movie, and everywhere *things*. That's the only way I could describe them; beautiful, valuable *things*. China and furniture and prints and little statues and glass and pictures and rugs and carpets. Pictures and rugs. To the right of the fireplace in the drawing room there was a Turner oil of what looked like a mountain; and it was beautiful. All colour and light. Say sixty thousand quid's worth. To the left of the mantelpiece was a Renoir: a little girl at the theatre. Only it was a copy. On a good day you might get ten quid for it. Once you saw the contrast you couldn't take your eyes off it. I went back to the master bedroom. On the right of the bed was a carpet. Persian silk it was. What they call a Heriz. Say twenty thousand quid. On the left of the bed was a white sheepskin. Very nice to stand on, but not the same. Not at all the same. I thought perhaps Ms Milligan had been careless. Certainly somebody had...

Time to unpack, then go into the kitchen, find the tea and biscuits and fresh milk, and a note from the concierge itemising the stuff she'd bought and telling me it would go on the bill. Donner could afford it. I made a brew, took it to the office and sat down on a leather swivel seat before a black wood desk that was covered with papers. There really was work to do. I called Melanie: I know I said I never did when I was working, but Donner was still paying, I was still reacting to connubial bliss...

The phone rang for a bit but I didn't hang up. Melanie's one who takes her time before she answers the phone. But at last she did.

'Hallo?' she said.

'Hallo yourself,' I said.

'Oh *Ronny*,' said Melanie.

'You sound a bit breathless,' I said.

'Well of course I am,' she said. 'I was just coming in and I had to run because the phone was ringing.'

'That was me,' I said.

'Oh *Ronny.*'

And a whole lot more stuff like that. Sickening if you don't love someone; perfectly understandable if you do. She was fine and her mother was fine and the car was fine. I hadn't a thing to worry about. Then I remembered that I too had a presentable relative.

'I went to see Anna Maria the day after I got back. Did I tell you?'

'No,' said Melanie.

'She said she phoned you a couple of times while I was in New York.'

'I *like* Anna Maria,' Melanie said. 'She's nice. Mum's bought a new mac.'

Whatever the row had been about it must have been a lulu. I'd just have to wait until one of them decided it was time to let me in on it.

'How long will you be away?' said Melanie.

I looked at the pile of papers on the desk.

'Three days,' I said. 'At least.'

'Oh *Ronny.*' But this time her voice was a wail.

'It's our living, love,' I said. 'Just give me a few more weeks and we'll have a holiday.'

'Where?'

'Anywhere you want,' I said.

*'Honest?'*

'Cross my heart,' I said, and why not? Mr Donner would be paying. And then there was a bit of what you might call chit-chat, and then we hung up and I could get back to my other love. Not that I ever thought of her as that. Not really. Not until I heard her speak.

But that came later. First I had to get on with my snooping. There was plenty of scope of course – a flat that size – but it wasn't anything like as rewarding as New York had been. This it was clear had been *her* place, her domain if you like. Donner's mark wasn't on the place at all: but hers was everywhere – furniture, curtains, that favourite rose colour of hers: it was all Jane Donner. Including the neatness. I've told you how finicking neat she was, and here in her own place everything was as precise as a guardsman's kit laid out for inspection. Which meant it was all available. Nothing hidden. Nothing secret. And where there's no secrets, who needs Ron Hogget?

Desk full of contracts and reports and business letters. So far as I could gather the businesses she was in were still making money – which meant her mother wouldn't approve, according to her father – and what use was that to me? I looked for photographs. One of mum, one of dad, one of Donner, all in expensive silver frames: and that was it. I went back to the business letters.

It just shows you it pays to be thorough. The business stuff was in big steel filing cabinets, with partitions divided alphabetically. When I got to XYZ – a contract for a writer called Bella Youngman, an offer from a publisher called Zulueta – I felt behind the partition just in case. What I came up with was a photograph. I'd found a snapshot of a young woman. Another thin, pretty one.

She wasn't exactly smiling, but she looked pleased with herself. She was on a beach somewhere, but no bikini for her, even though it looked good and hot. Slacks and a long-sleeved shirt, that's what she wore, because when you're on horse or smack or whatever it was she got her kicks from – shit's the commonest word for it and I think that's about right, though I'm not one for coarseness as a general rule – your arms tend to get a bit unsightly what with all those needles prodding and piercing. Still, for once she looked pleased with herself, as if she had a right to look pleased with herself. Maybe that was why Jane had kept it. I had no doubt at all about who it was...

Maybe I'd better keep it, I thought. There's no Ms Milligan here to argue. And then – oh dear oh dear. I remembered something. For once methodical, plodding Ron Hogget had slipped up, fallen down on the job. I already had a photograph of someone called Goody Müller, and I'd forgotten to show it to A. D. Carr... That's what wedded bliss can do for a man after he's been away too long.

I poked around the flat a bit more. No hidden cupboards, no wall-safe, the telly in the drawing room was just a telly, the music-centre just a music-centre. Might as well have a bit of music to lighten the gloom I thought, and pressed a button. It was the wrong button. 'My darling,' Jane Donner said, 'why has it been so long? I sit here in this incredibly chic flat and invent errands to get Cass out of the way and wait for the phone to ring and it never does. What's Jane done to upset you?' The last six words were in a travesty of a little girl voice that embarrassed me so much I pressed the stop button. Jane Donner should never have talked like that. But that was ridiculous. I was here to *work*, for God's sake, not worry about a dead woman's image. I pressed the button again. 'I love you, you know,' Jane Donner said. 'There's a dark side to

130

you, and I know you think I hate that, and I think so too. But hate and love are very close, my dearest, and my hate will always give way to my love in the end, so please, don't run away from me. I know I can't cure you – but I can live with you – I can make you happy. I know I can. I love you. Honestly.'

Then there came a sound like a sob and the tape kept running, but Jane Donner was silent. Silent as the grave. 'I love you. Honestly,' she had said. How else could she have loved whoever it was, and look where it had got her... Now hold on, Ron, I told myself. This was a bloke she loved. Why would he kill her? There was no answer to that, so I thought of Melanie instead, and for the first time I began to worry, I couldn't think why. And that worried me even more. I checked the rest of the tapes. There was nothing else to get excited about unless you like Schönberg, so I took out Jane's unfinished ode to a man unknown and put it in my pocket. As I did the door opened and Mr White came in and stood to one side, then Mr Black, who stood to the other side, then Mr Donner stage centre. All it needed was a fanfare by Schönberg. It wasn't one of my more fragrant moments. I had no idea if he'd seen me pocketing the tape or not.

'Why hello, Mr Donner,' I said. 'I thought you were in Perth, Australia.'

'I was,' said Donner. 'And now I'm in Paris, France. You want to know why?'

'To see me?'

'Not exactly,' said Donner. Seeing me was obviously not his idea of a good time. 'To hear how things are coming along.'

131

'The whole thing's beginning to look rather complicated,' I said.

'Stop talking like a limey fag' – I didn't know I had been – 'and cut out the bullshit. Where are you at?'

I gathered that Mr Donner was a little bit jet-lagged.

'I think I know how your wife was conned into going to Italy,' I said.

'So tell me.'

'She was friendly with a set designer called Frank Sokolny. He designed the set for *Honeyfall*.' I was looking at Donner straight on, but his face told me nothing at all. 'Sokolny was involved with a dancer called Mickey Wood.'

'What do you mean involved?'

'They were lovers.'

'Then say so, goddamit.'

'They were lovers,' I said. 'Wood was an addict – heavily involved in the drug scene. His pusher was an addict, too. A woman from the Austrian Tyrol – on the Italian border – called Gudrun Müller. She worked in a flower-shop. It was cover for the drugs they sold.'

'In the old days it was always a candy store,' said Mr Black.

Donner looked at him, and Mr Black looked as if he wished he hadn't uttered.

'When I want you to be nostalgic I'll tell you,' said Donner. 'What I want you to be now is silent.' He turned to me. 'Go on.'

'Wood and Sokolny – mostly Sokolny I would think, Wood probably stayed in the background – arranged for Jane to meet Goody. She felt sorry

132

for her. They knew that would happen. Your wife was known to be kind-hearted.'

'My wife was the softest touch on the Eastern seaboard,' he said.

'She also had great organizing ability and a streak of ruthlessness,' I said. His eyes looked down on mine.

'Think you know all about her, do you?' he said.

'Not all,' I said. 'I wish I did.' His eyes got angrier. 'It would help me to find her.'

There was a pause. 'Go on,' he said at last.

'Your wife got her out of New York. That took a bit of doing – lifting a pusher out of the drug scene right in the middle of New York.'

'Tell me why,' he said.

'You know why,' I said.

'Tell me anyway.'

'Because sooner or later if it's drugs in New York it's the Mafia. And nobody wants to take them on.'

'You think I'm scared of the Mafia?'

'I don't know about you,' I said. 'You're not on my agenda.'

'And cut out the bullshit. I already told you.'

'Mr Donner,' I said. 'All this is relevant or I wouldn't be saying it. Can't you please just let me tell it?'

I actually said these things. I just opened my mouth and out they came. Even Black and White looked awed. What the love of a good, dead woman can do.

'Go on,' said Donner.

'I don't know whether Mrs Donner was scared

of them or not, but she took them on,' I said. 'God help her.'

'What's that supposed to mean?'

'She took them on,' I said, 'and she won. The first round anyway. She got Goody to a place where she could be treated. My guess is it would be in Austria. Then later she went to visit her. Only I think they arranged to meet in Italy – in Riva del Garda because it's a holiday town where foreigners aren't conspicuous. Then she was kidnapped. Then she was killed.'

I didn't mention A. D. Carr's objection to all this: that Goody had disappeared twice. If I had Mr Donner might have wanted an explanation.

'You're saying the Mafia lifted her?' said Donner.

'I'm saying it's the most likely answer,' I said.

'For revenge?'

'For money,' I said. 'The revenge was just a bonus.' I hesitated.

'Maybe that's why they cut her head off and reneged on the deal.'

It didn't faze him. I doubt if anything could faze him.

'You figure these two guys – Sokolny and Wood – set my wife up for this?'

'Could be,' I said.

He turned to Black and White.

'Looks like we've got work to do,' he said.

'No,' I said. 'You haven't.'

He spun round on me, fast as a cat, jet-lagged or not.

'Mr Hogget,' he said 'I hired you to find things and that's *all*. You don't tell me what I can do and

134

what I can't.'

'I know I can't,' I said. 'But you can't touch Sokolny and Wood. They're both dead.'

'You sure?'

I nodded.

'By dead you mean murdered?'

'Yes,' I said.

He liked it, but not as much as I'd thought he would.

'So what happens now?'

'I go on looking,' I said. 'Paris, then Italy, the Tyrol.'

'OK.' he said. 'Go to it. I'm sorry if I was rough on you.' Martin Donner? Sorry? 'It's just that I'm jet-lagged to hell and gone.' He yawned and stretched. 'I'm going to get some sleep. I'll be at the Ritz tonight. We'll be back in New York to-morrow. If you've got something call me any time.'

'Don't you want to stay here?' I said.

'*Here?*' he sounded appalled. 'No ... I couldn't stay here. This was my wife's place.' He made it sound like a shrine. He looked then as if he were about to go, but there was one thing more. I thought there might be.

'Let me ask you something,' he said. 'You don't think Italian Reds could have done it? The Red Brigade? Some bunch of crazies like that?'

'No,' I said. 'I don't.'

'I talked to a lot of people in Italy,' he said. 'Politicos. Cops. They seemed to think Jane was just the target for those nuts.'

'They're scum,' I said. 'Violent, dangerous scum. But I don't think they kidnapped your wife.'

'Why not?'

'The Modus Operandi,' I said. If the Reds had done it they'd have hyped it for all the publicity they could get. Press statements, tapes for radio, tapes for TV. With your wife starring as the villain. A victory for the workers. A blow for capitalism.'

'The Italians said that, too,' he said. 'But–'

'Besides,' I said. 'There was no evidence against them at all.'

'You're sure?'

'Not a scrap.'

He scowled at me, realized I didn't deserve it, and switched the scowl to Black and White.

'One other thing,' I said. He realized by my tone it wasn't going to be good news, and the scowl deepened.

'In New York, somebody tried to kill me, too.'

'You're kidding.' He didn't mean to be insulting, I know that now.

'Once with a car. Second time two fellers setting up a hit – only I managed to lose them. That's enough for me. More than enough. I'm not sure I want to go on with this, Mr Donner.'

'You've got to go on with it.' I said nothing. 'You want more money?'

'If it's enough,' I said.

'Another fifty thousand dollars.'

'It's enough.'

'Maybe I'd better let you have some muscle, too.' He scowled once more at Black and White. 'Not these boys. They got other work. Besides they're dumb. They only know it's Sunday because that's when the church bells ring.'

'I'll get my own,' I said.

136

'Will he be any good?'

'He better be,' I said. 'It's my life.'

Donner nodded. Point taken. 'Put him on my tab,' he said. Then: 'Mr Hogget, I want you to take very good care of yourself.' He was absolutely sincere, I swear to God. In the next breath he added: 'You've got a jacket of mine. Where is it?'

'In London,' I said.

'I want it back soon,' he said. 'It's cashmere.' Then he turned to his two dumb heavies. 'Let's get some sleep for Chrissake,' he said.

I waited till I heard the front door shut then put on the chain bolt – an almost perfect example of locking the stable after the horse has gone – poured myself a cognac, Hennessy XO – and sat down, twitching, into a vast leather chair. I was shaking so much I had trouble swallowing my drink, but in the end I calmed down and looked about me. The carpet was that same glowing rose colour... My dearest Jane. If it hadn't been for you I'd never have done it but the point was I had done it. I'd won a round with Donner. Now all I had to decide was what to do next...

When my hands were steady enough I played the tape again, winced again at the sound of the baby-voice. It was what Sherlock Holmes would have called a clue, I suppose. It would have been even more of a clue if I'd known who she'd been talking to. Was the bloke alive or dead, for example? Little details like that... I went through the flat again from end to end, but there was nothing more. Just a snapshot and a tape, so I rang the concierge, told her to call me a taxi, and that I might be back soon. She managed to control her raptures. Then I called the Ritz, and asked the desk clerk to say to Mr Donner that T. R. Hogget would be in London for the next few days.

'Mr Donner is asleep,' said the clerk.

'You'd better whisper it then,' I said.

# 8

It wasn't just an excuse to get back to Melanie for a bit. I had to see A. D. Carr and show him some pictures. Mind you, seeing Melanie again was great, another bonus on top of the fifty grand I'd just stuck Donner for. And don't think he wouldn't pay. I'd written him a letter about it, and if he didn't reply there'd be no more action, *and* we both knew it.

Wedded bliss... You can't beat it. Especially as I'd remembered to buy her a bottle of Madame Rochas at Charles de Gaulle. Melanie said it was great. Wore it straight away. It did a lot for my love life. And hers. The best time of our marriage. At last she said: 'In the afternoon. We never done it in the afternoon before.'

'I wish we had,' I said. 'Too late now.'

'You're awfully serious,' she said. 'What is it? Work?'

I nodded. She turned on the bed and touched me. The Madame Rochas was all she wore. She was – very pretty.

'Is it too much for you?'

And there you had her. Pig-ignorant is Melanie, yet she comes up with the 64,000-dollar question without even trying. Of course it was too much for me, but how could I tell her that?

'Course not,' I said. 'It just takes a bit of thinking about, that's all.' Whenever I mention brain work Melanie thinks of food.

'I got a nice bit of steak for supper,' she said.

'I', you'll notice. Not 'I've'. And then she got off the bed and looked around for her robe and she looked prettier than ever. 'No rush,' I said. 'I've got to see Dave.'

'Is he going to work for you?'

'Yes,' I said.

She buttoned the robe in the wrong buttonholes and had to start again.

'It'll be dangerous then,' she said.

'Dave'll look after me,' I said. 'Don't worry... I've got to phone a bloke in the States as well.'

She didn't speak for a while, then: 'Do you *have* to do it? Truly?'

'I need the money, love,' I said. 'We both do.'

He was in the Mason's Arms drinking lager, like always. I bought him another one, gin and tonic for myself.

'You still want to earn?' I asked.

'I still want to go to the Dordogne.'

'What does that mean?'

'Working for you's the only way I'll get there,' said Dave. 'You still offering five hundred?'

'Minimum,' I said. 'Could be seven-fifty. Could be a grand.' He whistled. Suddenly I got ashamed of myself.

'Look Dave,' I said, 'last time we talked I wasn't all that – you know – honest with you. It is dangerous.'

'Bless your heart,' said Dave. 'Think I didn't know? The most you ever paid me in the past's been twenty a day.' He sipped his lager. 'When do we start?'

'How much have you had to drink?'

'One half of lager.'

'We'll start now,' I said. 'Anyway, as soon as we've seen our drinks off.'

Dave drank again, not gulping, just steady suction.

I kept my voice down. 'This time you may need a gun,' I said. He came out of his lager like a genie out of a bottle.

'Not for five hundred,' he said.

'Extra if you have to use it.'

'Ron, Ron,' he said. 'What are you getting into?'

'A geezer tried to kill me in New York,' I said. 'I think there was another try, too. I'm not sure – but I think so.'

His eyes were still on mine.

'You're not lying to me now, I know that.'

'Of course not,' I said.

'So just tell me this. What sort of chance d'you reckon you've got of doing this job?'

'With you – I reckon it's better than even money. Without you – no chance at all.'

'You always did know how to get round me,' said Dave, and sighed, then finished his lager. 'All right. I'll get the gun. You pay for it. I get another two fifty for carrying the thing – and another grand if I have to use it. OK?'

'It's a deal,' I said. And why not? For Donner this was bargain basement stuff.

'So where do we start?' Dave said.

'Shepherd's Bush,' I said.

'You're not much of a Romantic, are you?' said Dave. 'Who's there?'

'A. D. Carr,' I said.

'The writer?'

'You know him?' I asked.

'I've read him,' Dave said. 'Come on. Finish your drink and let's get going. I never knew you were an intellectual, Ron.'

The same street hanging on like grim death; the same kids with bikes and roller skates and trannies; the same rows of cars waiting for the knacker's yard, and at number seventy-three, the same gleaming motor-bike, the same Violet.

'A. D.'s not here,' she said.

'His bike's here,' I said.

'Sure his bike's here. He's at the BBC doing a telly. He's walking. I'll tell him you called.'

She shut the door, not without a sense of triumph. Hogget this time put to flight.

'What now?' said Dave.

'We find a phone that hasn't been vandalized.'

I'm supposed to be good at finding things, but believe me, in that neighbourhood it took some doing. We found one at last in a pub, and Dave bought a couple of beers just for the look of the thing – neither of us had the slightest intention of drinking them – while I got on the blower.

The geezer I was after was by the name of Lionel Pendleton, a documentary producer I'd done a job for once. What I'd found for him was a long-lost brother. He was doing a series about family life, and he needed a long-lost brother, and I found him one. And when he was re-united with his family they all started crying and carrying on, and so did the rest of Great Britain, and the show shot up in the ratings and had three repeats, and Lionel won an award. With him I was always welcome. He'd told me so.

'Ron sweetie,' he said, 'whatever it is, day or night, just call. Here's my home number. Just pick up the phone, heart.'

So I did. But of course, that had all been a year ago, maybe even fifteen months, and geezers forget. The trouble is he was resting, you see, and I sort of gathered he was helping his girl friend to rest an' all. He wasn't keen.

'You know it's funny,' I said. 'I was talking to a bloke about our programme only the other day. He'd got the idea *you'd* found the long-lost brother. As a matter of fact everybody seems to think that.'

Lionel Pendleton sighed. 'All right,' he said. 'Where are you?' I told him the name of the pub.

He didn't like the pub and he didn't like Dave, and he'd gone right off me an' all. He didn't like the car, either. Mind you I can't blame him for that. Dave's car has got mini-cab written all over it. Its springs nip like a pervert's fingers. All the same he got us past the security guard and into the BBC car-park, and Dave found a place to park because Dave always finds a place to park, then we went inside and he made a phone call from the reception desk and came back to us.

'He's in the club,' said Lionel Pendleton.

Dave snorted, and Pendleton blushed the sort of pink Jane had liked.

'Can you get us in there?' I asked.

'Of course I can,' Pendleton said. 'I'm a member.'

'We're mixing with the cream now,' said Dave.

We took a lift, and Pendleton signed us in, and we entered a vast room on two levels, patio outside, a bar that seemed to go on forever.

'Now what?' said Pendleton.

'Go back home and rest,' I said.

'You mean that's all?' I nodded. 'Why on earth couldn't you say so?' I didn't answer, and he turned and left.

I bought Dave a lager and me a tonic without the gin, and we went in search of A. D. Carr. He wasn't hard to find, sitting alone with four large brandies in front of him. Dave followed my gaze.

'Is that him?' He asked.

'That's him.'

'Strewth,' said Dave.

He had something there. A. D. Carr was in his best suit, probably his only suit, but he still looked every inch a mauler. I moved forward. Dave put out a hand and stopped me.

'Look Ron,' he said. 'I'm pretty sure I can handle him – unless he's learned a few tricks I don't know – but if I do it'll be vivid stuff. Page one of the *Daily Mirror*.'

'Don't be daft,' I said. 'He's a good guy.' I went up to him and Dave followed. 'Mr Carr,' I said.

He lowered his book. He'd quite obviously had several brandies before the ones in front of him.

'Mr Hawkshaw,' he said.

'Hogget,' I said. Carr picked up a brandy and swallowed, and then there were three.

'Pedant,' he said.

'I'd like to introduce you to my friend Dave.'

Carr looked at Dave. It was a very comprehensive look. 'Brought your minder?' he said. 'No need for that.'

'Don't be daft,' I said. 'Dave's a fan of yours.'

Carr's eyes never left Dave's.

'That's right?' he said.

'That's right,' said Dave.

Carr didn't believe him. 'Which of my multifarious works do you like best?'

'You've written four,' said Dave. 'I liked *Marsyas* best, but *Armour Pierced* was almost as good.'

'So you are a fan.' Another glass went to his lips. Two down and two to go. 'And doubtless you write yourself? Doubtless you have some choice morceau about your person you would like me to cast an eye over?'

'No,' said Dave.

'*No?*' A. D. Carr was so incredulous he forgot to drink. 'I can't write,' said Dave.

'"That never deterred any of the writers I know.'

'Well it deters me,' said Dave. 'So I read instead.'

'You're a very nice man,' he said. 'Quite possibly a unique man.' His face clouded. 'I've just done a telly,' A. D. said. This time he made it sound like having a bowel movement. He turned to me.

'How many of my works have you read?' he asked.

'None,' I said. 'I've come to ask you a favour.'

'Then buy me a drink.'

'What'll it be?' I said.

'Same again. Four brandies.' I turned to get them. 'And whatever you're having yourselves,' said Carr.

I brought back more drinks. Dave and A. D. (they were on first name terms by then) were discussing poetry, and I put four brandies in front of A.D.

'Sorry to interrupt,' I told him, 'but I'd like you to take a look at this.'

'While I can still see,' said A.D.

'Right.'

He cut loose with a laugh that turned every head in that enormous room, and I waited till the heads were in the right direction before I handed him the photograph I'd taken from the killer's hand in Sokolny's place. He looked at it upside down and I righted it for him.

'Do you know her?' I asked.

'No ... Wish I did.'

'You've never seen her anywhere – with or without Mr Donner?' He looked up at me then. He still looked drunk, but he also looked smart. Very smart.

'This couldn't be the lady who disappears at fortnightly intervals?'

'Not if you haven't seen her it can't.'

'Sorry, I can't help you.'

He made it sound like he meant it, and began on the first of my brandies.

'How about this one?' I said, and showed him the one I'd got from Jane's place.

'Clever, industrious Mr Hogget,' he said. 'She's

the one.'

He yawned and stretched. 'I'm knackered,' he said. 'Doing tellies always does this to me. Why do I do it, Hawkshaw?'

'The money,' I said.

'Right,' he said. 'This ludicrous obsession with food. And drink. And warmth in winter. Thank God lust is free.' He looked at the lines of brandy glasses, drawn up like soldiers.

'I'm touting for sympathy now. Sympathy I don't deserve, so withhold it, please. I did that telly by choice, just as I write by choice. That's all I have to say. Goodnight, sweet princes.'

Dave said, 'Will you be all right?' No answer. 'I mean – will you get home all right?'

A.D. said grandly, 'Of course I will. Somebody will take me home. They always do. Maybe I'll start to sing. Mussorgsky's *Song of the Flea*. Never fails. Four bars and they're helping me to the cab.'

'Good lord,' I said. 'Why on earth do they put up with it?'

A.D.'s look despised my intellect.

'For Christ's sake,' he said. 'This is the BBC. I'm a *character*. Of course they put up with it.'

We left him to it.


On the way back, Dave was silent for a while, and then: 'Poor sod,' he said.

I thought of Jane. 'He's had his share of happiness,' I said. 'Believe me.'

Dave said nothing for a while, and then at last asked me, 'What happens now?'

'I should get a letter tomorrow,' I said. 'When I do we're flying to Venice.'

'I like Venice,' said Dave.

'We're not going to Venice,' I said. We're picking up a car and going to Verona.'

Dave said placidly, 'I like Verona, too.'

When he dropped me off at my place I said, Want to come in for a bite?'

'No thanks,' he said. 'Got to catch up on my reading. Oh that reminds me – do me a favour?'

'What?' I said.

'Store a few books for me.'

'Pleasure,' I said.

There was a carton full. As usual. He wanted to carry them for me, but I said I could manage. I didn't want Dave to think he had all the muscle in the organization.

Where I store Dave's books is the garage. Big enough to take a Roller, that garage, and room to spare, and all I've got is a Datsun. So there's plenty of room for books. Just as well. The back of the garage looks like a bleeding library ... I heaved this carton on top of a pile of others, only I'm nowhere near as strong as Dave and it slipped and Burton's *Anatomy of Melancholy* hit the garage floor. No damage. Only it fell open and a bookmark dropped out. Very unusual bookmark. Lady's nylon stocking – and not a cheap one either. Christian Dior.

I went into the house. Melanie heard me come in and was in the kitchen, getting the steaks on. She didn't look too good. 'Everything go off all right?' she said.

'Something's upset you,' I said.

'Your dad's been.'

My father could upset a squadron of SAS men.

147

For him Melanie was a pushover. 'Money?' I
said. She nodded. 'How much d'you give him?'
'A fiver.'
'I'll go and see him in the morning.'
'It won't do no good, Ron,' she said.
'We can but try,' I said, and put my arm around
her. She leaned into me and turned the steak.
'Did you get anywhere tonight?' she said.
'I think so.' I began to fondle her.
'*Ron!*' she said. 'I'm *cooking.*' But she didn't
push my hand away.
'Got to go to Italy tomorrow,' I said.
'Don't you ever stay home?' said Melanie. 'I
wish you wouldn't keep going away all the time.'
'I'm taking Dave with me.'
'Oh,' she said, and brightened. 'That's all right
then. I mean if Dave's with you you'll be safe.
Bound to be.'

Donner's letter came next morning, delivered by
an outfit called Skybird Special. Five hours door
to door. It cost a fortune. I know because I'd sent
mine the same way. Donner added a PS to say (a)
he was leaving Paris for New York; (b) in future
we should use ordinary mail and avoid the phone
except in dire emergency; (c) he still hadn't got
his jacket back.
I phoned the travel agents and asked them to
book me two seats to Venice on the first flight
available, then I got on with the serious business
of the day: going to see my father. It was long
after eleven so there was a chance he was out of
bed. He was – just, but he wasn't any treat to look
at. The fiver he'd gouged out of Melanie last

night had all gone down his throat. He still has the house we were born and brought up in, Anna Maria and me. When my mother was alive it was shining-clean and smelled of basil and rosemary, Italian cheese and wine. Now it was just a dirty bottle bank that smelled.

My father in his dressing-gown was no delight to the eye or the nose. He looked at me blearily, all his reactions slowed down by booze.

'It's you is it?' he said.

'Clever of you to guess.'

He turned and walked into the stench, and I followed, to what had once been our living-room.

'To what do I owe the pleasure?' he said.

'What pleasure? You came to see me last night.'

'Did I?'

I know all his acts, and this wasn't one of them. He'd been too pissed to remember. 'I was out,' I said. 'You saw Melanie instead.' He thought a bit harder. 'Yes I do remember,' he said. 'We had a bit of a chat, you and your missus. She loaned me a fiver.'

'You won't do that again.'

'Won't I?'

I shook my head: no.

'Why not?'

'Because if you do I'll belt you.'

'Don't talk daft,' my father said, 'I'm your old man.' I didn't speak, and that worried him.

'I know what it is,' he said. 'You're the marrying type. Just like your mother.' I still said nothing, and that worried him even more because usually when he mentioned my mother I started screaming. Worry made him turn nasty. 'You know I

149

killed your mother,' he said. 'Crashed that old Austin into a lamp-post and she was killed and I walked out. I was drunk of course and she was sober. She got killed and I got three months.' He waited, and when I still didn't speak said: 'You had heard, hadn't you son?'

That had always been his best weapon: to boast about mum's death. It didn't work that day.

'We were talking about Melanie,' I said.

'So we were,' said my father. 'You said I was to stay away from her ... I don't think I will, though. I like a bit of a chat now and then with my nearest and dearest. Besides – we got a lot to talk about, me and Melanie.'

'You'll stay away,' I said, 'or I'll belt you.'

Without a word he grabbed a bottle from the table, came at me and swung. I swayed to one side, chopped down with my hand on his wrist and sunk a fist into his gut. He made a soft little noise and sat down on the floor. Like I say, Dave isn't the only heavy in our organization, I can beat up any sixty-two-year-old drunk my size. This particular one began to make some very odd sounds, but he was conscious. I crouched down beside him.

'Look,' I said. 'I'm going to be away for a bit – but if I hear you've been bothering Melanie while I've gone, I'll have you taken care of. Straight I will.' I took three cheques from my pocket, put them on the floor beside him. 'These are for twenty quid apiece,' I told him. 'Two of them's post-dated. That means you've got twenty quid a week in the hand for the next three weeks. Only stay away from Melanie.'

He continued to make strange noises while I went to the door, but when I reached it he managed to utter: 'Who've you got to take care of me? Your mate Dave?'

'I wouldn't let Dave soil his hands on you,' I said. 'These boys are villains.' He went back to making noises. The pater ... the dear old dad. Not that I had hired any villains. I just wanted Melanie left in peace.

On the way home I gave a knock on Dave's door and told him to stand by for a flight.

'And wear a clean shirt for a change,' I told him. 'We're flying first.'

When I got home Melanie was in a tizz, which is quite easy for her.

'You had two calls,' she said. 'The travel agent says to phone back; the other one was from Paris.' Paris was the tizz-maker; that was obvious.

'But Donner said he was off to New York.'

'I don't know anything about no Donners–'

*Any* Donners. *Please,* Melanie. But I didn't say it aloud. 'It was a woman,' said Melanie, not liking what she said.

'But I don't know any women in Paris,' I said.

'That's not what she thinks.'

Then at last the wheels began to turn.

'Was her name Madame Lenôtre?' I asked.

'How do I know?' said Melanie. 'I don't speak French.'

I had to yell at her. *'Was it?'*

She knows that when I yell I mean it.

'Something like that,' she said.

I got out my little book; found the number of Jane's apartment block.

'You're never going to call her,' she said.

'Well of course I am,' I said. 'She's the house-keeper of that place in Paris where I stayed.'

Melanie was disappointed: she'd been looking forward to a good row. All the same she hung about while I talked. It didn't do her much good though. All she heard from me was two yesses a no and a couple of grunts. I put the phone down. 'The apartment I stayed in's been broken into,' I said. 'I'll have to go and look at the damage.'

'I thought you and Dave were going to Italy,' she said. 'We'll go to Paris on the way.'

She looked at me, and for the first time, there was a kind of awe in the look. 'Oh Ronny,' she said. 'You aren't half getting high-powered.'

I dialled the travel agents to get ourselves re-routed.


# 9


Dave liked the first class on Air France; the cham-pagne and caviar, and seats where you could really spread – of course he did: he's not stupid. He liked the cab into Paris too – no pushing for seats on an airport bus – but most of all, he liked the 8th arrondissement, especially Jane's street. Its architecture alone, he said, was more than adequate compensation for Charles de Gaulle airport. I paid off the cab and Dave took out bags while I rang the bell that would fetch Madame. She appeared as if I'd rubbed the magic lamp.

'M. Hogget,' she said. 'It was good of you to come so quickly.'

The she took a look at Dave, and it was all on her face. This Hogget's no fool, her face said. He's brought his minder. And she approved. There could be no doubt that she approved.

'This is M. David Baxter,' I said. Well I could hardly say: 'This is my mate Dave.' 'He's by way of being an associate of mine.'

'*Bien sûr*,' she said. 'If you'll come this way please.'

No manservant to carry the bags this time, and she apologized for the fact. 'I think it best they do not know,' she said in the lift.

'Won't the police want to question them?' I asked.

She coughed. 'I think perhaps we should wait until we are in the flat,' she said. The door looked OK. It was even locked. I used my key on it and we went inside. The hall looked OK too. Madame stopped us there and we talked: mostly she did.

'I came in early this morning to check the place—'

'Why?' I asked.

'It is part of my duties, monsieur. Part of the security. I do it with all empty flats. Then I find – what you shall see. But how did they get in? It is supposed to be impossible. Anyway – I at once phone Monsieur Donner in New York, and he says I must phone you to come at once and on no account to contact the police unless you tell me to do so, M. Hogget.'

'And you'll do as M. Donner says?'

'Of course,' she said. 'The police do not pay

me. M. Donner pays me. Please call if you should need anything at all.'

I went straight in the room used as an office and I had guessed right. The place looked as if a tribe of baboons had been let loose in it. They always do, after that kind of caper. Behind me Dave gasped aloud. There was paper everywhere; every drawer had been emptied, every filing cabinet forced. They'd ripped up cushions, the backs of chairs, even the hems of curtains. They – or he? That wasn't my problem. My problem was 'why' not 'who'.

Dave said, 'Somebody's had a ball.'

'This is nothing,' I said. 'You should see what geezers like this can do when they're really trying.'

'So what do we do now?' said Dave.

I showed him where the kitchen was. 'You make some coffee,' I said. 'I need to have a bit of a think for a minute.'

He went out and I looked at the disaster area and tried to figure it out. I must have missed something, by the look of it – and the first question was, had the other lot got it? I started sifting through the stuff on the floor, but that was daft. They'd thrown that junk away because they *didn't* want it. I was after something they did want.

I looked again round the room. Desk, swivel chair, a couple of filing cabinets, three Barcelona chairs for anyone who happened to drop in, secretary's swivel chair with an arm-rest for when she was taking dictation: and all slashed, smashed, bashed beyond repair. It was a damn shame, particularly the Barcelona chairs. I picked up the secretary's chair to set it to rights. Something glinted on the bottom of the seat; a metal tag giving the maker's name. 'J-P. Rampollion et Fils, Lille'. What had caught my eye was that one of the screws holding the tag in place was loose. I got out the Swiss army knife, struck the screwdriver blade under it, and pressed. The metal broke, and a small piece of paper came free. It was folded once, then again, and I opened it up. 'Eduardo Guardi,' I read. 'Via Raffaello 15, Verona.'

I went to the phone and rang my sister in London.

'Anna Maria,' I said, 'this is Tommaso. I'm phoning from Paris.'

'From Parigi?'

'Si,' I said. 'It costs a lot of money so I'll make it quick. You know Verona?' She should, she went back there every chance she got. 'Who lives in the Via Raffaello?'

'Nobody nice,' she said. 'You stay away from there.'

'What sort of nasty people?'

'Students,' she said. 'Reds. They have what they call communi. You know, communes. All live together. Everything in common. Including beating up my brother if he doesn't watch himself.'

'I've got Dave with me,' I said.

Anna Maria thought it over then, 'That's good,' she said. 'That's very good. But take care anyway.'

We exchanged a few more kind words then I hung up just as Dave came in with the coffee.

'Sorry to take so long,' he said, 'but all they've got here is filters and they can't be rushed.'

'That's all right,' I said, and took a cup. Dave makes smashing coffee, always did.

He sipped. 'Where do we start?' he said.

'We're finished,' I said, and he spluttered a mixture of Brazilian and Colombian, twenty francs the kilo.

'All we do now is – I make a phone call – and you tidy this lot up.'

'But I've no idea where it belongs,' he said.

'Just bung it out of sight.'

'And the furniture?'

'We'll hold the funeral tomorrow.'

I headed for the living-room, to make my call in private.

'Pity about the Barcelona chairs,' said Dave.

Call me at any time you think you've got something, Donner had said. Well I'd got something, and to hell with what the time was in New York. I dialled. The geezer who looked like Mohammed Ali's successor said: 'Mr Donner's asleep.' He sounded pretty whacked himself, and far from happy. I proceeded to make him even less so.

'Wake him,' I said.

'*What?*'

'Look,' I said. 'My name is T. R. Hogget. Mr Donner told me to call him any time.'

'Gee, I don't know,' Mohammed Ali's successor said.

Then I realized something. Mr Donner must be sleeping in company. 'Look,' I said. 'Just give me his extension. It'll be all right – if you don't you'll be out of a job.'

It took a bit more, but at last he put me on to Donner's extension. The extension phone rang five times, then I was treated to a blast of profanity that would have done credit to a sergeant-major, but then I found out later that Martin Donner had *been* a sergeant-major, or at least a master-sergeant, which is much the same thing.

I bawled my way over the monotonous stream of filth he used for reproof. 'Hogget,' I kept saying. 'J. R. Hogget.' At last it got through.

'Jesus,' Donner said. 'Do you know what time it is?'

'You said to call any time if I had something.'

'Oh,' said Donner. 'Just a minute, will you?'

Faintly I heard the word 'Hon', then the mouthpiece was covered while hon was sent to make coffee or a fresh bed or something.

'OK,' said Donner. What you got?'

'In a minute,' I said. 'I gather you know about the burglary?'

'Sure,' he said. 'That sexy French janitor phoned me right off. I said she should call you.'

'She did,' I said. 'I'm here now.'

'You didn't call the cops?'

'Of course not,' I said. 'You left word not to. Only–'

'Only what?'

'What about the damage? Some of this place is a shambles.'

'Leave it.' He sounded impatient. It was only say twenty thousand dollars after all. Probably what he made per hour, and tax-deductible at that.

'Glad to,' I said.

'What I found,' I said, 'was a name and address.' I read it to him. 'Eduardo Guardi, Via Raffaello 15, Verona. It's on a sheet of plain, cheap paper and it's typed.' But not on the machine in the flat. I'd already checked. 'Mean anything to you?' No answer. 'I've got a contact I use sometimes,' I said. 'A woman. I phoned her. She was a bit reluctant, but I finally got it out of her.'

'More money,' said Donner.

'I think you'll find it's worth it. It's a commune.'

'A what?'

'A students' hangout,' I said. 'A Left Wing Students' hangout.' And indeed it was bound to be, if my sister was right, because the whole street was.

'Left wing?' said Donner. 'Like the Red Brigade?'

'Could be,' I said.

'Whoever broke in,' Donner said. 'Do you think they found that address and just left it to fool us?'

'No,' I said.

'Why not?'

'Even I had to look for it twice.'

'You really hate yourself, don't you?' Donner said.

'It's why you hired me... Because I can find things.'

'Now you're going to find this Guardi?'

'Right.'

'Go to it.' It sounded like he was going to hang up, so I yelled: 'Mr Donner!'

'What now?'

'Who knew you were going to Paris?'

'Does it matter?'

'I was here for almost two days and nobody bothers. You look in for ten minutes and this happens.'

'It matters,' said Donner. 'Let's see … I flew straight to Paris from Perth, Western Australia, so a whole lot of Australians know. They kept joshing me about it.'

'Who else?'

'Nobody,' said Donner.

'Oh come on,' I said.

'Why should I lie? I'm paying you good money. It's the truth I'm after. Nobody else knew. Just me. And my secretary, and Black and White of course. And – oh yeah – Cass Milligan. In case you phoned her and were trying to reach me… What else did you find?'

'Nothing,' I said.

'I guess what you've got is enough. Anything else?'

'That's all for now,' I said. 'Sorry if I–'

He hung up on me.

I went back to Dave. He still had an awful lot of tidying up to do. 'Keep at it,' I told him. 'You're doing fine. I'm going out for a while. When I come back I'll take you out to dinner.'

I went out thinking that at least Anna Maria's new winter coat was taken care of. None of your rubbish either. Harrods. And she deserved it too. One of the best, my sister Anna Maria.

When I got back Dave had bunged all the loose papers out of sight. The room still looked awful, but what could he do about it? He looked at me, and the parcel I was carrying. 'What you got there?' he asked.

'It's a piece of crystal sculpture,' I said. 'Present for my Aunt Agnese.'

'Those things cost a fortune. You must love her dearly.'

'She's all right.' I said. 'The thing is I may want her to do things for us and she wouldn't take money, me being family... Mad on crystal, she is.'

'You really plan ahead, don't you Ron?' said Dave.

'I have to,' I said. 'Which reminds me, I better arrange to get you a gun. I'll have to phone a bloke in Rome...'

'No worries,' said Dave. 'I've got one with me.'

'*You what?*' If I was screaming, I reckon I was entitled.

'Well of course I did. You said I'd need one.'

'You great steaming berk,' I said. 'You mean you took it through customs? Twice?'

'Just once,' said Dave. 'I packed it in my case.'

'Well of course you did,' I said. 'If you hadn't we wouldn't be here.'

'But nobody checks your baggage these days when you come through the green,' said Dave.

'Nobody could break into this place, only somebody did,' I said. I mixed a gin and tonic. Dave had got the ice out. There was even a slice of lemon from the fridge.

'I'm sorry, Ron,' Dave said. 'I should have checked.'

'You bloody should,' I said.

'It's a good gun,' said Dave. 'Only hand-gun I've ever used, come to that. Want to see it?'

'Why not?' I said.

He went out and rummaged in his luggage and came back with this mean looking bastard of a revolver.

'Colt Python .357 Magnum,' he said. 'Use it right and you'll kill your enemy every time. Use it wrong and you'd do more good chucking it at him.'

He offered it to me but I backed away. I hate guns.

'Ever use it on anybody?' I said.

'No,' he said. 'Not that one. I've used others.'

His eyes suddenly weren't seeing me any more, and he was remembering Northern Ireland.

'But you're saying that's the only hand-gun you're really happy with?'

'It's the only one I've ever fired. You remember – that pistol range I used to go to?'

I remembered. I remembered what I'd been told about the bloke in Rome, too. Get you a gun quick, any time, but you couldn't argue about what kind. You took what you got. Once you got specific it might take days...

'We got it this far,' I said. 'We'd better take it all the way.'

'Thanks, Ron,' he said.

'Where did you get it, anyway?'

'The Falls Road, Belfast,' said Dave. 'It's a souvenir.'

'Let's go and get something to eat,' I said.

Usually when you say that to him it's like 'Bring on the dancing girls'. He's got a real good appetite, Dave. But this time he shuffled from foot to foot and looked sheepish.

'I brought extra ammo as well,' he said.

'I'm surprised you didn't pack a tank while you were at it,' I said. 'Let's go and eat.'

'Shall I take the gun?' he asked.

'Guns are for Italy. We're still in France,' I said. Which goes to show you I was as daft as he was.

I took him to a place Jane had mentioned in her appointment book. Four courses and a bottle of Burgundy later, I reckoned we'd earned our walk home. I called for the bill looked at it, and at once saw Donner's face, heard his screams, when he saw the item in the expense account. But in the end he'd pay...

We walked through a maze of streets that would have been baffling if I hadn't got a street map and Dave a good sense of direction. Twenty minutes of cheerful chat and the worst – or best if you like – of the blow-out beginning to work off. Almost home, in fact. Just cut through an alley like a London mews and we're back on our own street. Then suddenly Dave says, not even breaking stride, just strolling home: 'We're being followed.' Don't ask me how he knew, ask Northern Ireland. But he did know. I very nearly did stop on account of I was appalled, but his hand took my arm, urged me on.

'Just keep moving,' he said, 'and do as I say. Got it?' Then he laughed. I thought he'd gone bonkers.

'What the hell are you laughing for?' I said.

'To show how carefree we are.'

'Oh ... yeah!' I said. So I laughed, too. It sounded like a loony being tickled on the feet with wire wool.

'You're a terrible actor,' said Dave.

'I'm a first-rate coward,' I told him.

We kept on going round a bend in the alley. Two blokes stood between us and our road.

'Split up,' said Dave. 'How much change you got?'

'You couldn't bribe these blokes with change.'

'Fill your hand with it and make a fist,' said Dave, 'then you've got a club. Here – take mine as well.'

He handed me a load of coins then pushed me into the shadow of a wall and took off like a sprinter before I could say 'Ta'. Headed straight for the blokes at the top of the street. The two geezers came towards him of course, but Dave was up in the air before they could get anywhere near, and his body twisted in the air so that he was parallel with the ground and his feet shot out in a snap kick that caught one of the geezers on the chin. I could hear it even where I was. The geezer went down, of course, and Dave had worked out precisely where he was going to fall – the way a lumberjack knows just where a tree will drop. He fell across his mate, and while he was busy doing it Dave lands on his back, head tucked in like a boxer's, shoulders and arms breaking the fall.

Meantime two other blokes were racing up the alley towards Dave and they had things in their hands I didn't like the look of. But Dave bounced up like the Michelin man and linked his two hands together and cracked the bloke who was still entangled with his mate on the back of the neck, and again I heard it. Nasty.

The first of the other two had reached him by then and I saw that the thing in his hand was a knife: saw too that he was circling round his resting comrades so he could stick it in Dave, who was using his first two victims as a barricade. Then there was number four, moving in behind. I groaned to myself, but I had no option, did I? Dave was my mate. I moved up in the shadows towards number four, who only had eyes for Dave, as the song says.

Suddenly number three lunged and Dave's body swerved, the knife flashed past him and Dave's arm bent, his elbow smashed into number three's throat, and at the same time number four got set to lunge at Dave with his knife, only I said a short prayer, and swung my arm like a club, and to my immense surprise number four went down as if I'd pulled the rug from under him and my hand began to hurt like hell.

'And you said we wouldn't need a gun,' said Dave. 'Thanks mate.'

'I feel sick,' I said.

'What a waste of good food,' said Dave. So I wasn't.

Dave lined them up neatly, like sardines waiting for the can.

All they had on them was a lot of money, which we kept.

'Hired muscle,' I said, and Dave nodded, and went over them again, then tapped the one he'd kicked.

'This one's dead,' he said. 'I broke his neck.'

Again I wasn't sick. God knows how I managed it. I sneaked a glance at Dave, but he didn't look sick. All he did look like was a man who'd just done a good job. And he had. But I'd had no idea he was that good. I mean, Dave had been my minder before, several times, but all that meant was showing his muscles – a swift kick in the balls at most.

'What I don't understand,' I said at last, 'is why that last geezer didn't go for me.'

'They wanted me out of the way first,' said Dave.

'But I could have run out of the other end of the alley.'

'They probably hoped you would,' said Dave. 'There'd be another one waiting there. Maybe more than one.'

'So where are they now?' I asked.

'Scarpered,' Dave said.

'I wouldn't blame them,' I said, and looked at the fallen.

When we got back, Dave said he was hungry. He was apologetic about it, considering the dinner I'd bought him, but all the same he had to eat.

'I'm sorry,' he said. 'But fights always get me like this.'

The fact that he had just killed a man seemed to bother him not at all. I felt a twinge in my right hand and looked at it: it was a rather nasty shade of purple and about twice the size of the left.

'Got just the thing for that,' said Dave.

He disappeared, and came back with a bottle and some cotton wool, dabbed whatever was in the bottle on my hand. Almost at once the twinges stopped, soon I could move the fingers.

'It'll be fine by morning,' he said.

'Thanks,' I said. 'Go have a look in the fridge. I've still got a bit more work to do.'

'Better you than me,' said Dave, and went into the kitchen.

I went to the study. What else did you find? Donner had said – I'd found nothing because I thought there was nothing – but then Guardi's address had turned up. Jane had been good at hiding things, when all was said and done. A private person who valued her privacy. I went back to the study, but there was nothing there. What I was after was sewn into the base of the sofa in the living-room, and what I'd found was a piece of microfilm. Unfortunately I didn't have anything to read it by.

I went into the kitchen. Dave had found Brie, and butter and biscuits, and had now moved on to peaches in brandy. I had some myself, then went to the fridge and got out a bottle of champagne.

'We shouldn't,' said Dave. 'If we finish that I'll be pissed. I can't fight when I'm pissed.'

'You won't have to,' I said. 'Not tonight anyway.'

'You're sure?'

'Certain,' I said. Dave went to get the glasses and I sat and wondered why we were drinking. Celebration? Consolation? We were in need of both. Then Dave came back with the glasses and I gave up wondering and just drank.

# 10

We didn't catch the earliest flight to Venice, not the way we were feeling, and had a very light lunch on the plane, and another glass of champagne apiece for medicinal purposes.

In those days the Venice customs only had the one right bastard, but he was hell on wheels. I know because I used to go to Venice a lot, what with having a lot of relatives in Verona, and Melanie liking that part of Italy. I'd never crossed him because as I've said before, the business I'm in, it pays to keep your nose clean with the customs, but I've seen him in action. Oh dear, oh dear.

Everything depended which exit he covered, the green or the red. Either way he'd be opening suitcases... He was on the green. I took Dave's suitcase and the crystal vase and headed for the red. Dave took mine through the green. The geezer I saw looked at the vase and was impressed, then he looked at the bill and was even more impressed. I told him – in English: nothing sticks in the memory of officials more than an Englishman speaking fluent, if inaccurate Italian – that the only other stuff was the duty frees. Extra cigarettes for Dave, under protest; cognac for Uncle Pietro. He charged me twenty thousand lire and wished me a nice trip. At that I had to wait for Dave. The monster had stopped him, and when he didn't find anything he got so mad he went through all my stuff twice...

We needed a car. That meant the Piazzale Roma. Dave was looking hungrily at signs that said 'Vaparetto Grand Canal', but that was for tourists. We were working men, and that means the Piazzale Roma. It's a weird place, so big it's monstrous and lined with bus-stops and garages, and noisy with the clangour of internal combustion engines. Nothing to do with Venice at all.

Cars are tricky. Hire cars I mean. You have to fill forms in and show passports and sign for things. I was after something you could buy. Something comfortable enough – and fast enough – to take care of long distances – and yet not too conspicuous, not too flash.

There was a garage I'd heard Uncle Pietro speak well of in the past, and I nosed around till I'd found it, and sure enough, there was a possible. Lancia Flavia, three years old: well used, certainly, but not clapped out.

I said to Dave, 'What d'you think?'

'It'll cost a fortune,' he said.

'Can you drive her?'

'A damn sight better than I drive that heap of scrap I use for cabbing,' he said. So we went inside and I used my fast, inaccurate Italian to get Dave a test drive, and Dave was impressed. He was even more impressed when he drove the Lancia. She was a lady, a fast and elegant lady.

We went back to the garage and I paid cash from a wad of notes that would have choked an ostrich, and this time Dave wasn't impressed: he was awed.

'When did you get that?' he asked.

'Yesterday. When I went to buy the vase.'

We drove to Verona. It's a good, fast road, mostly autostrada, and Dave and the Lancia loved it. When we got to the suburbs he eased off and got in lane, and I was glad he'd driven in Italy before. The first time you feel as if every man's hand is against you, and it is. But Dave knew how to cope. I guided him past the arena, where they have opera nowadays, (mostly Aida, complete with camels and elephants) past the prefecture, and the streets full of fashionable shops, into a quiet corner of uncompromisingly bourgeois housing, to my Uncle Pietro's house, which is as uncompromisingly bourgeois as he is.

My Uncle Pietro had three jobs that I knew of. He was an accountant, he wrote a political column for a Social Democratic paper, and he bought and sold houses and shops. In his spare time he watched football. He used to play it when he was a young man, and pretty good he was, too. Aunt Agnese hadn't done a damn thing since she married Uncle Pietro except run the house, but she manages to make that into a twelve-hour day. I'd phoned to tell her I was coming, so she was out to the door pushing the maid aside before my thumb was off the bell-push.

It's always hard seeing Aunt Agnese after you've been away from her for a while, because she looks so much like my mother. A little shorter, a little fatter, but the same brown eyes with a special light in them, the same small, high-bridged nose, expressive mouth and even more expressive hands. But Aunt Agnese never gives you time to brood. 'Tommaso!' she said, and hugged me as if it were three falls or submissions to decide the winner. I struggled free and introduced her to Dave, and it was now his turn to impress me.

'*Piacere di fare la sua conoscenta, molto lieto,*' he said. To the manner born.

Aunt Agnese was enchanted.

She hustled us inside, and took us into her living-room, that looked more like Aladdin's cave than anything else. I've never seen so much stuff packed in per cubic foot outside a packing case. Even so the maid was in straight after us with plates of cakes, and Aunt Agnese was pouring Marsala wine. I told Dave in English to watch his step and he said he saw what I meant. That room had everything from a reproduction in miniature of Michelangelo's David to a row of ivory elephants.

I gave Aunt Agnese the piece of crystal and wondered where on earth she was going to put it. Unperturbed, she tore at the string and wrapping, and when all was revealed went into raptures. '*Chè bella. Bellissima.*' The she bellowed 'Claudia! Claudia!' And the maid came on the run. Then she went into raptures too, though I can't think why. It was just one more thing for her to dust. Carefully the two of them moved the elephants closer together on their shelf, eased three Meissen saucers together till they overlapped – and there was a home for the vase. If I hadn't seen where they'd put it, it would have taken me a week to find it.

Then Claudia went back to carry on making the evening's pasta, and Aunt Agnese said: 'I may speak in front of your friend?'

'Of course,' I said. 'He is also my partner.'

'In business. I thought so. You are a dear, sweet boy Tommaso, with a lovely wife and a terrible father, but there has to be a reason why you give me this.'

'I have also a wonderful aunt,' I said.

She chuckled. 'It is true,' she said. 'But even so... Why, Tommaso?'

'David and I are here on business,' I said. 'We have – certain enquiries we must make about a missing person. We may want your help a little. This is just to say "Thank you" in advance.'

'What help?'

'Just information. From you and Uncle Pietro. Maybe Adriana too.' (Adriana was the daughter uncle Pietro was worried about.)

'Who is missing, Tommaso?'

'A young woman,' I said. 'A kind, pretty, intelligent young woman.'

I could feel Dave's glance on me. He was not to know whether I lied or not. She looked at me hard, and it worried me. Aunt Agnese's blend of shrewdness and intuition were very like my mother's. She looked again at the vase.

'I will help you Tommaso,' she said. But it wasn't just that incredible lump of glass: as a family we liked one another enough to help when asked.

'Where are you going to stay?' she asked. I'd already told her we couldn't stay with her.

'Somewhere not too conspicuous,' I said. She phoned a place a little way out of town which, she was sure, was just what we needed, and found us a bed. *Commendato per Dottore Pietro Calvi,* I heard her say, brandishing her husband's name like a weapon. But it got us a room.

'About those questions,' I said.

'We wait for Pietro,' she said. 'You go to your hotel and relax and come back here at eight. Then we eat and talk. Me *and* Pietro.'

She wouldn't budge, I knew, so I kissed her on the cheeks, and Dave took her hand and bowed, and we went to the hotel Aunt Agnese had booked for us. It was one link in an enormous chain of hotels that stretched all over Western Europe. All the same, all anonymous, and just the place for us. The hotel was stacked with youngish, eager, slightly worried-looking geezers just like us, sales reps, technical reps, promotional consultants. We melted right into the landscape.

It wasn't bad, though. Telly, two three-quarter beds in the one big room, (which made me feel more secure) and a mini-bar.

'What now?' said Dave.

'We relax till we eat. Then we ask my aunt and uncle to suss out this Guardi geezer.'

'Do I take the Colt?'

'Do me a favour,' I said.

'You did say it was for Italy,' said Dave.

'In the glove compartment,' I said. 'But for God's sake make sure you immobilize the Lancia properly. The Italians are the best car-thieves in the world.'

'It's because they love them so much,' said Dave. 'Don't you worry. I don't intend to lose her.'

Aunt Agnese and Uncle Pietro had dressed up nicely, so I was glad Dave and I had changed too. Uncle Pietro is handsome and slim and elegant, even at his age, which is well into the fifties, and

Aunt Agnese adores him. But being slim doesn't mean he was on a diet. Aunt Agnese had cooked quite a meal. Dave ate rather more than his share and my aunt and uncle watched appreciatively, piling up his plate. At last it was time for coffee and strega. Uncle Pietro put the bottle of cognac I'd brought on the table, too, but we both said no. Uncle Pietro looked relieved.

'You're a generous young man, Tommaso,' he said. 'Your aunt tells me we may be able to be of help to you.'

'Just some information about a man we're trying to trace. It's connected with the case we're working on.'

'The pretty, intelligent young woman?'

'That's the one.'

'Who is he?'

'Eduardo Guardi,' I said. 'Via Raffaello 15.'

He made a face.

'Not a nice neighbourhood?' I asked.

'The worst,' said Uncle Pietro. 'Red students. Squats. Communes. Raffaello ... Guardi. Two nice painters. Why do they have to give their names to such people, such places? What do you want to know?'

'Who he is. Who else lives at number 15. Any scraps there are, really.'

'It will have to be tomorrow,' Uncle Pietro said. 'I can reach my contacts only in the daytime.'

'Fine,' I said. 'Just tell me where it is and we'll drive through the street on our way home.'

'Not in your car,' Uncle Pietro said.

'What's wrong with my car?'

'Nothing in the world,' said Uncle Pietro. 'Your

aunt has told me about it. It is a very fine car and I wish I had one like it.' (A polite lie. He drives a Mercedes 250.) 'What you must do if you wish to go there is speak nicely to Claudia and borrow her little Fiat and go in that. You will give her some money, too – not too much,' he added sternly. My aunt and uncle did not believe in corrupting servants with over-indulgence.

And that's what we did. Dave studied the street map Uncle Pietro produced, and we set off in Claudia's baby Fiat, which moved with the same kind of erratic urgency as Claudia herself, down the wide elegant streets once more, and the shops full of silk and perfume and crocodile leather, the restaurants full of the rich and replete, then on past rich houses, middling houses, blocks of flats, tenements. On to the worst tenement of the lot, which was Via Raffaello. It was the bottom. Obviously nobody who lived there paid rent, so none of the houses were maintained. By maintenance I mean such things as glass in the windows, water in the taps, tiles on the roofs. The only electric light was the street lamps, and half of them were broken. Inside they used candles, and the soft, warm light they made was the only pretty thing in that whole hideous street.

The people who lived there seemed to be either tramps, students or drunks, and quite a lot of the students looked like junkies. Long hair and jeans, and a tendency to scratch because if there isn't any bath water there can't be any baths. Dave slowed as we reached number 15. Much like the rest, except outside it there seemed to some kind of political meeting going on. A geezer in a red shirt was raising a clenched fist, and a joint was being passed from hand to hand. Donner would have loved it. Suddenly one of the joint-passers saw us.

'Bourgeois!' she yelled. In *that* car?

Dave put his foot down, and we passed out of their lives...

'You saw?' Uncle Pietro said, when we returned home.

'More than enough.'

My uncle sighed. 'It is a sad thing. A disgraceful thing. But there are too many students and not enough jobs – so what are we to do?'

'Talking of students,' I said. 'How's Adriana?'

'Better than when I last talked to your sister. She does well at her studies,' Uncle Pietro said. 'And she is not quite so – political as she once was.'

Adriana had been a roaring Lefty since the age of twelve, so this was news indeed. 'Where is she now?' I asked.

'At the university. At Padua.'

'But surely this is the vacation?'

'She wishes to study a little more. I begin to be quite proud of her.'

At this point Aunt Agnese began to show Dave her photograph album, with special reference to Adriana from the age of three weeks on. I lowered my voice.

'Do you have access to a telex, Uncle Pietro?' I asked.

'Of course.' Who doesn't? his voice seemed to say.

'Could you send something and get a reply

without anyone else knowing?'

'Is it legal?'

'Oh yes,' I said. 'Perfectly legal. Just confidential.'

I handed him a sheet of paper and he put it away carefully.

Then there was one more coffee and strega and it was time to go. Aunt Agnese embraced me, Dave bowed to her and Uncle Pietro, then my uncle came out to look at the Lancia.

'Not for the Via Raffaello,' he said. 'Not in a thousand years.' How right he was. Then he shook hands with Dave, and he embraced me in a formal way.

'Goodnight, *Dottore*,' I said.

He aimed a mock blow at my chin and went back into the house.

'What's all this dottore?' Dave asked when we got to the car.

'Just a kind of flattery,' I said. 'Only with Uncle Pietro and me it's a joke. Doctor's sort of a title. I don't mean like a medical doctor—'

'Doctor of Philosophy, Doctor of Literature, that sort of thing?'

'Right,' I said.

'And is he a doctor? Your uncle, I mean.'

'Of course he's not,' I said. 'It's just that Aunt Agnese thinks he ought to be.'

'This is the first time I ever heard of a self-inflicted doctorate,' said Dave.

Next morning I waited till Dave went to take a shower, then put in a call to London. The geezer I was after was a bloke called Horace Betterton Lumley – Horry if you wanted something out of him. So he was Horry to me. Very upper class was Horry, and bent as a corkscrew. It all started at Cambridge, where he was thrown out. Very difficult to get thrown out of Cambridge these days, Dave reckons, or any other university come to that, but Horry managed it. All on account of horses. He had a great flair for picking losers, and at last the time came when he'd run out of money, so he borrowed a bit of the college silver and popped it. Purely as a loan, he kept telling the fellows and professors and tutors and that, but they wouldn't listen. They invited him to leave. He wasn't sent down, on account of his uncles are all generals and air vice-marshals and chairmen of the board, but they didn't beg him to stay on either. Which was a pity in a way. They all thought he'd do brilliantly: end up as a research fellow himself. Well at least he's doing research. It was him I got Uncle Pietro to send the telex to, and the rates he charges, he's bound to be making more money than he would at a Cambridge College. Must be ... I heard the phone ringing.

'Hello!' he said, in the sort of voice that says I just got out of bed with a hangover, so watch it.

'Horry,' I said. 'This is a mate of yours.'

'So you say.'

'I found that diamond ring you lost.'

(He'd gone and got engaged when he was drunk, and given the girl a ring that belonged to one of his uncle's wives. The idea was he should have it cleaned, not get engaged with it.)

'Oh,' Horry said. 'I suppose you are a mate then.'

Not very gracious, but I needed a favour.

'You'll be getting a telex from me soon,' I said. 'A bit of research I want you to do for me.'

'Why don't you tell me on the phone?'

'You know how shy I am,' I said.

'Oh...' said Horry. 'Like that is it. How much are you offering?'

'A grand,' I said.

'*A thousand pounds?*' He was my mate now all right.

'It's a rush job,' I said.

'I'll drop everything.'

As he spoke, Dave came back into the room. He's the fastest shaver and showerer I ever came across. Must be the army training.

"Where'll I send it?' Horry asked.

'The address is on the telex,' I said. 'Be seeing you, Horry.'

'You really are a mate,' said Horry. 'Goodbye.'

He was ecstatic, and so would his bookmakers be. I turned to Dave: he didn't look happy.

'Don't you trust me or something?' he said.

'Dave, I–'

'Because if you don't, just say so and I'll pack up my Magnum and go home.'

I tried again. 'Dave, I–'

'I thought we were supposed to be mates,' said Dave. Just like me and Horry Lumley. 'Partners. And all the time you're doing things behind my back.'

'Dave,' I said, 'I don't–'

This time the interruption was a knock at the door, a floor waiter with toast, rolls, butter, marmalade, coffee and milk. He put it down and I showed him out.

'Don't try telling me it's a coincidence that you never make a phone call till my back's turned – because I bloody well wouldn't believe it.'

'Of course it isn't bloody coincidence.' I yelled it, and it stopped him. 'I don't want you to know more than you have to,' I said.

'Don't you think that's obvious?' said Dave. Sarcastic. Trying to wound. And then he went and spoiled it by buttering a roll and lathering it with marmalade. Always hungry, Dave.

'You *should* thank me,' I said.

'Should I indeed?' Dave bit into his roll as if it were an enemy.

'That's right. You should,' I said. 'I'm in this thing deep,' I said. 'Very deep.'

'Don't tell me,' he said. 'I don't even know what thing.'

'It's a dangerous thing,' I said. 'Extremely dangerous.'

'So I suppose. That's why you're paying me so well.'

'The more you know, the more dangerous it'll be,' I said.

'More dangerous than the other night when those blokes came at us? I killed one of them for you, Ron boy. Or had you forgotten?'

'I'll never forget,' I said. 'I–'

'And while we're on the subject – have you told your boss about that?' I shook my head. 'Why not? Had it slipped your memory – or do you consider it too trivial to mention?'

No doubt about it, Dave really was mad.

'I can't tell him,' I said.

'Can't?'

'If I phone him he'll take over,' I said. 'Tell us what to do. I can't have that. We've got to do this my way. It's the only way I know.'

I put my face in my hands, and I think Dave realized that the strain was getting to me. 'Look,' he said. 'Let's have some coffee.'

'All right,' I said. 'And while we're having it I'll put you in the picture.'

'You don't have to. I was just letting off steam. And anyway you're the boss.'

'I do have to,' I said. 'You could have died the other night. You're at least entitled to know why.' And I told him the lot. Everything except the way I felt about Jane. When I had done he said, 'Jesus ... I'm glad it's your problem and not mine.'

Probably the nicest compliment Dave ever paid me, but it was still my problem. 'You do the fighting,' I said, 'and I'll do the worrying. Let's stick to what we're good at... And talking of fighting,' I said. 'They really teach you in the Paras, don't they? All that jumping about and that.'

'That wasn't the Paras,' said Dave. 'That was karate. I belong to a club.' He poured coffee. 'Ask me what for.'

'What for?'

'Because I'm good at it,' he said. 'Because I enjoy it.'

'You enjoyed the other night?'

'I was scared all right,' said Dave. 'But I conquered that and the adrenalin flowed and I knew how good I was. Yeah ... I enjoyed it. It's nothing to be proud of, but it's nothing to be ashamed of either.'

'I'll stick to worry,' I said. Then the phone rang.

It was Aunt Agnese. Uncle Pietro would like us to join him for coffee at eleven-thirty. Café in the Piazza. That just gave time for Dave to take a look at Juliet's balcony in the Capulet house in Via Vappello. He reckoned it was a fake.

It was some American geezer who said that Italy is a poor country full of very rich people. There are plenty of poor ones too, of course, but he was right about the rich. The Piazza dei Signori is bang in the middle of that section that runs from the Piazza della Erbe to the Town Hall, the open-air opera arena just round the corner, and smells of money. Big old buildings in golden stone, wide streets with trees, the kind of shops that wouldn't have looked out of place in Bond Street, or even the Rue de la Paix. And this in a small provincial city that nobody would ever have heard of if it hadn't been for Shakespeare. We had trouble parking too, among all the Mercs and Alfa-Romeos and Ferraris. The Lancia didn't look poor, but it didn't look opulent either.

Uncle Pietro had seen us coming and had signalled for coffee. Espresso. If you don't like coffee stay out of Italy.

Aunt Agnese wasn't there, so Uncle Pietro spoke in English.

'I have news for you,' he said, and looked at Dave.

'That's all right,' I said. 'Dave's my partner.'

'That's good,' said Uncle Pietro. Whether he meant it was good that I trusted my partner or that he was big and strong, I still don't know.

'I have news about Eduardo Guardi ... Comrade Guardi.' The Comrade came as no surprise.

Uncle Pietro noticed that.

'You knew about his politics?'

'We had an idea,' I said. 'And in that neigh-bourhood–'

'It's true,' said Uncle Pietro. 'Reds or derelicts. They live in squalor, even in filth. There was a time when I thought my Adriana–' he hesitated, then his hand moved again: a dismissive gesture this time.

'Eduardo Guardi is rich,' Uncle Pietro con-tinued. 'His father owns a textile factory in Milano. A very big factory. He is worth at least three million dollars American. Eduardo is his only son. He also has four daughters, but Eduardo is his *son*. In Italy this is very important, even in these days. He is twenty-three years old, clever, not bad-looking. I got you a picture.' He handed up a photocopy of a newspaper photograph. Not bad-looking about summed it up. Robert Redford he wasn't.

'Nice work, Uncle Pietro,' I said.

'I got it from the newspaper I write for,' Uncle Pietro said. 'There were no difficulties... Your Guardi lives in the squat to show solidarity, but he is not like the others.'

'In what way?' I asked.

'He is active, energetic, and he is also clean. And fit.'

'You're saying he is an activist?'

'I am saying only what I tell you. It is said that he is a very competent planner and administrator – just like his father. The irony is that ten years ago an attempt was made to kidnap him – only his father's bodyguard saved him.'

'Reds?' I asked.

'The Camorra,' Uncle Pietro said. The Camorra, also known as the Gentlemen, are a sort of mainland Mafia who specialize in kidnapping.'

'Is Guardi in the squat now?' I asked.

Uncle Pietro shook his head. 'He is in Padua,' he said. 'I could not find out where – but here is the name and address of someone who will tell you.' He handed me a sealed envelope.

'That information cost me a quarter of a million lire,' he said.

I paid up like a man.

On the way to the car Dave said, 'Your cousin Adriana's in Padua, too.'

'I know,' I said.

'She used to be a Red.'

'You think I'd forgotten?'

'Well then?' said Dave.

'Well then what?' I said. 'She's my cousin. Family. And she's Italian. And so am I. Or the best part of me is.'

'Sorry,' said Dave. 'I only thought–'

'I know,' I said. 'It could have saved us days.'

Then we stopped at Aunt Agnese's house to take formal leave because that's the way they do things in Italy. This time she embraced us both. Dave certainly had something going for him and it wasn't just his appetite.

As we left she said, 'Your uncle phoned. He tells me you are going to Padua. He says to remind you to look up your cousin Adriana – as if you'd needed reminding to call on your own family. She's in the Via Petrarco – Number 83. A nice little house. But so bare.' She looked with pride at the heaped up treasures in her living room. 'Now don't forget to come to us again before you leave Italy.'

'Of course not, Aunt Agnese,' I said. More hugs and kisses, a handshake and a ten thousand lire note for Claudia and we were off to Padua.

When we were back on the autostrada Dave said, 'What's your cousin Adriana like?'

'You saw her photographs,' I said.

'Yeah, I know,' he said. 'But what's she *like?*'

That needed thinking about. 'Clever,' I said. 'Restless. Last I heard she was rebellious, too. She must have changed.'

'Your uncle seemed to think so.'

'He did indeed,' I said. 'He's given us permission to ask her about Guardi.'

'You think so?' said Dave.

'I know so,' I said. 'He phoned Aunt Agnese to tell us that – and you remember he gave us the name and address of someone who'd put us on to Guardi? It was Adriana's name and address.'

'Well, well, well,' said Dave. 'Is she beautiful? She looked beautiful.'

'Who? Adriana?'

'Of course Adriana.'

'Depends how you look at her,' I said.

'In the eye of the beholder?' said Dave.

'Something like that. She's tough and she's supposed to be brainy, according to her mother, so there've been times she wasn't at all feminine. On the other hand there've been times when she was.'

'Did you ever fancy her?'

'She uses too many long words,' I said. 'Anyway – last time I saw her she was just a kid. Spotty. A bit of a podge.'

'She isn't like that now,' said Dave. I let it lie.

# 11

Padua is a university town – one of the oldest in Europe; and quiet and sedate the way university towns are, except when they're having student riots. We found a room in an ancient albergo that Uncle Pietro had recommended. From outside it looked as if the last person to have stayed there could have been Garibaldi, but inside it was great. Big room, comfortable beds, old, easy furniture. And a courtyard at the back just made for the Lancia. We ordered dinner, and while we had our aperitifs – if you can call Dave's lager an aperitif – I phoned Adriana.

'Tommaso hello,' she said. 'Pappa said you would phone.'

Did he indeed? I thought. You always were a crafty one, Uncle Pietro. Just what are you up to?

'Me and my mate Dave just got in,' I said. We were wondering if you'd like to have dinner with us.'

'Oh Tommaso, I can't,' she said. 'Not tonight. I have a date for dinner. But if you are free for coffee–'

'Of course,' I said. 'Do you want to come into town?'

'No.' She was quite firm on that. Then, more gently: 'I am on the Abano Terme road. It's pretty there at this time of year. Could we go there?'

'Sure,' I said. 'Pick you up?'

'That will be nice,' she said. 'Here at nine thirty?'

'Look forward to it,' I said. 'Ciao.'

Being a woman she forgot to tell us how to get there, but it didn't worry me. The hotel had sold us a street map. I went back to my campari and soda, no orange.

'After dinner we pick her up at her place,' I said.

'Why not dinner?'

'She has a date.'

'You mean she's got a bloke?'

I remembered what Anna Maria had said. 'Of course not,' I said. 'She's a student.'

After supper we backed the car out of the cobbled courtyard. It was half past eight. Far too early, really, but we had to allow time for getting lost. The Via Petrarco took a bit of finding at that, but we tracked it down at last and made a bit of a detour, and pulled up at Number 83 at five past nine.

It was a neat, stone-built house, nine or ten rooms, and Adriana rented two of them. Maybe fifty years old, perhaps a little more, with big windows and a verandah, and a garden with an olive tree, a few oranges and lemons, and roses, gladioli, geraniums. Adriana was in the garden, too: her black hair worn long, summer dress of white with huge green spots, arms, legs and shoulders darkly tanned. In her hands she carried a white cardigan, a green handbag. For this evening at any rate, Adriana had decided to be beautiful.

Dave said, 'You're driving on the way back,' and I quite saw what he meant. I got out of the car and went to meet her and she said, 'Tommaso. It's been so long.' Her English, I noticed, was excellent. Then she embraced me just like her mother, only the effect wasn't the same. It wasn't the same at all. I took her up to the car, and she was impressed, and so she should be, the amount Donner had paid for it, then I introduced her to my mate Dave.

'Miss Adriana Bonetti,' I said. 'This is my friend and colleague Mr David Baxter.' David started to tell her in Italian what a pleasure it was. Meaning it too, but she choked him off.

'Oh please,' she said. 'Do let's speak English. I need the practice.'

Then she got in the car with me and talked all the way to Abano Terme in Italian.

Abano Terme is a little town that is built on mud. Not literally – the mud is somewhere up in the mountains – but in terms of economics certainly. The mud is hot and comes coughing up from deep down in the earth's surface, together with a lot of boiling water which comes in very handy for the swimming pools. The swimming pools are for the guests of the hotels. There must be at least a score of them; all full of people queuing up to be daubed with the mud, then hosed down with therapeutic water.

It's a pretty town. Not much in the way of buildings, but some nice gardens. There's a café in one of them and that's where we sat. Coffee and Vecchia Romagna brandy for Dave and me, just coffee for Adriana. She continued to chatter away in Italian: how was my sister? wasn't it about time I became a father? how much she still missed my mother – all that, but at the same time she was keeping an eye on Dave, getting his reactions; and the silly berk didn't twig: just kept on looking more and more mopish. Love at first sight, I thought. That'll never do.

I said in English, 'Your father suggested I should look you up.' She blinked at me and said, also in English: 'Of course... So nice to see you ... both.' She fished in her handbag for a cigarette and Dave was there at once with his lighter. She blew smoke. 'Pappa warned me you'd be coming,' she said.

'Warned?'

'You are like my professor, Tommaso,' she said. 'Always the correct word. Told me then.'

'Did he tell you why we're here?'

'Only that you and–' she looked at my mate.

'Dave,' I said, before the pause got too long.

'That you and Davide,' she pronounced it in the Italian way, 'are doing something here and I can help you perhaps. But I don't see how.'

'Do you mind if I ask a few questions?' I said.

'Let us see.'

'First the obvious one... Why are you staying in Padua in the vacation? Why aren't you at home?'

'Because with – what do you say – the best will in the world, I am not ready to live with my parents again, no matter how much I want to. Not yet.'

It sounded like she meant it.

'You used to be very political,' I continued, and

188

she nodded. 'Are you still?'

'No,' she said.

'Not at all?'

'Not that.' She snapped her fingers. No English rose could have done it: scorn, disgust, rejection; all in one gesture, one sound.

'Why?' I said.

'I don't see that it is your business,' she said.

'Adriana,' I said. 'My business is both dangerous and important. I can only work with people I can trust.'

'You don't trust your own cousin?'

'Not if she won't answer my questions,' I said.

'Oh Tommaso.' Her voice was a wail, her lip quivered.

Dave said, 'Take it easy, Ron.'

'Belt up,' I said, and he stayed quiet because just for now I was the guv'nor, and anyway Adriana was just trying it on. She knew she'd have to answer eventually, because Uncle Pietro had told her to, and she was daddy's girl again, but she was having her bit of fun first. One poor little girl at the mercy of two hulking great men. At last her lip ran out of quivers.

'Tell us Adriana,' I said. 'Or else we all go home.'

She went back to Italian then, to tell me what she thought of me. Dave enjoyed that. Then the fun was over. She took another drag on her cigarette and was ready for business.

'For three years I was a Communist,' she said. 'For eleven years I sympathized, but for three I was *involved*... And I believed it all – if necessary we would use violence to overthrow society...'

'What got you into it?' I said.

189

'I told you,' said Adriana. 'I'd been flirting with the idea ever since I began to have tits.'

Dave winced: he didn't like the idea of his beloved in the massed ranks of liberated womanhood.

'There's got to be more than that,' I said. 'What got you into all this pure destruction?'

'A man,' she said. 'What else?'

'You care to tell us his name?'

She hesitated a moment, but now she was daddy's girl.

'Eduardo Guardi,' she said.

Dave grunted. He was new to this game. Also, he didn't know Uncle Pietro.

'How did he do it?' I said.

'There was a meeting,' said Adriana. 'Sort of seminar. What I think you call a discussion group.' She looked at Dave, and he nodded. I've no idea how she'd figured out that he'd been to university too, but she had.

'I was – was chairperson,' she said. 'Eduardo was guest speaker. Only he didn't speak first. He spoke last. For two hours he sat and listened while my friends and I talked about street corner meetings and slogans on walls and mingling with the workers. Then he got up and made a speech about fighting in the streets.'

'Then what happened?'

'We were thrilled,' she said. 'Of course. This was all the words we wanted to hear. I cannot tell you how thrilled we were. Especially me.'

'Why you?'

'We became lovers,' she said. 'It was reckoned to be a great honour – to be screwed by Eduardo.

190

So ... I have been honoured. Frequently.' She sipped her coffee. 'He wasn't a bad lover at that.'

I looked at Dave. He was hating it.

'Then what happened?'

'I became aware in the world of student communism, there were herring and there were sharks. I was a herring. I talked a lot about the toiling masses and how bourgeois my parents are – but that's all I did. Talk.'

'Eduardo?' I asked.

'Eduardo was a shark. In fact Eduardo was king of the sharks. He began his life by hating his father – why I don't know – and ended by hating every rich man in Italy. In the world. He even formed his own unit – the Red Commando – to do something about it.'

'What *did* he do about it?'

'He attacked them,' Adriana said. 'Bombs in a rich man's car, a machine gun on a rich husband and wife coming home from the opera, a rich man's child kidnapped.'

'Did he do all these things himself?' I asked.

'Of course not. There were others. I told you. The Red Commando. Two girls. Three more men. But he led. Without Eduardo they were nothing.'

'How do you know?'

'I was the messenger,' she said.

'A dangerous job,' I said.

'Not particularly. Students drift around a lot.'

There was a silence.

'Are you going to do something about Eduardo?' she asked at last.

'Depends on whether he pulled another job or not.'

'There was one more.'

'Who?'

She leaned forward. 'Tommaso – if I tell you, I must be protected night and day.'

'You will be,' I said. 'I promise.'

She leaned forward, and even there, with two of us protecting her and nobody within twenty feet, she whispered.

'I think – I am sure – he kidnapped Mrs Donner.'

'Who?' I said, before Dave could speak up and blow it.

'The wife of that rich American who was kidnapped. They – they cut her head off.'

'You're saying Guardi did this?'

She nodded. 'He and his gang.'

'Can you prove it?'

'Of course I can't prove it,' she said. 'If I could I wouldn't be sitting here with you now. But I took the messages, I heard the whispers, I was there when Eduardo spoke on the phone. I *know.*'

'Let's see if you do,' I said. 'Where was Mrs Donner kidnapped?'

'Riva del Garda.'

'What day?' She told me. That she could have got from the papers, but not the next one. 'How many were in on it?'

'It only took three. Emilia and Bruno and Guiseppina. Guiseppina to get close to her, Bruno to drive the car. Eduardo to keep Mrs Donner quiet. He would enjoy that. Keeping a pretty bourgeoise quiet.'

'Go on,' I said.

'Off to Bolzano. Two men and two girls. On

holiday... And if one of the girls is sleepy – maybe she drinks too much. It was so *easy*.'

'Where did they lift her?'

'She'd been to a restaurant,' she said. 'They got her as she left.'

'Ristorante Cesare,' I said. Not asking her. Telling her.

She nodded. 'You know too much, Tommaso. Maybe you are in danger, too.'

I remembered the French thugs. How right she was.

'Once we get him we'll none of us be in danger,' I said.

'He has friends.'

'So we'll get them too... Where is he how? Still in Padua?'

'No... He left this morning. That is another reason why we can talk like this. He is in Riva del Garda. He owns a house there.'

'He owns property?'

She smiled. 'Eduardo likes to be comfortable. He has a flat in Rome, too. He says there is no crime in enjoying the capitalist system so long as you work hard to destroy it, too.'

'But in Verona he lived in a squat,' I said.

'Oh Tommaso, Tommaso,' she said. 'Do you not see it? In Verona, in Padua, he must be at one with the revolutionary students, so that they may worship him. And besides, if he did not, where would his safe houses be? But to be poor is not Eduardo's way.' She touched the bodice of her dress. 'He bought me this,' she said.

I reckoned Dave had suffered enough.

'Just one more thing,' I said.

'Why I left him?... He cut off that poor woman's head. I think maybe he raped her too – he and Bruno.' This time it was my turn to suffer. 'Then he took the ransom and never gave her a chance. That was when I started thinking. Only I couldn't leave him right away. I had to wait until he found another girl. Another messenger.'

'He's done that?'

'Before they kidnapped Mrs Donner. For a while he ran both of us – then suddenly I was out and she was in ... I was the lucky one. They are in Riva del Garda now, discussing Engels' Communist Manifesto in between bouts of screwing.' The irony finished there. She shuddered. 'You said you will protect me, Tommaso.'

'Guaranteed,' I said. 'Let's take you home.'

I drove back. In the back seat Adriana and Dave began a long discussion about some geezer called Benedetto Croce. With Melanie and me it was usually Frank Sinatra. Then after a bit they started snogging so this Croce geezer must have his points. When we got to her gate she wanted Dave to start protecting her straightaway, but she would keep till the morning and we all knew it. Dave saw her inside, then came back to the car and drove.

'Funny isn't it?' he said.

'I could do with a laugh,' I said.

'You know what I mean,' Dave said. 'I come out here on a job – I mean crumpet's the last thought in my head – then I meet up with a little belter like that. Good mind, too. A bit crude now and again, but that's the company she's been keeping. She'll get over it... She's beautiful, you know that, Ron? And not only that, she turns out to be a key piece in your jigsaw, too. See what I mean? Funny...'

'Yeah,' I said. 'Sometimes you could die.'

# 12

In the morning Dave still thought it was all funny. Of course she'd have to get rid of all that women's lib lark and stop talking coarse, but all the same there was a pattern in it somewhere. He knew there was. I didn't have the heart to tell him that Uncle Pietro's daughter would be interested in a mini-cab driver who preferred reading to driving only on a very temporary basis indeed.

'You think she'll be all right?' he said.

'Why don't you call her and find out?' He would do it anyway.

'Maybe I should go over there. Stay with her.'

'You've already got a date. Riva del Garda,' I said.

He sighed. 'You will take care of her, Ron?'

'Of course,' I said. 'Without her we've got nothing.'

He glared at me. That wasn't the right answer. Then he made his call and felt better. After twenty minutes of Croce he said to me, 'She wants to talk to you.' He even sounded jealous.

'Right,' I said. 'Go and have a look round while I'm talking and see if anybody's watching us. If not, get the Lancia filled up then come back and pack.' I gave him some money, and he went.

Reluctantly, but he went. I spoke into the phone. 'Adriana?' I said.

'But what a splendid friend you have,' she said. 'Such muscles. And so clever.' I gathered that Dave would be acceptable on a very temporary basis.

'Dave's OK,' I said. 'How are you?'

'Afraid,' she said.

'Want to get out of Padua?'

'Please,' she said. 'I know it's silly–'

'Maybe it's not,' I said. 'How about staying with my sister for a while?'

'It will be very boring.'

'It will also be safe,' I said.

There was a long pause. 'All right,' she said.

'Stay away from the Italian Club,' I told her. 'Don't even go to an Italian restaurant. Stay out of Soho too.'

'Such an exciting time I will have.'

'With your face unmarked and your throat uncut.'

She gasped aloud. 'Don't say such things, Tommaso.'

'Don't make me say them,' I said.

'All right,' she said again, and this time it was like any other Italian woman who knows the man's the boss.

'We'll put you on the first plane,' I said. 'Phone your father at his office and tell him what's happening. Let him explain to your mother.'

'You really are *very* clever, Tommaso,' she said.

'You better believe it,' I said. 'Get on with your packing. *Ciao*.'

Then I phoned my sister and she said definitely

no students, not even if they were relatives and I told her how much I was paying, and she said OK.

Naturally David thought I'd done it on purpose, which of course I had, but it was to preserve Adriana, not louse up his love-life, and at last he admitted it, but it didn't make him any happier. Still, I drove to Venice and he sat in the back with Adriana. He must have made the most of it, because when we said goodbye at Marco Polo airport she kissed him full on the mouth. He watched her go.

'That's some lady,' he said.

I could think of a lot of words for Adriana. 'Lady' was well down the list.

We pushed the Lancia a bit, and made it to Riva del Garda in time for a late lunch at the Ristorante Cesare. Eduardo Guardi was there. He looked as if he'd been there for hours and would be there for a few hours more. Three others were with him: a very pretty girl, a very handsome girl who looked like a dyke, and a short, squat man with a lot of muscle, a sort of scaled-down version of A. D. Carr. Eduardo Guardi took a look at us when we came in, but we didn't look at him, and besides we had 'tourist' written all over us and he looked away again. We hid behind the menus and took a good look.

'What d'you reckon?' said Dave.

'The pretty girl's his new love-life,' I said. 'Emilia. And from what Adriana told us the dyke is Guiseppina, known as Bo-bo, and the heavy is Bruno. They were in on the job.'

'Bruno's got a lot of muscle,' said Dave.

'So had those Frogs.'

'He could have taken two of them,' Dave said. 'Maybe even three.'

I didn't argue. This was what Dave calls his own field of expertise.

We ate a leisurely lunch too but they seemed set for the afternoon. Coffee and brandy after coffee and brandy. They drank a hell of a lot for Italians, and while they were drinking I left Dave with the bill and drove to a hotel I knew. Not far. Nowhere is very far in Riva del Garda. It's a pretty hotel and it once belonged to an Emperor of Austria, when Austria owned that part of Italy. Not so austere as the place in Verona. More rounded, more comfortable – more feminine I suppose. I booked us a double then walked to a sale-room down the road and bought a Fiat 1200 off the peg like buying a shirt. Only I knew it would be all right because the geezer who sold it to me was the hotel receptionist's brother, and the receptionist owed me a favour ... Italy ... I love it.

When I got back to the restaurant, Dave was sitting on a wall, sunning himself.

'Have they gone?' I asked.

He shook his head. 'They're paying the bill,' he said. 'But there's only four other people left. I thought it was time I went.'

'Good boy,' I said, but he was looking at the Fiat.

'You've never sold the Lancia,' he said. He sounded disgusted. First I took his girl away, next it was his car.

'Relax,' I said. 'We're a two car family now.'

'Blimey,' he said. 'You're splashing it about, aren't you?'

Then he ducked into the Fiat as Guardi and his

pals came out of the Ristorante and got into a Ferrari.

'I'm not the only one,' I said.

The Ferrari moved off, smooth and easy, and I followed. Bruno was driving the thing of beauty in front, and he was driving well, no matter how many brandies he'd drunk. They'd be wary as cats, I knew, but there was plenty of traffic, and every other car was a Fiat anyway.

'Hear anything?' I said.

'Tomorrow it's lunch in Sirmione.'

'Get the restaurant?'

'The Grifone.'

'We'll be there,' I said. We were following the Ferrari along a road that twisted and turned round a lake that really was sapphire blue, scored with white where the power-boats slammed across it, dotted with the multicolours of the sails of dinghies. There was even a touch of comedy: an elderly ferry waddling its way to Sirmione. But the rest was all beautiful: the beauty of the lake and the mountains beyond.

The Ferrari disappeared. We were following it down a tree-lined bend and when we reached the straight it had gone. It was Dave who spotted the gap in the road: just about wide enough to squeeze in a Ferrari, but you'd have to watch out for the paint. I drove on to the next turn off that led to the ruins of a villa and a couple of abandoned cars rusting to death.

'Turn round and go back?' I said.

'Turn around,' said Dave. 'But it's better if we walk back. Nowhere to leave the car.'

So we did, and very nerve-wracking it was the

way Italians drive. Dave led the way, and again I could see that feline wariness, the caution that masks the need to strike. The road was mostly broken rock, which the Ferrari wouldn't like at all, banked with earth dried hard in the Italian summer, bare except for the kind of weed that nothing can discourage. Dave followed its curve and I followed Dave, and when we reached the straight Dave dropped flat and I did the same, and banged my knee on a stone. Cautiously Dave moved into the shelter of the right bank, and I joined him. Before us was the house. No sign of the Ferrari.

Nice house it was, bigger than the one where Adriana stayed; bigger garden too. Olives, lemons, oranges. The kind of flowers that are well looked after, so a gardener must be on the pay-roll too. All white, the house was, with a verandah the length of the house and a vine creeping up by the front door. It could have been a hundred years ago, except for the air-conditioning units dotted about, and the eight-foot wire and concrete fence around it.

'I could use a suggestion,' I said.

'We wait,' said Dave. 'Till it gets dark.'

For this kind of thing he was the guv'nor, so we waited. Waiting's something I can't stand, but it comes easy to Dave on account of having been in the army. He just lay there, completely relaxed, had a couple of fags, then began to breathe slowly, rhythmically.

'What you doing?' I said.

'Yoga breathing,' he said. 'Helps the relaxation.'

I tried to kip but the ground was too hard...

But at last it got dark. There was a bit of a moon

– not too much – and Dave reckoned we could give it a go. He wriggled his way to the fence, and I followed. About a yard from the fence we stopped, and listened. Nothing but a steady thumping sound from the back of the house.

'Looks like he's got his own generator,' said Dave, then all of a sudden his glance flicked to the fence. Concrete slabs up to six feet, then heavy wire, three horizontal strands six or seven inches apart, stretched between concrete posts.

'Not too bad,' I said. 'At least it isn't barbed.'

There was a tree close by, a discouraged-looking lime tree, and Dave went to it, snapped off a piece of branch already dead, and lobbed it at the wire. There was a jagged flash like lightning, a sort of metallic hiss, the smell of burned wood.

'Mr Guardi likes his privacy,' said David.

I should have been prepared for it, but I was disappointed. 'That's it then,' I said. 'Let's go and have a drink.'

I was moving off when Dave stopped me.

'*That's it,*' he said. 'Don't you know the Paras' motto? *Utrinque Paratus* – Ready For Anything.'

'Very likely,' I said. 'But I can't get past that.'

'Maybe not,' said Dave. 'But I can.'

Then before I could stop him – and anyway, how could I have stopped him? – he climbed up that tatty lime tree like a small boy after birds' eggs, tested the branches till he found a live one, and moved out to its edge. He must have been a good fifteen feet up, but he was a long way short of the fence. Three feet easy. Suddenly he was kneeling on the branch, steadying himself with his hands, and then he was on his feet erect, just for a couple of seconds, like a tight-rope walker, and then his knees bent, the branch sagged and pushed back up, and he used its momentum to take off like a diver, straight into a patch of grass, going into a forward roll as soon as he touched the ground. Rather him than me.

I was watching him from the word go, *and* there was a moon, but when he reached the orange trees I lost him, and I was left alone with my thoughts, which were mostly how scared I was, but I'd left a little room for Sirmione... Why Sirmione? It's a nice town, nicer than Riva del Garda, on the lake, and hotter too, being that much further from the mountains. But they've got the lake for coolness and trees for shade, and it's beautiful. But why would the Reds be going there? Another job, seemed likely. Sirmione is wall-to-wall bourgeois...

I switched to feeling scared again, and I'd graduated to sheer terror when at last I saw Dave again. He'd emerged from the orange trees and was coming towards me, but how on earth was he going to get out?... He made it look so easy, but I knew that all I'd have to do was try it once to break every bone in my body. What he did was shin up another tree, an elderly olive this time, and tough as old boots, do his balancing act again, then another flying leap, only this time he went straight for the branch of the lime-tree, grabbed it with his hands so that it bowed with his weight and lowered him downwards. He dropped to the ground. As he came over to me he looked at his hands. They were scratched and bleeding.

'Getting soft,' he said. 'Now let's go for that drink.'

We chose a bar where the music was so loud I could hardly hear Dave, never mind anybody else. We drank brandy, I remember. In my case it was purely medicinal.

'Weird set-up,' said Dave. 'They've got a greenhouse round the back – they grow marijuana in it. A lot of marijuana... The house is furnished with a lot of good taste and a lot of money. What I could see of it anyway. They were in a sort of drawing room. Big, comfortable chairs, nice pictures...

'Mostly they talked Italian, and they talked quickly. So I didn't get it all – but what I did get was that Bo-bo owns a house in Sirmione and that's where they're going to be staying. They're lining up another job. Really big this time, Eduardo said... Wasn't a million dollars enough for him?'

'What sort of job?' I said.

'They didn't say. Or if they did, I didn't get it.'

'When will it be? Soon?'

'The Autumn,' said Dave. 'They said the Autumn... I tell you what, Ron – that bird Emilia's in a lot deeper than Adriana ever was. She heard every word. Put in a few herself.'

Maybe love is blind, I thought, and maybe you're right. Adriana was much too smart to get in deep. And then I remembered something else.

'You said mostly Italian,' I said. 'What else did they speak?'

'Mm?' said Dave. 'Oh yes. Very peculiar that was. It was when they were talking about Autumn. The dyke–'

'Bo-bo,' I said.

'–she suddenly spoke English. She said:

"Seasons of mists and mellow fruitfulness.
Close bosom-friend of the maturing sun
Conspiring with him how to load and bless
With fruit the vines that round the thatch-eaves
   run."

And the rest of them all started laughing like
lunatics. They couldn't stop.'

'Poetry?' I said.

'Not just poetry,' said Dave. 'John Keats... Why
would they laugh?'

I didn't know the answer, so I suggested we eat
instead. Dave looked at me, sort of old-fashioned.

'You've also got to make a couple of phone
calls,' he said. 'We've got to make sure Adriana
got to Anna Maria's OK.'

'Indeed we do,' I said.

'And you've got to phone Donner, Ron. You've
*got* to. So much has happened.'

But I was ready for that one. I was still scared
of Donner so I'd decided to call Cass Milligan
instead. All the same I left it till after dinner.
Watching Dave work made me hungry.

Adriana first. Anna Maria answered the phone.
She didn't care a lot for Adriana, I gathered, but
her husband did. For an Assistant Bank Manager
Sydney Muspratt had quite a thing about Italian
ladies. But she could cope with that, and anyway
Adriana was good with the kids so it sort of
balanced out. If only she'd watch her language...
Then Adriana came on. She'd got to Heathrow
OK. No problems, and Anna Maria had met her
and taken her back to Putney. She wasn't exactly

crazy about Putney, but she could stand it so long as she was safe. Only would I please hurry up and straighten this thing out, because she wanted to be back where the action was, and she hoped Dave was all right. The two statements were not unconnected. I asked her if Bo-bo had ever studied the poet Keats. She said they'd all been interested in the romantic movement, Bo-bo especially, but they preferred Shelley because he was a revolutionary. Then I put Dave on, and I went to the bathroom to let it get more personal.

When I came back he was hanging up and looking at me. I fidgeted like he had when he'd told me he'd brought a gun.

'Dave, I'm sorry,' I said. 'I can't phone Donner with you listening. I'm too nervous. I'll tell you all about it afterwards, but I can't handle it with you listening.'

He didn't hesitate. He's a real mate. 'I'll go and put the cars away,' he said, and I felt rotten as I picked up the phone because I was going to lie to him.

Cass Milligan said, 'Who the hell is this?'

'Ron Hogget,' I said.

'Have you any idea what time it is?'

'It's ten forty-five p.m. in Italy.'

'Well it's going on for five in the morning here and I'm tired.'

'Don't hang up,' I said. 'I mean that.'

There was a pause. 'OK, so you mean it.'

I pictured her there in that neat and tidy bedroom in that neat and tidy bed, the one I'd helped her into; trying to tell myself she was tough, and not believing a word.

'Where's Donner?' I said.

'Didn't they tell you at his place?'

'I couldn't get through.' Couldn't – wouldn't. What's the difference? 'He's on his way to Silicon valley. He'll be thirty thousand feet above the Middle West by now.'

'I've got news for him. Can you give him a message?'

'Wait till I get the pad...'

'Don't write it down,' I said. 'Just memorize it... First off – my associate and I were attacked by four thugs in Paris. My associate is Vice-President in charge of mayhem. He killed one of them. We chased off the other three.' With that last sentence I sounded rather smug.

'Your – associate – *shot* a guy?'

'He killed him with his hands.'

'Mother of God,' she said. I bet she hadn't said that in ten years at least.

'So we've got enemies,' I said. 'We've also got a lead. A hot one.' And now I came to the bit I hated to have to say.

'It could be I'll have to see Mr Donner soon,' I said. When is he due back?'

'Tomorrow,' she said.

Jet-setter indeed. 'Tell him I'll be in touch,' I said. 'Pleasant dreams.'

'Wait,' she said. 'Do you really think you're getting close?'

'Yes,' I said.

'Aren't you scared?'

'Are you crazy?' I said. 'Of course I'm scared. Goodnight.'

I hung up, and fidgeted around the room until

Dave came up. I told him the lot, and felt good, because I didn't have to lie after all. Well, not much.

'You'll have to call him in Silicon Valley tomorrow,' said Dave.

'Nobody calls him in Silicon Valley,' I said. 'Standing orders.'

'But this is about his wife.'

'Silicon Valley's about money,' I said. 'His money. And anyway – it's better we hang loose for a couple of days. That's why I didn't leave an address. Like I say, if Donner could reach us, he'd be trying to run the show from the States. It's bad enough running it from here.'

Dave nodded, because I was making sense. 'Let's get some kip,' he said.

Next day we drove both cars into Sirmione long before lunch-time, and I parted with large sums of money to a car-park attendant to leave the Fiat handy to the exit near the restaurant for as long as we wanted. Then we went to look at the Roman ruins and Dave walked for miles and I got a suntan. Then we paid more bribes to park the Lancia and sat outside a café drinking Americanos and looking at the restaurant.

It's a nice place, the Grifone. Right by the lake in the shadow of a castle. Mostly outdoors, but shaded with a sort of false roof covered with vine-leaves, smart waiters, good wine, and food you wouldn't believe. Dave was drooling just looking at it... Quarter to one and the Ferrari came. We got up at once and moved away before they could see us. They headed straight for the bar, all four of them. We got into the Lancia and Dave drove off before they could turn around.

'Same as yesterday?' said Dave.

'We've got to see her house after lunch,' I said.

'Shouldn't be worse than yesterday,' he said.

'Except it's the second time,' I said. 'They've seen us once. Stop at a bookshop.'

He found one and pulled up, and I bought a paperback called *Libro Gastronomica In Italia*. I checked the Cesare in Riva del Garda; it was there, and so was the Sirmione.

'When we go in we talk about this,' I said. 'We're on a gastronomic tour – and tomorrow we're going to Venice. We can't make up our minds between the "Graspa de Ua" and the "Ristorante àl Conte Pescaor".'

'I wish that was our only problem,' said Dave, and looked at the book.

They were still in the bar, watching the street, when Dave and I drove up in the Lancia. They'd seen us before and didn't like it. They'd have liked it even less if we'd driven up in a different car. So they knew who we were. I took out the book as we entered and I began to talk about food, then Dave took over. Dave can talk about food till it gives you indigestion. He talked about Alfredo's in Rome and Sabatini's in Florence and Giannino in Milan and he'd never eaten in one of them; just read it in the book. We sat in the bar and had another Americano and Dave went on and on till our four new chums couldn't stand any more and went to a table. They were drinking whisky, and ordered more. After a bit we went to a table, too.

I should have been too nervous to eat, but that food was something else. Dave had second helpings of everything, but even so we were drinking coffee long before Guardi and his mates had finished. They seemed to have a lot of wine left, too. It was becoming a pattern. We paid up and went out arguing where we'd eat in Venice tomorrow, and Bruno decided to go to the 'Gents' and followed us to the door and watched us drive off in the Lancia. Sirmione was full, as it usually is in summer-time, and it cost a lot of money to find another place to park. Then we walked back to the Fiat, and changed our shirts for T-shirts of a rather vulgar nature. I wore a white linen cap, and Dave one of those American golf-caps with a long visor. We both wore different sun glasses.

After half an hour we were cooking in the Fiat, even with all the windows down, then Bruno went out of the restaurant and came back with the Ferrari. Bruno had drunk about twice as much as the others, but you'd never have guessed.

'That geezer could be a problem,' said Dave, and switched on the ignition. The other three came out of the restaurant, laughing merrily as they climbed into the Ferrari, then we were all off to Bo-bo's place. At least I hoped we were.

# 13

Again the pattern repeated itself: through the town then out on to a secondary road. This time Dave was taking no chances. In the town he tailed from two cars back, and even on the back road he managed to lurk behind another Fiat that was busting a gut trying – and failing – to pass a Ferrari. Then, just as the day before, the Ferrari disappeared, but this time we saw it happen, watched it turn into a gap in the road like a rabbit into a burrow. We kept on going till Dave found a turn-off, and debated whether they'd drunk enough to stay where they were for a bit. If not we'd need the car. In the end we decided they were too drunk, and set off to walk. Before we did so I opened the glove compartment and took out a pair of Japanese binoculars. Dave lifted an eyebrow.

'You bring guns,' I said. 'I bring binoculars.'

'So where were they yesterday?'

'I forgot,' I said.

This seemed to cheer Dave enormously.

'At least it proves you're human,' he said. 'Ready?'

'You're not taking the gun?'

'This is just a recce,' he said. 'The binos are all we need.'

Back down the road to the gap in the road, along another dusty track, lined with cypress trees this time, and another sizeable house, not as big as Guardi's, but older-looking, with smooth, yellow stone and wrought-iron verandahs, the iron painted black and tipped with gold. There was a black wrought-iron fence all round the house, tipped with golden spear-points that could do you all kinds of mischief, and there was a garden, too, just like before. Roses that looked exhausted in the heat, and gladioli neatly staked, geranium borders and azaleas like trees. And olives, lemons, oranges, just like before. No people. No Ferrari either. Just a garage with the doors tight shut.

We edged round the garden. Behind was a field of Indian corn, waiting for the harvester. We plunged into it and were powdered with golden dust as we worked our way to the back gate, which was as high and firmly padlocked as the front one. As we neared the back garden Dave slapped my shoulder and we dropped. Guardi was talking from the garden to the back of the house. He had something in his hands. I got out the binoculars and took a look, just before he disappeared. The something looked like a folded newspaper, not new ... I began to take a look at the back garden – kitchen garden really. Strawberries, asparagus, fennel, onions, and herbs in pots that were big and very old, a vine climbing over what I took to be the gardener's shed. No marijuana. I handed the glasses to Dave, and he looked as I had done, but for longer, much longer. At last he touched my arm and motioned us away. We crawled our way round to the front of the house where we could watch out for signs of people leaving, dash back for the Fiat.

I looked at Dave: he was as golden as a statue, gilded with corn husk, and somehow it brought out the power of the man, the menace behind the grace. Strip him and gild his body as his clothes were gilded, and you'd have one of those gods he'd been looking at that morning: Mercury say, or Achilles. No, not Achilles. He had no brains. Apollo. The god Apollo in a Yankee golfer's hat. We began to slap the corn dust off ourselves, comb it out of our hair. Then Dave crouched down, careful, where the smoke wouldn't be seen, and lit a cigarette.

'I think I know where Mrs Donner's head is,' he said.

I just gawked at him. He was telling me he'd found something I hadn't even begun to look for. Me. Ron Hogget. The geezer who could find one twig in a forest, according to Donner. I must have been looking a right nana, but Dave didn't say anything, just crouched there and smoked.

'You feel like telling me?' I said. He looked at me. 'Where her head is?'

'Where I think it is,' he said. 'I'm sorry, Ron. It's such a bloody awful–' he broke off. 'I better just tell you. Yesterday Bo-bo quoted Keats. Right? His ode *To Autumn*.'

'I remember you telling me,' I said.

'Keats wrote another poem and it was looking at the kitchen garden reminded me of it. Did you notice the herbs?'

'In those big old pots,' I said. 'I thought one of them might be hash, but there wasn't any.'

'Marjoram,' he said. 'Chives, tarragon, two or three I didn't know. One of them was Basilico –

in English it's called basil.'

'So?' I said.

'This other poem of Keats is called *Isabella, or The Pot of Basil*. Ever read it?'

'Not that I remember,' I said.

He sighed. 'I was hoping you had. It's based on a story of Boccaccio... This really is the hell of a thing... It tells the story of Isabella, who falls in love with a bloke called Lorenzo, only her two brothers disapprove. They murdered Lorenzo out in a forest or something, and Isabella goes crazy with grief. Then she has a vision of where her brothers buried him and digs him up and preserves his head in a potful of herbs. Basil in fact. Isabella goes mad when she finds out and cherishes the pot as if it were her lover.'

'Dear God,' I said.

'Of course it may not be that at all—'

'But it could be,' I said. 'Having seen that lot. It certainly could be.' Dave smoked on for a bit, waited till I got my ideas in order. Guardi had been walking away from those pots when I'd seen him.

'I've got to get in that house,' I said.

'I'd better see what they're up to,' said Dave. He took the glasses and shinned up a cypress tree. No Barnum and Bailey stuff to get inside, not this time. Just straight-forward peeping Tom. And just as well. I needed Dave. This was no time for him to have an accident...

At last he came down. There was a funny look on his face, as if he couldn't believe what he'd just seen.

'What they doing?' I said. 'Smoking pot?'

'No,' he said. 'They've done that. They're having an orgy.'

'Oh,' I said, trying to play it cool. 'Bit hard on Bo-bo isn't it?' She'd be the odd man out so to speak.'

'Not the way they've paired off,' said Dave.

'Jesus!'

'I don't think they'll leave the house tonight,' said Dave.

'We'll have to make them,' I said. 'I've got to get in there.'

'Let me think a minute,' Dave said, and at last began to talk. It took a while.

'You're taking a hell of a risk,' I told him.

'It's what you're paying me for. Besides I happen to agree with you – you have to go in there – and you can only do that if I draw them off. Only I can't use the Fiat, Ron. That Ferrari would be on me in minutes. You'll have to drive her back to town and fetch the Lancia. I should be able to manage with that – especially if I take care of Bruno first. You'd better fetch the Magnum as well.'

So I did just that. Brought back the Lancia, the Magnum and a flask of brandy, put the Fiat where the Lancia had been and went back to Dave. He wasn't there. I sat and sweated for twenty minutes, then he came out of the garage, crossed the garden and came up to me. So he'd got inside, golden spears or no golden spears. I handed over the Magnum, and he took a swig of brandy.

'I've fixed the Ferrari,' he said. 'She's good for ten minutes and that's it – which means they'll be all of ten miles away. I'll try to lead them away from transport. You'll have plenty of time.'

'Suppose they call the coppers?'

'How can they? I'll cut the telephone wires.'

'With what?'

'Nice little tool chest in the garage. Anyway it's my guess they'd never dare call the coppers. They've got too much to hide. Besides,' he grinned, 'I'm not just going to be a burglar. I'm going to scrawl Fascist slogans all over the place.' He looked up at the sky. 'Dark enough,' he said. 'Bring the Lancia here, and leave the keys in the dash.'

I brought the car and he grinned at me. There'll probably be only three come after me,' he said. 'But don't worry about Bruno. He'll be resting. See you, Ron.' Then he gave me a Heil Hitler type salute which was all wrong for an Italian Fascist, but it wasn't salutes he'd be handing out inside ... I felt all kinds of a bastard, but I let him go.

He told me later all the windows were wired with burglar alarms, but the tools in the garage took care of that. He opened a ground floor window and went in: he was lucky. They were all four resting between rounds so to speak, and that helped. Emilia and Bo-bo were tucked up together, but Guardi and Bruno had split. Dave went into Bruno's room, and belted him a good one, no messing, with the butt of the Magnum. Then he took the aerosol of paint he'd found in the garage, the one that was there for touching up the Ferrari if she ever had a crunch, and wrote: 'Now We Are Avenged'. He didn't know what it meant, but it

215

gave them something to think about. The paint was green: the downstairs walls unsullied white. Carefully, lovingly almost, Dave sprayed on the walls in letters a foot high: 'Long Live The Italian Fascists', 'Death To All Reds', 'Slaves Of The Kremlin Live Here'. This last was a particularly dirty crack, as Guardi's mob hated Russia every bit as much as the Fascists did.

When he'd had his fun he went through all the papers he could find downstairs. There wasn't much on offer except a few far-left magazines, so he sprayed them too, then put them in the middle of the floor and set fire to them. It was the smoke that woke them upstairs – all except Bruno, and they came tumbling down grabbing for light switches, but Dave had fixed the lights, too. All the same, the magazines gave enough light for them to see the slogans. Guardi grabbed a vase full of flowers, threw away the flowers, and dowsed the fire, all the time yelling for Bruno, and Dave deliberately broke cover before Guardi could go upstairs and look for his bedmate. He went through the window in a flailing dive, and the others were after him like hounds. The thought of getting their hands on a Fascist was all the incentive they needed.

Guardi saw Dave's car in the moonlight, and sped off to the garage. Emilia followed, but Bo-bo produced an automatic and blasted off at Dave. I saw him stumble, but even so he reached the railings and was out like stepping over a stile. Then he got in the car and deliberately stalled the engine, waiting till the Ferrari came out. As it did, the front gates opened. There must have been an electronic device in the car. Emilia was already aboard and Bo-bo scrambled in and as she did so, Dave's engine started, the Lancia shot away and the Ferrari followed. I was free to enter. The gates were flung wide as they say.

The trouble was I didn't want to enter. I was scared. But in I went because it was either that or not get paid. Up the drive – the very best kind of gravel, hand-picked by the sound of it, then round to the back where the Hoggets of this world belong, and there it was. Sort of waiting for me. Third from the left, after the chives and oregano. And I noticed an odd thing. The basil had just been watered: none of the others. And there was a trowel, and a knife with a long, thin blade – all nice and handy. Water to loosen the soil, tools to lift it out. I didn't have any choice. All I could do was get to work.

The tools went in nice and easy, and the soil and basil lifted out all in one piece like a big plug: a sort of stopper in the bottle. I put them down carefully and took a look at what was left. A plastic bag: the kind with a seal that makes it airtight. My hands were shaking even before I lifted it out to have a look at it, but somehow I did get it out; somehow I did look.

It was Jane, or rather it had been Jane. Now it was just a decomposing mess of horror. The neck was jaggedly severed and she had been terribly beaten and burned about the face. I was in such a hurry to put it back I nearly missed what had been underneath it, but I spotted it in time. Another plastic bag. I could taste the fear in my mouth, it was like a rusty knife-blade, as I took out the second bag, but all it was money. Maybe three-quarters of a million dollars worth, neat bundles of bills, twenties, fifties, the occasional hundred, divided into portions of fifty K a time, each one wrapped in newspaper that was beginning to show its age. Just like the one Guardi had been carrying ... I put everything back the way it had been, then took a turn into the house via Dave's window and poked around a bit, first taking a look at Bruno. He was alive, but far from well, and unconscious. That was the main thing.

Like I said, I looked around for fifty grand. For Guardi it had looked like spending money. OK I would spend it. Child's play really. It was in a desk that looked like a work-room. I opened it with my knife, then took a look around. Dave had been there with his spray, so my next move was obvious. I locked the desk again, then bashed it open with the poker, tore and smashed everything the desk contained. There'd really be a punch-up with the local Fascisti now, I thought. It couldn't happen to two nicer sets of bastards. Then I remembered Jane, and no longer felt cheerful...

Up in the turn-off, waiting for Dave, I tried to figure out my next move... No. That isn't quite right. I was trying to figure out a way of avoiding my next move, but there wasn't one. By the time he appeared I'd given up.

'You OK?' I asked him.

'Never better,' he said. 'I feel great.'

'But that bitch shot at you. I saw you stumble.'

'All in the script,' he said. 'Gave them another incentive to chase me.' He chuckled. 'It just isn't their night,' he said. 'Guardi's nothing like the driver Bruno is. With a Ferrari you've got to be stern. Master the brute.' I wondered how many Ferraris he'd driven, but I didn't ask.

'I took a corner blind,' said Dave. 'Nothing else for it, only four-wheel drift and prayer. Round the other side there's an outcrop – rock. I missed it by four inches. Guardi hit it head on. Smack on the bonnet. I needn't even have bothered fixing the engine.'

'Anybody hurt?'

'Only their feelings,' he said. 'Dip your beak time tonight, eh Ron?' I didn't answer. 'All right,' said Dave. 'Let's have it.' His voice had lost its note of triumph. He was that kind of mate.

'You were right,' I said. 'I found her. Under the basil. It was the most horrible thing I ever saw... They'd tortured her. Burned her face... Maybe that's why they cut her head off. I don't know.'

'Poor old Ron,' Dave said. 'You had the rough part.'

'We both did,' I said. 'Just like we both did our jobs. I also found Donner's money – or most of it.'

'That gives him two reasons to be happy,' said Dave. 'What now?'

'I'm sorry, Dave,' I said, 'but I'll have to go to see him.'

'Want me to come with you?'

'Yeah,' I said. 'But I can't. You'll have to stay here.'

There was also the fact that Donner wouldn't want Dave around anyway. He makes me braver than I am. Then there was the further fact that he'd taken more than his share of risks, considering the money I was paying on Donner's behalf. I'd have to up it, even if it had to come out of my share. All in all, Dave had to stay and watch Guardi's lot. He'd even be safer...

'What do I do here?' said Dave.

'Watch Bo-bo's house. If they look like packing up phone me immediately. But I don't think they will. I think they'll declare war on the Fascists. It'll be Montagu and Capulet time.'

'OK.' said Dave. 'Just that.'

'I shouldn't be long,' I said. 'Couple of days.'

'No rush,' Dave said. 'I can cope – if they sit tight. You've wrapped it all up nicely.'

'Thanks to you and your degree in English,' I said. 'But it isn't wrapped up yet.'

'But surely,' said Dave, 'Donner will–'

'Donner will be over here like a shot,' I said. 'And he'll bring Black and White with him. This will be no place for sensible blokes like us, Dave.'

'Suits me,' said Dave. 'Myself, I fancy a trip to Putney. It's pretty this time of year.'

We had a little brandy to celebrate, then went to watch the house from cover. After an hour, the three of them came back in a taxi. They didn't look in the mood for orgies. Guardi paid off the cab and they went inside. I gave it four minutes, and then the howl came. The howl of pain of a Communist urban guerilla who's just been robbed of fifty thousand dollars he obtained by extortion. Ten more minutes, and Bo-bo came out, backed an Alfa-Romeo Guilia from the garage and was back in ten minutes.

'What d'you think?' said Dave.

'Phone call,' I said. 'You cut the wires.'

Half an hour later an ambulance arrived, and Bruno was taken away. Emilia went with him. Half an hour after that she came back, with coppers.

I yawned. 'That won't be her idea,' I said. 'Whatever hospital they took Bruno to would report it. They'd have to.'

The coppers stopped two hours. I was nearly asleep, but Dave looked as if he'd just got up... We watched and waited, and one by one the lights went out. We took turns sleeping.

Next morning a man came to mend the telephone, but nobody stirred. We drove into Sirmione and got a barber to shave us, then I sold the Fiat and actually made a bit on it. I would have sold the Lancia too, but Dave begged me to let him buy it out of his share. I bought another Fiat instead, with a bit of punch in the engine. New outfit for Dave, too. Very trendy. Track suit and training shoes. And a tent and canned food and bottled water and a spirit stove. All that. Dave the happy camper. That's for if he was seen. But what I wanted him to do most was stay out of sight. Then we took both cars for a look at the house. Nobody had left, but a Volkswagen bus load had arrived. Communist Maoist muscle.

I told Dave I thought we might need reinforcements, and he huffed and puffed a bit when I told him who I had in mind but who else was there we could trust? And in the end he agreed, so I left him to it and kept going for Riva del Garda, told them to keep the room for me and booked a second one for three days' time. That was the only piece of optimism I allowed myself.

Then I went to a travel agent who was only too happy to oblige when I told him what I wanted, especially when I paid in cash. Dollars.

So I sent a telegram to Donner and another to A. D. Carr and went to a library then back to the hotel. An express letter had just arrived. The name on the envelope was H. B. Lumley. Bit of luck, that, but then I deserved a bit of luck. Time for one quick black coffee to keep me awake, then I drove the Lancia towards Venice, found a garage for her in Piazzale Roma, and took a cab to Marco Polo airport. I had just fifteen minutes before the flight, but I got aboard OK, downed a quick brandy and slept all the way to Heathrow, where they woke me up and threw me off: politely, because I was first class. I fumbled my way to the Concorde Departure Lounge or Hospitality Room or whatever it is, and was just nodding off when a very polite young lady shook me and said I was Mr Ronald Hogget. I agreed and she said, 'A Mr A. D. Carr is calling.' Then just to make things clear she added, 'On the telephone.'

I went over to it yawning.

A. D. Carr said, 'Are you really going to fly Concorde?'

'Half an hour from now,' I said.

'Sleuthing pays a lot better than convoluted prose,' he said. 'What's up? Something to your advantage it says here.'

'I got that out of a detective novel,' I said. 'It's what the solicitor wrote when he put an ad in the paper to find the missing heir. Mind you, it could be to your advantage at that.'

'What could?'

'Are you still concerned about what happened to Jane?'

I should have said Jane Donner, but I was too tired, and anyway he didn't notice.

'Of course. What's up?'

'Meet me at the Hotel du Lac, in three days' time and I'll tell you,' I said.

'What *is* this?'

'What I say it is. Three days from now I shall reveal all, as my detective novel said, and if you want to get involved any further you'll be very welcome.'

'You mean it?' said A. D. Carr, then: 'Stupid question. Excuse it, please. What would be the point in lying?... I'll come.'

'I'll cable your plane fare from New York,' I said.

'No,' said Carr. 'No need. I'll take the bike. There's plenty of time. Only I'll have to ask you to give me back the petrol money. It's the rent.'

'No problem,' I said. 'Drive carefully. We need you.'

'You know you really are a fascinating person,' Carr said. 'I haven't begun to get you yet.'

Then we both hung up, and I ate peanuts till the flight was called.

All I remember about Concorde was that I ate and read Horry's letter and slept. I remember eating because caviar was involved, and that was the first time I ever ate the stuff. When we touched down it was five hours later than I thought it was, but my time-clock was in such a mess anyway it didn't seem to matter. And at least I'd had some sleep. I was halfway towards the queue for immigration before I realized I hadn't phoned Melanie, and I felt awful, but US Immigration and Customs helped me to forget it. They *were* awful.

Mr Black and Mr White were waiting for me. In New York it was over eighty degrees, with humidity in the high seventies, but they still wore the suits that were as much a part of their trade as dungarees to a joiner. Mr Black took the one light grip I'd brought.

'Nice trip?' he asked.

'Restful,' I said.

'You don't get too much of that these days,' said Mr White.

Then they eased me out through the mob to where the Rolls-Royce waited, and the New York sun snarled down; I put on my Italian sunglasses.

'Smart,' said Mr Black.

'He looks really good,' said Mr White.

'And so he should,' Mr Black said. 'Mr Donner's *pleased* with him.'

I closed my eyes and dozed off till we got to the fortress on the upper Eighties on the corner of Fifth Avenue, and when I opened them again I knew that I was awake enough to risk facing Donner. Whether I had the guts for it was quite another matter.

He was in the same enormous room, but this time there wasn't any fire, thank God. He got up as I came in and if he was pleased to see me he didn't show it. Not at first.

'Where's my jacket?' he said.

'In London.'

'Why isn't it here?'

'Because I didn't know I was going to be here myself,' I said. 'Not until I got what you were after.'

Then I really had him. Then he was pleased.

'You mean you've *done* it?' he said.

Which just goes to show that, multi-millionaire or not, he wasn't as smart as A. D. Carr. It didn't dawn on me that the question was stupid.

'I've really done it,' I said.

Donner said. 'Get Ron a drink. What'll it be Ron?' and I said 'Brandy,' and White brought a little bottle of Remy Martin Fine Champagne and Black brought ice and soda, and I put four cubes of ice in the glass like a goldfish bowl, covered then with brandy and topped up with soda because that's the kind of house it was.

'Tell us about it, Ron,' said Donner.

I looked at Black and White.

'That's all right,' Donner said. 'These gentlemen will stay. They're involved.'

Black and White didn't like it, but they had to take it.

'Red students took your wife,' I said.

'I knew it! I *knew* it!' said Martin Donner. I let it pass.

'I don't know yet quite how they did it–'

'Never mind that,' Donner said. 'So long as you can prove it.'

'The proof is where they are,' I said. 'In a house just outside Sirmione.'

'You mean you left it there?' Donner said.

'The house is being watched,' I said.

'I should have known,' said Donner. 'I'm sorry. Go on... What proof did you get?'

That was the question I hadn't been looking forward to. What was I supposed to answer? The hacked-off head of your wife?

'You remember when Mr White found the body,' I said. 'The head was missing?' I looked at White. He remembered all right. 'It's in this house in Sirmione,' I said.

'My God!' said Donner, in a voice of total bewilderment.

'It – I hate to tell you this,' I said. 'But she'd been tortured... The marks still show.'

Suddenly he was on his feet and yelling.

'No!' he screamed. 'No! No! No! No! No!'

Then he covered his face and sat down. His two goons moved towards him, but he sensed their movement, waved them away.

'Just give me a minute, will you?' he said.

Horry Lumley had written: 'My goodness Ron, you do pick 'em. Sixty million on the hoof, and one day he'll make it ten times that. Rags to riches, too. Straight out of Samuel Smiles. Born Youngstown, Ohio, 1941. Lots of bad boys in Youngstown, but Martin Thaddeus Donner stayed legit so far as is known. Vaguely successful salesman of electrical goods before the draft got him in 1963. Straight to Vietnam, poor sod. Infantry. Did all right though. Promoted corporal... Distinguished Service Cross and Purple Heart. That means a wound of course. He could have been discharged but he actually volunteered to stay on. Attached to supply in Saigon. Promoted Master Sergeant ... On the fiddle I fear me, Ron, or how could he afford to start an electronics business when he came marching home? But don't say it out loud, Ron.

226

He is reputed to be, and I quote: "a mean bastard". You'll have read about his wife of course...'

Donner lowered his hand. His eyes were wet.

'I'm sorry,' he said. 'It was just – I wasn't set for the punch.'

'It's me that's sorry,' I said. 'I just couldn't think of an easy way to break it.'

Donner said to Black, 'Get me some rye. Straight.'

'I found something else, too,' I said.

'Wait,' said Donner, and Black put a glass in his hand. He took a swig. 'OK,' he said.

'I found your money,' I said.

'Well I'll be damned,' he said. 'You did?'

'Not the whole million,' I said. 'Some of that's gone. But I should think three quarters of it's still there.'

'You're a marvel, that's what you are,' said Donner. 'A twenty-two-carat fucking marvel.'

'I managed to swipe a few of the notes,' I said, and took from my pocket two twenties and a fifty, gave them to Donner, who handed them on to White. 'Get on to it will you?' He turned back to me. 'Just where are these – things?' he said. I told him.

'And how many people are involved?' I told him that, too.

'You'll take us there, Ron.'

'Of course,' I said.

'You'll take us there, and then you're out of it. You can go home... You'd like that, wouldn't you, Ron?'

'Very much,' I said. Then White came back.

'They're the right notes,' he said. 'They're part

227

of the ransom money.'

'Ron,' said Donner. 'Soon I'll owe you a hundred thousand dollars.'

'When you take delivery,' I said. 'I know.'

'You're an honest man,' said Donner. 'There should be more like you.' And then: 'You look tired.'

'I'm whacked,' I said.

'We've booked you in the Plaza again, OK?' Donner said. 'Go there and rest.'

'When do you want to go to Italy?' I said.

'It can't be this week,' said Donner. 'Sunday's the earliest.'

'I want to be back in Italy on Friday,' I said. 'Keep an eye on things.'

'No problem,' said Donner. 'You keep an eye on things till we take over. Goodnight Ron – pleasant dreams.'

The Roller, and the same elegant chauffeur were waiting. I hadn't lied to Donner: I really was exhausted. But I knew I couldn't sleep. I went up to my room and switched on the telly, contemplated a quiet night and knew it just wasn't on: not a chance. First I phoned Doctor Richard Gregory, who said he'd be delighted to see me any time, so we made a date. Then I called Ms Milligan and she was in so I didn't have to leave a message.

'Guess who?' I said, and she said, 'Oh God,' so I knew we were on the same affectionate terms.

'Not quite, but you're getting warm,' I said roguishly. 'This is Ron Hogget. I have to see you.

'I can't right now,' she said.

'I don't want to see you right now... Dinner tomorrow?'

'Where?'

'You choose.'

'My God,' she said, 'are you that rich?...The Four Seasons.' It seemed to be the only restaurant female New Yorkers had ever heard of, 'OK,' I said. 'Pick you up at seven.'

'What do you want to see me about?'

'Just a few questions, Ms Milligan,' I said. 'Just a few questions.'

She hung up and I did, too. Then I looked at my hands. They were shaking. No doubt about it, I was falling apart. But I couldn't fall apart. Not yet. I looked at my watch instead and did sums. It was OK to call Melanie, so I did. She answered at the second ring, snatching up the phone as if it were against the law not to.

'Hallo?' she said.

'Hallo yourself,' I said.

'Where are you?'

'New York,' I said. 'I flew here this morning from Italy.'

Not the complete truth, but enough to keep Melanie happy. 'Are you all right?'

'I'm fine,' I said, lying like a gentleman. 'Listen. My cousin Adriana from Verona's staying with my sister. Why don't you nip over and see them?'

'Oh lovely,' she said. She didn't bother asking how I knew all this ... that wasn't the point. The point was she didn't want to go.

'Might be a bit dodgy getting over there,' she said. She made Putney sound like John o'Groats and she must have twigged it because she said: 'The car's due for an overhaul.'

The car had had an overhaul four hundred

miles ago, but I let it pass.

'How are you keeping?' I said. 'Missing me?'

The conversation got a bit personal after that, until we reached goodbye time, then: 'Oh, I nearly forgot,' she said. 'How's Dave? Keeping you out of trouble?'

'That's what he's for,' I said. 'He's doing a great job... He's got a new girl, too.'

'That's nice,' she said. 'You better go, Ron. This call's costing a fortune... Give Dave my love when you see him.'

'Will do,' I said. 'God bless, Melanie.'

'God bless,' she said. And then I was alone again. Alone and afraid. Even talking to Melanie hadn't cured that. I thought about some red snapper and Riesling, but the thought of that made me feel sick. It would have to be the bar and brandy and soda. I hate mogadons.

# 14

I should have taken a torch. I've never met a Brit yet who's got used to the darkness of American bars; and the Plaza's no exception: only more comfortable; and it should be. It's the *Plaza*. I moved to a stool at the bar like a blind man who's lost his white stick and said, 'Brandy and soda.'

'Yes, sir,' the barman said. 'Hine? Courvoisier? Martell? Hennessy? Vecchia Romagna? Carlos Primero?'

'Yes,' I said. 'With ice.'

Beside me somebody chuckled. It was so damn dark I couldn't even see who it was, except that by the chuckle it was female. 'Mr Hogget,' she said. 'The married man.'

Dave says that's very nearly a quotation from Shakespeare. All I knew was that it was Lenora Buell.

'Hell,' I said. 'Can I buy you a drink?'

'You certainly can,' she said. The barman brought me some kind of brandy with ice and a siphon. She said to him: 'Champagne, Bollinger. Non-vintage.' The barman went off with something suspiciously like a flounce, but in the end gave her a glassful.

'Still finding things, Mr Hogget?'

I remembered that she was a friend of Mr White.

'No,' I said. 'I've found them.'

Her voice dropped.

'You've found out about Jane?'

'Yes,' I said, and drank whatever it was the barman had given me. 'Why aren't you working, Miss Buell?'

'You mean you didn't hear?'

'I've been away,' I said. 'In Italy.'

'Of course,' she said. 'On account of Jane. But nobody's told you?'

She seemed to take my ignorance as a personal affront.

'I left *Honeyfall* just after our lovely lunch,' she said. 'That redhead intellectual phony should have *told* you.'

'Cass Milligan?'

'Right... As a matter of fact it was your fault.

Your doing anyway.' She told me why before I could ask her.

'I loved that play,' she said. 'But it was killing me. You remember I told you it was killing me? And all the time there was this big hassle about me having to go to London and Milligan telling me I owed it to Jane. I admit I thought so too at one time, but after she made her pitch I decided I didn't owe Jane a goddam thing. Or her memory.'

Aren't you the lucky one, I thought.

'She gave me a job and I did it, and I realized I'd had enough. So I gave a week's notice. It's in my contract. All the notice I had to give was a week. You'd have thought I was spitting on the flag. You sure you didn't hear about it?'

'Cross my heart,' I said.

'What sort of papers do they have in Italy for Christ's sake?' She was lovely and warm and alive, but I was feeling bad again. I didn't have very much small talk left in me.

'You're on your own,' I said.

'There's nothing much escapes *your* hawk-like gaze,' she said. 'I am on my own. And I'll tell you why, Ron Hogget, married man. I've been stood up. Well. Not exactly. I mean I had a date with a producer. He's got a new play he wants to talk to me about and he says why don't we meet at the Plaza for cocktails then we'll eat somewhere and I'll tell you all about it, and I thought why not? It'll be nice to go to the Four Seasons for dinner for a change. At lunch I never dare drink enough champagne.'

I had to use both hands to get the glass to my mouth. I also had difficulty in finding my mouth.

'Then just as I get here and order champagne and put it on his tab – I mean it's not as if I'm working – he has the gall to ring up from New Hampshire and says he may be a teeny bit late on account of his car won't start. I asked him what kind of car he drives and he said a Buick. A *Buick*, for Christ's sake. And he has the nerve to call himself a producer.'

I began to laugh, and that was OK. What she'd said was funny. The trouble was I couldn't stop laughing, and my laughter, I knew, had nothing to do with amusement. For once Lenora Buell stopped talking. There was a book of matches in front of her. She struck one, looked at me, then blew it out at once, and touched my arm. 'Ron... Baby,' she said. 'What is it?'

But I couldn't stop for long enough to tell her, even if I would. Her hand moved down to my wrist, and I felt the sharp sting of her nails as she pressed.

'Now you just stop that,' she said, 'or Lenora's going to haul off and bust you one in the kisser. I mean that.'

I believe she did, too. Anyway, I stopped.

'That's better,' she said. 'Now you can tell me all about it. But not here. I just love an audience' and here she scowled at the barman, '–but not when they haven't paid for their tickets.'

She took my arm and led me out. In the bright light of the lobby I looked terrible, and I knew it.

'Where would you like to go?' I asked.

'What have you got here?'

'A suite,' I said.

'Let's go up to your place,' she said. 'You can

phone down for drinks. I mean – we couldn't do that if you had just a room, but if it's a *suite*–'

So we went up, and I phoned for drinks. Bollinger NV, one bottle and two glasses. No more brandy. I was in enough trouble.

She wore scarlet, I remember, low in front and full in the skirt, an ivory white silk stole on her shoulders, ruby clips in her ears. She looked like a Cleopatra carved out of ebony as she walked round the room, took a look at the park, and subsided at last on the sofa. I stayed on my feet till the floor-waiter came and opened the bottle, labour so demanding he got five bucks for it. I poured without spilling and it took some doing, gave her a glass, held on tight to my own.

'You want to talk about it?' she said.

'I'm sorry I'm behaving like this,' I said. 'Lucky too – if you hadn't been there–'

'So was I lucky,' she said. 'I was only stood up for twenty minutes before I got a new date.' She smiled, but I couldn't. 'What's wrong, honey? Go ahead and tell me. I can listen when I have to.'

'I suppose it's all because I'm not as tough as I thought I was,' I said. 'Most of us find that out sooner or later,' I thought of Donner, and of Dave. 'Not all of us – but most...You didn't like Jane, did you?'

'I remember I told you that,' she said. 'I admired her – but I didn't like her.'

'She was too cold, you said.' Lenora nodded. 'That wasn't the picture I got of her, but she had other qualities that came before warmth, being outgoing. Whatever it's called, she was honest and scrupulous and she believed in justice. A very straightforward system of ethics inside that beautiful head–'

Then I realized I'd used the word head, and nearly gagged. Lenora waited.

'She was one of the doers of this world,' I said. 'She made things happen.'

'She had the money,' said Lenora.

'She also had the will. Drive. Energy. She made work for people.'

'That's true.'

'She was a – good person. She was beautiful and she was good.'

'You're in love with her.' She blurted it out unthinking, then her hand went to her mouth.

'I could have been, certainly,' I said, 'and much good it would have done me.'

But I was just playing with words. I *was* in love with her.

'She's dead, Ron.' Lenora's voice was very gentle. 'Don't let it become a – fixation or whatever it is. You'll get hurt.'

I am hurt, I thought, but I'm going to finish it.

'I want to tell you something,' I said.

'Sure.'

'But it's just between the two of us.'

'Don't worry,' she said. 'I can keep a secret. That's OK.'

My face was still grimacing, and I willed it to be still. Things had to be said.

'This cool, ethical, brilliant, beautiful, work-making lady,' I said. 'I found her head.'

She shot up as if I'd rammed a needle into her.

'Oh my *God*,' she said.

'It was in a white plastic bag – almost transparent, hidden at the bottom of a pot of herbs. It was dark – but there was a moon. I could see her quite well. She was beginning to decompose but not too much because the bag was hermetically sealed. I could see her face. She had been tortured.' Lenora cried out: champagne slopped from her glass.

'Maybe that's why they cut her head off,' I said, though I knew it wasn't. Then suddenly it was all too much for me and I cried out as loud as she, and covered my face in my hands and wept.

She came over to me at once, and her arms came round me, she rocked me like a child. 'Ron, baby. Sweetheart,' she said, but the tears kept on coming.

She pulled me to my feet and led me into the bedroom, and undressed me like a child, took off her own clothes, got into bed beside me. She was warm and yielding and clever, and infinitely desirable. She knew things, if you'd told Melanie about them she'd have thought you were kidding – but I made love to her as if it was somebody else doing it, somebody else who was all body. I was all mind; thinking of Jane and what they had done to her. At last the body could do no more, and she looked at me again, an appraising look, like a doctor's after therapy.

'Feeling better?' she said.

'Yes nurse,' I said. She slapped me, not too hard but hard enough.

'Now you stop that,' she said. 'I'm fussy who I sleep with. You should be flattered.'

'I've got a funny way of going courting,' I said.

'Now that's enough! It was good, wasn't it?'

'Great,' I said.

'Me too. You married men when you cut loose – you sure know how to give a girl a good time.' She chuckled again. 'You ever done it with a black lady before?'

'No,' I said.

'Well you're going to lie there and rest for a while and I'm going to bring the champagne. And after we've had a glass we'll take a shower together then we're going to do it all over again.'

I wished I had her optimism but she was right. She was a very determined lady... While we drank together she told me how she understood all about why I felt the way I did but what I had to realize it was all over and there was just no *good* in thinking about it. And I said yes, I could see her point, but she hadn't seen the head...

Then we went to the shower, and she dried me and I dried her, and that time my body and mind belonged to the same person and that person was me, and it was great, a meaningful experience, sexual acrobatics of Olympic standards, and if the earth didn't move we certainly did. And I felt grateful for all her trouble and that's all I felt.

'What you thinking about?' she said.

'I'm not thinking,' I lied. 'You've done that for me. I shan't forget it.'

She kissed me then: the kiss was kind. Then she went into the bathroom and I thought about Martin Donner.

I knew he thought I was stupid, but this routine put me in the well-nigh certifiable class. I was down there with the idiots. Lenora Buell stood up, then going to bed with Ron Hogget after just two drinks? Not that she'd done it badly. She'd been very good. And very kind, too, I remem-bered. She'd done a good job on me. And if actions were any indication, she'd enjoyed what she'd been doing. All the same she'd been made to do it, I was sure of that. Money wouldn't have done it, not for her. Donner must have had some hold on her. Maybe it was all tied in with her fling with Mr White...

She came back with a towel wrapped round her, then shed it and began to collect her clothes. She really had a very pretty body, I thought, but no prettier than Melanie's. Then I wondered if she'd believe me if I told her that. But she was telling me, and I was too polite, and too grateful to interrupt. Relax, she was telling me, forget all this. It's over.

As she talked she put her clothes on: that took about three minutes. But after that she had to renew her makeup, and that was serious busi-ness. I lay on the bed and watched her, and remembered Horry Lumley's letter.

'After Nam he took off like a rocket. He had the money, you see. But where from, Ron? A humble sergeant with nothing but his gratuity pay and a twenty-five-dollar-a-week disability pension? Where from? Could it be, as I suggested before, that he was moon-lighting in Nam? He'd become a key figure in that stores dump where he worked. Dispatching goods all over the place. Dispatching others things, too. But nothing proved, do you see, Ron? They even brought the CIA in but nothing proved. And now the CIA just loves him. Those delectable microchips he makes. What a turn on for the CIA...'

She turned from the mirror at last. 'How do I look?' she said.

'You just saw in the mirror,' I said. 'You look beautiful.'

'You are really *something*, Ron Hogget,' she said. 'I could go for you in a big way.' I hoped, even prayed, that she was telling the truth as she came over to me, looked down into my eyes, 'Now you just remember what I told you,' she said. 'It's over.'

'Yes, Lenora,' I said.

'I'm serious,' she said. 'It is over, isn't it? There's nothing else you have to do for Jane?'

I lied a second time. 'There's nothing else I can do for her,' I said.

She put a finger first to her lips, then to mine, so as not to smudge her lipstick. She had to be off to phone Donner; tell him T. R. Hogget had finished his labours...

'Goodbye, Ron,' she said and headed for the door.

'Goodbye, Lenora,' I said. 'And thanks ... I hope you catch up with that man with the Chevrolet.'

'It was a Buick,' she said.

In the morning I took a cold shower. I hate the things, but brandy and champagne and Lenora Buell and no supper are the wrong mixture if you want to avoid cold showers. A nice lady, Lenora, I thought as I scrubbed with the towel. But she mixes with the wrong people and refuses to sit in judgement. Not like Jane. That reminded me. I phoned the desk and asked them to send somebody out for a tape-recorder, and being the Plaza they did. While I was waiting I called Dr Gregory and reminded him we had a date for eleven thirty, then I had breakfast and watched television so I could think. Then the tape-recorder arrived, and I played Jane's tape instead. Her little message of love. Over and over.

'My darling, why has it been so long? I sit here in this incredibly chic flat and invent errands to get Cass out of the way and wait for the phone to ring and it never does. What's Jane done to upset you?'

Those last six words really bothered me.

At eleven I put on a fresh shirt, a sincere-looking tie and a lightweight suit and went to call on Dr Gregory. The cab had air-conditioning, so I felt no pain all the way to 79th Street, only misgivings. Hunches were all very well in their way, but if this one was wrong...

The manservant said, 'The doctor will see you.' He sounded surprised. Maybe it was the suit. We went straight to the study.

Dr Gregory sat, wearing a lightweight suit much better than mine, smoking his pipe. He was glad to see me. He said so, and motioned me to a chair.

'What can I do for you?' he said. It was a question he must have asked a million times.

'Answer some questions,' I said.

'What about?'

'Your daughter... Your son-in-law.'

'Oh,' he said. 'I'm not sure I–'

'You told me you wanted to help,' I said.

'Certainly I want to help. But not gossip.'

'We never call it gossip,' I said. 'Facts. Inform-

240

ation. Inferences. It's a way to get to know things, Dr Gregory. Sometimes it's the only way.'

'The way to what?'

'The way to the people who murdered your daughter.'

I was gambling that he hadn't heard from Donner, but it was odds on that he and his son-in-law never ever spoke to each other. I was right. He took the pipe from his mouth and looked at it as if wondering what it was.

'Ask your questions,' he said.

'You never did tell me why your daughter married Donner,' I said. 'Not properly.'

'Only she could answer that,' the doctor said. 'But unfortunately she can't.'

'Why do you think she did?'

It was still like pulling teeth, but I'd gone there for answers. He knew what he had to say all right, but he didn't want to say it. 'Maybe your wife could tell me,' I said.

'No!' It wasn't the sort of sound Dr Gregory should make. A crude sound, vulnerable, like an animal in pain, and he knew it at once.

'I'm sorry,' he said. 'But I won't have my wife involved.'

'You tell me then.'

'Very well.' He shuddered. 'She was in love with him. She adored him. Couldn't live without him. She told me so.'

'How long did that last?'

'With him it never started. With her – right to the end.'

'She had lovers.'

He glowered at that. 'She was not promiscuous.'

'I didn't say she was.'

'I'm sorry,' he said. 'But she was my daughter. She was all I–' He broke off. 'Donner tires of women very easily. He changes them the way you and I might change cars.'

Oh the rich, the rich, I thought. I'd had my car eight years.

'He'd never married before because he hadn't felt the need.' Gregory said. 'But now he'd grown rich he thought he needed a little respectability. Jane provided it. The right background, Bryn Mawr, all that. Her devotion was a bonus. Essentially Jane was there to go to the right cocktail parties in New York, the right dinners in Washington. She never let him down. Even when he began to look elsewhere.'

'When was that?'

'Six months after they were married... She stayed celibate for quite some time – channelled the drive of her needs into her work – but needed the companionship of a man, just as I need that of a woman.'

Me too, I thought. Me too.

'Not just sex,' he said. 'Being together. She was very like me in that.'

Maybe she was very like her mother, too, I thought. But I didn't say it.

'So she turned to other men,' he said. 'I think not many.'

'Two,' I said.

'You're sure of that?'

'Virtually certain,' I said. 'Both were the artistic type. One of them is a writer of great distinction.'

'You've met him?'

I nodded.

'What's he like?'

How to describe A. D. Carr?

'Maybe he's a genius,' I said. 'Some people say so. Not handsome, but forceful. Quite poor. He never took a penny from Jane. He even helped her – when she tried to do somebody a good turn.'

'I thank you for that,' he said. 'And the other–'

'Sort of an artist,' I said. But he hadn't finished.

'The other was Frank Sokolny,' he said.

'That's right.'

'Would you have told me?'

'Only if I had to,' I said.

'You appear to be a nice man,' said Dr Gregory. 'Far too nice for the business you're in.'

'How did you know about Sokolny?'

'Stick to the facts,' he said. 'Is that what you're telling me?'

'If you don't mind,' I said.

He looked at his watch.

'I'm not working today,' he said. 'How about a little Scotch?'

'Brandy,' I said. 'With ice and soda.'

He poured as he talked.

'I work part-time now,' he said. 'Financially speaking I don't have to work at all, but I like to keep my hand in. Most of what I do these days is charity – a lot of it with drug addicts. Especially heroin addicts. Most of it is a colossal waste of time. You get them on methadone for a while – that's a heroin substitute that allays the craving – but there's no kick in it. No high. And a lot of them dislike it because there's no risk of death in methadone. Heroin addiction's slow suicide, Mr Hogget. Do you think the poor wretched addicts don't know that? So as I say, it's almost certainly a waste of time. But only almost. And so you persevere in case, just for once, you've got one who still hopes.'

'Jane asked you to treat Mickey Wood?'

'Not so fast,' Gregory said. 'Men of my age hate being rushed ... Bosco. He called himself Michele Bosco... Not one of my successes. Jane brought him to me, yes. He gave up after the third visit. I never saw him again. Then I read in the newspaper that he'd died.'

'He was murdered,' I said.

'Can you tell me why?'

'He knew about Sokolny,' I said. 'And so it seems do you.'

'I'm not particularly proud of this,' said Gregory, 'but I was curious about the connection between my daughter and this Bosco. I hired a private detective to find out.'

'And he told you it was Sokolny.'

'Yes.' He sipped at his Scotch. 'As you say– Bosco was murdered because he knew about Sokolny. And as you also say – so do I.'

'But you don't run around saying so,' I said.

'On the contrary.'

'All the same, I'd consider a holiday if I were you. Or a check-up maybe. In a hospital... Were you ever in the Army, doctor?'

'World War II,' he said, and smiled. 'An incredible time. I was with the medical unit on Omaha Beach.'

'Not later?'

'No,' he said. Three years was enough. I took my discharge in 1945.'

'Then it must have been the junkies,' I said.

'I'm afraid I don't follow,' Dr Gregory said.

But I began to relax. He followed all right. I nodded at a gadget on his desk. 'I see you've got a microfilm reader,' I said.

'Certainly,' he said. 'I keep a lot of files. Microfilm saves space.'

'Maybe your daughter got the idea from you, then.'

'Very possibly,' he said. 'But I want to know what you meant about my army service – and junkies. Never mind the microfilm.'

'They're connected, doctor,' I said. 'Just be patient. You'll see. D'you mind if I use that thing?' I nodded to the reader.

'If you really must,' he said.

'It's the quickest way to get rid of me.' Cheeky that, but I could afford to be cheeky now. I set up the film as we talked.

'I've only seen this film once before,' I said. 'Yesterday. In a library in Riva del Garda.'

'Was it only yesterday? It had cost me a fifty thousand lire bribe, whenever it was.

'I've told you before, I've never been to Italy,' said Gregory.

'This is nothing to do with Italy. Well not directly,' I said. 'But it's important. Believe me.'

I adjusted the focus, and there it was. 'Come and look,' I said.

He came. Reluctantly, but he came. He'd already sensed he wouldn't like what he saw.

They were pictures of drug addicts. Dozens of

them. Some long shot, some full face. Some clothed, some naked. The ones who were naked were particularly ghastly. They showed wasted bodies, the dirty sores an unsterilized needle causes. Sometimes, instead of a naked body, there was a close shot of an arm or a leg. They were even more ghastly: emaciated, filthy, ulcerous. Every subject on view was male.

Dr Gregory got about a quarter of the way through.

'Is it all like this?' he said.

'More or less.'

He leaned back. 'If you don't mind, doctor,' I said, 'I'd like you to go all the way through.'

He went on viewing, then leaned back at last.

'I know it's tragic, I know it's appalling,' he said. 'That's why I do the work I do.'

'You saw that the last but three was Mickey Wood – Michele Bosco?'

'I'm not blind.'

'Was he the one who told you?'

'Either stop talking in riddles or get out,' Gregory said.

'I think you compiled these pictures,' I said.

'How could I possibly take pictures like that?'

'Not took,' I said. 'Compiled. Brought together. It shouldn't have been too difficult. You work in the field of drug addiction anyway. Getting hold of pictures like this wouldn't be a problem. With your background you could open any files you liked.'

'But why in God's name should I?'

'In a moment ... I suppose Mickey Wood told you he'd been in the Army?'

It was another bit of cheek, another bluff, but by now he was easy meat.

'Yes,' said Gregory.

'And that he'd been in Vietnam?'

Again, 'Yes.'

'And that he'd started his habit there.'

'Poor little bugger,' said Gregory. 'What chance had he got? Not just a fag but a ballet-dancer. In the infantry.' He sighed. 'It wasn't like that in my war.'

And maybe it wasn't, at that, I thought. They'd have had more sense than to take him to Omaha Beach.

'I can't prove this next point,' I said, 'but I will if I have too... All the others were in Vietnam too.' Gregory was silent. 'That's why there are no women.' No answer from Gregory, either. 'Isn't that so, doctor?' Not a word.

I tried again. 'Your daughter held on to the letters she wrote,' I said. 'Don't ask me why. She just did. And if she replied to them she had a habit of writing the gist of the reply on the original letter. I came across one from you.' I dug in my pocket, fished out my notebook. 'Sent to Paris, it was. All very loving and paternal. But there was a PS. "You still haven't replied about the contents of my last letter," you said. Your daughter wrote underneath: "Told dad I was still thinking about it. He has caused me a lot of grief but it's not his fault... What on earth am I to do?" That's what she wrote,' I said, and put the notebook away.

'She got that habit from me,' said Gregory. 'Summarizing a reply at the foot of her letter. But

I never sent her that.' He nodded towards the microfilm.

'Of course not,' I said. 'Look at your PS "Replied about the contents of my last letter." Why not just "Replied to my letter"? – Because there were enclosures. Eight by ten glossies I would think. You really wanted to ram it home, I bet. But Jane used another of your habits. She put it on microfilm and got rid of the originals... Then she hid the microfilm. Hid it well.'

'Only you found it,' said Gregory.

'It's what I'm for.'

Gregory got up and made us both fresh drinks.

'It wasn't Bosco,' he said. 'Bosco went to Vietnam ... Nam he called it. They all did – long after Donner was so honourably discharged. It was another of those fellows in that microfilm. It doesn't matter which one. He told me when he was dying.'

'That Donner was his pusher?'

'Pusher?... He was running the whole damn syndicate. Supplying the addicts in the whole army corps.'

'That meant money, all right.'

'Of course it did. It also meant bribes and pay-offs – not to mention a working arrangement with the Vietcong to make sure the supplies got through. They were delighted to oblige, of course.' He gulped at his drink. 'This was the man who'd married my daughter, and my daughter was besotted with him. I had to *do* something. What I did was start to compile a dossier on him. Looking in my files, as you said. Seeking out the men who'd served in that particular army corps... God knows there were enough. As you say, the fact I'd been in the army helped... I asked about pushers, the men who controlled them, about supplies, about payment. And in the end I had quite a document.'

'You sent it to Jane?'

'I sent it to the CIA. I named Donner, of course.'

'And?'

'They sent it back by return. Nothing but hearsay, they said. Suggested I bear in mind that what I'd done was libellous... Hearsay! It was circumstantial evidence of the most damning kind.'

'Why do you think they did that?' I asked.

'Because Donner and his microchips are important to them,' Dr Gregory said. 'Those poor damn drug addicts are history.'

'So what did you do next?'

'I sent it to Jane,' he said. 'To Paris. Dossier and all.'

'The dossier isn't there,' I said.

'And yet she microfilmed the photographs,' said Gregory. 'Why not the dossier?'

'Because the dossier might have been what you said it was – circumstantial evidence,' I said. 'The pictures are just – very sad human interest.'

'Then why keep them?'

'To think about it,' I said. 'Your daughter was a great one for thought before action.'

Gregory knocked back his Scotch, saw I still had a full glass and poured himself another. 'Do you think'- his voice shook –'d'you think what I did had any bearing on my daughter's death?'

'I'm afraid so,' I said.

'But she was murdered by Terrorists, wasn't she?'

'Yes,' I said.

'Well then?'

'Doctor,' I said. 'It's nearly over. Keep all this to yourself for another week – two at most. Then I swear to you I'll explain the whole thing.'

'Explain my involvement in my daughter's murder? Do you really think I want to know?'

'Yes,' I said.

'You're a smart man, Hogget,' he said. 'I'll keep quiet. Might even go away for a bit.'

'I should,' I said. 'Have that check-up I suggested.'

'When you have something to tell me they'll always send on a message from here.' He looked at his watch. 'Is there anything else?'

'Did you ever give your daughter the name of a doctor who specialized in addiction cases and lived in the Southern Tyrol? Austria maybe?'

Gregory opened an address book and read out: 'Doctor Joachim Neumann, 17, Kaiserinstrasse, Linz, Austria.'

'Why did she–'

'Jane told me she'd found an addict who needed help. It had to be outside the United States. She asked me for the name of the best man available. I put her on to Neumann. He is the best.'

'Did she tell you why?'

'No ... Jane could be secretive at times. All she said was it was a fortunate coincidence it was Austria, but she wouldn't tell me why.'

I thought of Goody. Another word for secretive was discreet. 'Do you know this Dr Neumann?'

'I visited the clinic a couple of years back. He's one of the most outstanding psychiatrists I know.'

'Tell me about the clinic?' I said.

'What would you like to know?'

'The way he functions,' I said. 'The daily routine.'

He told me, and when he had finished he got to his feet. 'One more thing,' I said. 'I need a sleeping draught.'

'What kind?'

'The kind you dissolve in water. Also the strong kind.'

'Why do you want it?'

'Because I can't sleep.'

His look said he didn't believe me, but he wrote me something. 'Now if there's nothing more,' he said, and as he did so his wife came in.

'Richard,' she said, 'you're keeping poor dear Jason waiting and he's brought *all* his new anti-poems. Perhaps you and Mr–' Her voice faded. She looked at the glass in my hand, then at the glass in Gregory's.

'Oh sweetheart,' she said. 'You've been *drinking*.'

I left and nobody noticed. I'd asked all the questions I could. Somehow I couldn't bring myself to ask a bereaved father which of his dead daughter's lovers liked her to speak in baby talk. I went to the Choc' Full O' Nuts instead and had ham and eggs and coffee. For dessert I tried to figure out what an anti-poem was.

# 15

It was time to go to Bleeker Street. Not that I
wanted to. I had to. Bleeker Street was the only
lead I had to Gudrun Müller – both the Gudrun
Müllers. So I took a cab and told it to slow as it
passed the flower-shop, and we drove down past
the neat, brick houses with their inappropriate
wrought-iron work, past the cute people in cute
shops that sold cute things, and on to the
florists'. It was closed. No flowers in the window,
no plants in tubs on the sidewalk, just a big sign
in the window: Closed. I've never been more
relieved in my life. The cab took me on to the
Plaza and I went up to my room and turned on
the telly – a bearded geezer in a kaftan describing
to a fascinated blond how yoga cured his acne;
with all that fuzz on his face, how could you tell?
– and settled down to think about the pieces Dr
Gregory had given me and where they fitted. At
four o'clock, being British, I phoned for tea and
bikkies, and at five I reckoned I'd thought
enough for one day and took a walk as far as
Saks' Fifth Avenue and thought of buying something for Melanie, then remembered I was going
to Italy, and bought myself a suit instead. After
all I did have a dinner date.

I presented myself on time, showered, new-
suited. I'd even bought her an orchid at the hotel
florist's – or Donner had.

'What's this? Irony?' she said.

'I thought it would suit you,' I said. It certainly went with her dress, which was of a subtle, grey-green colour, the colour of the fields of her ancestors. The orchid's cream and brilliant yellow were just what it needed. She pinned it into place.

'Why thank you,' she said, when she saw its effect. 'Would you like a drink?'

'At the table,' I said, remembering her thirst, and off we went to spend even more of Donner's money. The table we got wasn't bad, but not being habitués it wasn't good: much too far from the pool. Still, that didn't affect the food and Ms Milligan enjoyed every mouthful. And the wine.

'Do you know how many times I've been here before?' she said. I shook my head. I was drinking Romanée St Vivant '71 and refused to gulp.

'Not once,' she said. 'Never. This is very kind of you. When I said the Four Seasons I was–'

I finished swallowing. 'Being ironic?' I said.

She flushed. It is a bad thing for redheads to do.

'I owe you another thank you,' she said.

'Eat your nice steak,' I said. 'It's getting cold.'

'No honestly. You remember, when Frank was – killed, and I was worrying about the cheque I signed – you said if the police asked I was to say I was sending him to London to set up *Honeyfall?* Well they did ask and I said just that and that's the last I heard of it.'

'My pleasure, Ms Milligan,' I said.

'You're a good person, Ron,' she said, 'and I wish you'd call me Cass.'

So I called her Cass, because it was a new experience, and I knew it wouldn't last.

Then Lenora Buell came in, with the sort of producer who's never owned a Buick in his life, and she saw me and waved, and I waved back. My companion became alert at once like a terrier getting his first sniff of the rabbit.

'That black bitch,' she said.

'Come come, Cass,' I said. 'Colour prejudice? From you?'

'Nothing of the sort,' she said. 'She's black, isn't she? Well she's a bitch as well. Or don't you think so?'

'I hardly know her,' I said.

'You don't act like you hardly know her,' she said.

'I gave her lunch here once,' I said. (Always tell the truth when it helps.) 'Now tell me why she's a bitch?'

'I offered her *Honeyfall* in London,' she said. 'She not only refused to go, she left the New York production too. Talk about ingratitude...'

'You offered her?' I said. 'You make the decisions?'

'No Godammit,' she said. '*She* made the decision,' and then: 'I put up the ideas and send them to Donner. So long as we stay in the black he just rubber stamps them.'

'No interest in the theatre?'

'Or in art, or music, or literature, or anything else. Only money.'

We chose dessert. A chocolate mousse that strained the waistband of my new suit, and a glass of Muscat des Beaumes de Venise to help it down.

'You sure know how to give a girl a good time,' said Cass.

I looked at her. Lenora had said that – in a rather more intimate situation. Was it some kind of password? But Cass was wiping her mouth with her napkin, and not even looking at me.

'My pleasure,' I said. 'But now I'm going to have to spoil it by asking questions.'

'Sure,' she said. Not even indignant.

'First there's something I have to tell you – only keep it to yourself or Mr Donner's going to be very angry.'

'You know who did it?'

'It's just about sewn up,' I said. 'A few loose ends.' I made the kind of fluttering gesture that Anna Maria makes, to show how insignificant the loose ends were. 'For instance, you know I checked up on Jane Donner's lovers?'

'Yes,' she said, and her lips began to tighten at once.

'Now now,' I said. 'Remember we're supposed to be chums... If I hadn't done that, I wouldn't know why she was killed, or who killed her.'

'All right,' she said. 'You had to do it. All right.'

'She was no nympho,' I said. 'From what I gather Donner lost interest in her sexually almost as soon as they were married. She was good to have on his arm when he went to important parties and that was it. All the same she only ever had two lovers – no matter how you define the word.'

'Frank Sokolny and A. D. Carr,' she said.

'That's right... You know Carr?'

'I've met him a few times.'

'You would say Jane loved him?'

She frowned, trying to get it straight: trying to be honest.

'She was – easy with him,' she said. 'Never any strain. They were like an old married couple. It was crazy. Jane with all that money – and him with nothing, living in a Black Ghetto, and they were happy. Relaxed.'

'Not like Frank Sokolny?'

'With Frank it was always quarrel and reconciliation.'

'Would you say they were both mature men?' I asked.

'No artist is mature,' she said. 'None that I've met, anyway.'

'Did either of them go in for baby-talk? You know – tootsy-wootsy, snooky-ookums.'

'No,' she said at once. 'Neither of them. It would have been undignified – and neither of them could stand that.'

'When did you begin to work for Jane?'

'Five years ago next fall.'

'And did you live here before that?'

'No,' she said. 'I was running a little theatre in San Francisco.'

'Thanks,' I said. 'Just one or two more. But not here... Just in case.' I signalled to the maitre for the bill. 'Care to make me a cup of coffee?'

She hesitated.

'That's all I'm asking,' I said. 'I won't take advantage–'

She relaxed. 'You didn't last time,' she said, 'and I was in no shape to put up a struggle if you had. OK. Coffee.'

I paid the bill in cash. The maitre looked as if it were something he hadn't seen much of just lately...

In the cab I tried to imagine A. D. Carr's reactions if I were to tell him he lived in a Black Ghetto, and decided to leave him in ignorance. Cass, mindful of the taxi-driver's presence, prattled on about the dinner she had had... In her flat she got to work at once, and there was much grinding of beans and filtering of coffee. There was cognac, too, and I sat on a sofa and sipped it while I waited. What I had to say next was going to strain our new friendship to its limits.

When she came back at last, there was coffee and the right kind of cups on a silver tray. She poured the coffee, topped up my brandy, and poured one for herself.

'Now,' she said. 'Ask away.'

'What are you going to do now?' I said. 'When it's over, I mean.'

'Is that relevant?'

'It could be,' I said. 'Please answer.'

'Well,' she said, 'I've had New York. It's time I moved on.'

'Back to San Francisco?'

'Further,' she said. 'Much further. The Mediterranean. That's where I want to be. A blazing sun, nice wine, good food... Some place where the ruins are really old. Not made last week.'

'What would you do?'

'I'd find something,' she said. 'Us old Bryn Mawr girls always find something.'

And it was true. Jane had been a Bryn Mawr girl too.

'Where would you live?'

'I'd find somewhere,' she said. 'Ron, what is this?'

'It may be the end of our beautiful friendship,'
I said. 'You're looking for a villa, aren't you?
Around the eighty thousand dollar mark – maybe
a bit more.'

'How in the name of...?'

'Last time you passed out, but I didn't. I took a
look at those brochures.'

'Get out,' she said softly, then her voice rose
each time she repeated it: 'Get out, get out, get
out.'

'You don't mean that,' I said. 'And keep your
voice down or your neighbours might get interested ... I also found what you proposed to use
for money.'

This time she didn't yell: just threw her brandy
glass at me. But it was empty and missed by a
foot, hit the cushion next to me. I picked it up,
poured brandy in it and gave it back to her.

'One Persian rug,' I said, 'what they call a Heriz.
And a small oil by Turner. Do you have any idea
what they're worth?'

'No doubt you'll tell me,' she said. 'Goddam
snoop.'

'But you always knew that,' I said. 'Now listen.
The best place to sell the Heriz is Switzerland.
The Swiss are crazy about them. Only don't take
a penny less than thirty-five thousand dollars.
You should get more.'

'You mean you'll let me keep it?'

'How can I stop you?' I said. 'It might be yours.'

'And the picture?'

'There you have a problem,' I said.

'I might have known.'

'You should have thought,' I said.

'I just know it's going to be worth more than the rug.'

'Certainly,' I said. 'It would fetch around two hundred thousand dollars – if you could sell it.'

'Why shouldn't I sell it?' she asked.

'Cass,' I said. 'May I still call you Cass?'

'What's the use,' she said. 'Go ahead.'

'Thank you, Cass,' I said. 'But have you never heard of provenance?'

'Of what?' she said.

'And you a Bryn Mawr girl. Oh dear. When you go to sell an authentic picture, the first thing the dealer will ask for is its provenance. That's the names of all the previous owners as far back as they can be traced, plus the bill of sale or whatever from its last owner. Without that he wouldn't look at it.'

She swigged at her brandy as if it were beer.

'You really do know about this, I suppose?' she said.

'Certainly I know. It's my business to know,' I said.

I sounded pompous, which meant I was getting drunk, so I eased off the brandy and poured more coffee.

'Let's have a look at it,' I said. She made no move. 'Please, Cass.'

'Why do you have to be so fucking polite?' she said and went and got it, propped it on a chair.

It was beautiful of course, but its beauty was a kind that only Turner could create. One of his Alpine scenes: all vague masses never quite realized, and the beauty was in the light, the way it fell. The shapes it made...

'Hey,' said my friend Cass. 'You've been staring at it for three whole minutes.'

'It's that kind of picture,' I said. 'Did you know Turner used to be a lather boy?'

'I don't even know what this is,' she said. 'No provenance, huh? You saying I should give it back?'

'Good lord no,' I was shocked she laughed aloud. 'I'm saying you should give it to me.' The laughter died.

'You can stop calling me Cass right now,' she said.

'I can get a provenance,' I said. 'That's half the deal. You've got the picture. That's the other half. We split fifty-fifty. Say it makes two hundred grand ... that's a hundred for you plus your thirty-five or more for the rug. One hundred and thirty-five plus thousand dollars. You could buy yourself a very nice castle in Spain for that. What d'you say?'

'Let me think about it.'

'No,' I said. 'If you don't tell me now there's no deal.'

'And you'll tell Donner?'

'Stop turning me into a monster,' I said. 'All I'll do is leave you on your own – and you'll do something stupid and wind up in jail, and Donner will get the picture back. Is that what you want?'

It was the last thing she wanted, and we both knew it. 'It's a deal,' she said, and held out her hand. We shook.

'I don't like the idea of leaving them in that cupboard,' I said. Where can I keep them?'

'In your bank.'

'Stolen goods?' She giggled. She loved the idea.

'They're so pompous in the bank,' she said.

I got up to go, and she got up too, tripped on the carpet and fell against me. I held on to her. She was nice to hold on to.

'I'm a little drunk,' she said.

'Me too.'

She sighed. 'Then now is not the time.'

''Fraid not.'

'Pity,' she said. 'A great pity. I like you very much, Ron Hogget.' Then she began to sag, and I pulled her up and aimed her at the bedroom.

'I'll let myself out,' I said.

'You do that,' said Cass. 'And let yourself in again real soon.'

I had to go outside. The thought hit me and I wasn't ready for it. I felt sick. Last time I had left this house two men had been waiting for me down below, and I'd got away by the fire-escape, and then across the roof-tops. But I was far too drunk for any mountain goat stuff that night. I wished Dave was with me, but if wishes were horses beggars would ride, as they say, and all I could do was get on with it, walking on the edge of the pavement close to the roadway, away from the shadowed doorways, sweating at every step till I reached the corner and a cab came by and I got back to the Plaza and passed out cold...

Next morning I phoned Donner's fortress and requested an audience and was granted one right away. No cracks about cashmere jackets, just hundred proof geniality oozing down the phone. 'Come on over,' he said. 'There'll be coffee waiting.'

I went on the jump. The coffee was terrible, but he smiled at me.

'What can I do for you, Mr Hogget?' he said.

'I've come to say goodbye – well, arrivederci anyway,' I said. 'I'm going back to Italy.'

'So you are,' he said. 'Concorde again?' I nodded. 'I wish I could have loaned you the Grumman Gulfstream,' he said, 'but I'm due out in Silicon Valley again tomorrow. We'll fly out to Italy ourselves from there.'

'We?'

'Myself. Mr Black. Mr White,' he said. 'We'll handle it between us. Now you go and keep an eye on that place for us–'

'Right,' I said.

'And make sure that's all you do.'

'That's what I'm getting paid for,' I said. 'Which reminds me – I need a little money.'

He looked reproachful. 'On delivery, Mr Hogget. You said so yourself.'

'Not my fee,' I said. 'Of course not. I stand by my agreement. But I've had rather a lot of expenses.'

'What for?'

'Bribing people – to get close to Guardi and his friends. And then there's my minders. I've got two now.'

'Your what?'

'My bodyguard. They cost a thousand a day.'

'Kind of high, isn't it?'

'The way one of them flattened those heavies in Paris he's worth it, Mr Donner. He has to be. And the other's good too. If they weren't I wouldn't be here now tying it all up for you.'

He had to admit it. It was true.

'How much do you need?'

'Thirty-seven thousand.'

Never give them round figures: it makes them suspicious. 'Jesus,' said Donner. 'Who did you bribe?'

'A journalist, a land-dealer and an accountant,' I said. That took care of Uncle Pietro. 'And somebody who could get themselves killed for telling what they knew about Guardi... People put a high price on their own necks, Mr Donner.'

He wrote out a cheque.

'Phone the Hotel du Lac at Riva del Garda,' I said. 'Chances are I won't be there but you can leave a message at the desk. I'll keep checking. Make the message nice and simple. Just the time of your arrival and how much you're looking forward to the visit.'

'It'll be the truth,' he said. I didn't dwell on it.

'Would you like me to book you into the hotel?' I said.

'What kind is it?'

'The best,' I said.

'Two rooms and a suite,' said Donner.

There was still one more question. Not that it worried me: I was just curious.

'Mr Donner,' I said, 'Are you going to kill Guardi?'

'I'm going to kill all of them,' he said.

'But – but you'll be arrested,' I said. 'You can't possibly hide the fact that you're in Italy, not when you arrive in your own private jet.'

'You're a nice man, Mr Hogget,' Donner said, 'to worry about me like that.'

So many people were telling me I was nice I

was beginning to believe it.

'But do you really think I hadn't thought about this? It's going to be all right, Mr Hogget. Just you leave it all to me.'

He was paying, after all, so I left him to cash my cheque at the bank, and signed my bill at the Plaza for Mr Donner to pay, then it was caviar and filet mignon concorda, and champagne on the 737 to Venice, but not too much because I had to pick up the Lancia at the Piazzale Roma.

She started with no trouble at all, the way all good Italian cars do when the weather is warm, and I took off for Sirmione, drove past the house and, I hoped, past Dave. He was nowhere in sight. I went to the turn off, parked and began to walk back. Dave seemed to rise out of the ground to meet me.

'That's far enough, Ron,' he said. 'There's quite a crowd back there.'

I didn't answer for a minute. I was too busy gawking at him. He hadn't shaved since I'd left him, and, not to put too fine a point on it, he stank.

'You look a bit rough,' I said.

'I haven't had much sleep,' he told me.

'I should have got Carr out here sooner,' I said. 'It was too much for just one man. I'm sorry.'

'Not to worry,' he said. 'I managed.'

'What happened?'

He grinned. 'They're all still here, including the heavy mob.'

That took care of my main worry. Dave went on grinning.

'What's so funny?' I said.

'Between the two of us,' he said, 'we've started a war.'

'Tell me,' I said.

'Well the Reds had no doubt at all that the Fascists had done it. That's why they moved in that bus load of heavies – to guard their base. And also to make what you might call retaliatory strikes.'

'Where?'

'A bomb in the Fascist HQ in Milan. They also broke up a rally they were holding in Verona. So naturally the *Fascists* thought the *Reds* had started it. So *they* put a bomb in their newspaper in Mestre, then beat up a couple of blokes selling propaganda sheets in Turin. Then yesterday both sides had a head-on clash in the Piazza del Duomo in Milan. Fifty a side. It was better than a Manchester United-Chelsea match. According to the car radio they beat the shit out of each other.' The thought pleased him.

'Guardi and his mates get involved?' I asked.

'Of course not,' said Dave. 'They're staff officers. Staff officers never get involved... What now?'

'We sweat it out till Sunday,' I said. 'That's when Donner gets here – and Mr Black and Mr White.'

'Ah,' said Dave.

'In the meantime – if you could just hang on here till I go and pick up A. D. Carr? We ought to have a meeting.'

'Sure,' said Dave. 'Take your time. I'm enjoying myself.'

I went back to the Lancia. There was my mate, planting false evidence, belting blokes, inciting riots. I began, like Frankenstein, to wonder just what kind of monster I'd created...

A. D. Carr got to the Hotel du Lac about an hour after I did. He'd done the eight hundred miles in twelve hours, and looked a hell of a sight fresher than me and I'd come by plane. I took him to the Ristorante Cesare, and as we ate I filled him in, told him the lot.

When I'd finished he looked at me a long time, then swigged at his Barolo, and I knew he still hadn't got me.

'You take some big risks, Mr Hogget,' he said.

'Call me Ron,' I said. 'Where's the risk? If you told me the truth about Jane and you – there isn't one.'

'You know I like you, Ron, I really do,' said A. D. Carr. He said it as if liking people was something he did about once in five years. 'And by the way – you can call me A. D. Have you any more to tell me?'

'Ask you,' I said. When you were a boxer – you said you were terrible.'

'Hardly ever won a fight,' he said.

'Why not?'

'I was always being disqualified for fouling.'

'Let's go and talk to Dave,' I said.

He insisted we go on his motor-bike, which reduced my life expectancy considerably. Just my bad luck he had a spare helmet. But at least it cut out the chat. Mind you, to be fair he cut the motor a few hundred metres or so before we reached the house and sort of coasted in.

Dave was waiting for us, and we hid the bike in

a gully. We followed him to a hide he had constructed that gave a clear view of the house.

'I've told A. D. the lot,' I said. 'Now it's up to us to decide what to do next.'

'You mean you'll take a vote on it?' Dave said.

'No,' I said. 'I mean you can bow out if you want to. I'm going to finish it.'

'Bow out?' said Carr. 'I only just got here. Bow out of what?'

'Murder,' I said.

Dave lit a cigarette, fingers cupped round it, shielding its glow from the gathering dusk. 'Whose?' he said. 'Those creeps in there? You think Donner's going to kill them?'

'I know he is,' I said.

'So what?' said Dave. 'They'd hang anyway, if Italy still has the death penalty. Does it?'

'No,' I said.

'It ought to,' said Dave.

A. D. said, 'I should like them to die. I wouldn't mind killing them myself – I mean rather than let them get away with it. Go free. But if Donner thinks he can do it – then let him go ahead.'

I remembered A. D.'s face when I told him about the severed head, the torture marks. He meant what he said.

'How about you?' Dave asked me.

'I'm with you.' I said.

'Then as I see it,' said Dave, 'all we have to do is keep them here till Sunday. What time?' he asked me.

'Donner reckoned mid-afternoon,' I said.

Dave looked at his watch. 'Say another forty-three hours,' he said.

267

'Has their Ferrari come back?' I asked.

'Not the way I fixed it,' said Dave. 'It'll take weeks. They've got a BMW now, the big one. And the Alfa of course. But neither of 'em'll do better than the Lancia – not with Guardi driving – and that bike of A. D.'s'll lose them.'

'How is Bruno?' I asked.

'Walking,' said Dave. 'Still not a hundred per cent. Maybe by tomorrow, though. He's a hard one–'

He broke off. There were visitors. First a police car, all flashing lights and futuristic noises, and behind it a bus with so much armour on it was more like a tank. Car and bus were jam-packed with men.

'What on earth–' said Dave.

'Riot police,' I said.

A geezer jumped out of the bus. He looked as elegant as a tailor's dummy and as hard as nails. He also looked like the bloke in charge. When nothing happened he signalled to the car, and someone inside began to play a spotlight on the house, probing it room by room, till at last the door opened and Bo-bo came out, and the spot stayed with her till she reached the gate, then she and the hard, elegant geezer began to argue, and the geezer gestured at the bus.

'He's telling her if she doesn't open up he'll ram the gates with the bus,' said Dave. 'He will, too.' He was lost in admiration.

But he didn't get his treat. Bo-bo opened up and the car and bus poured in. The bus parked cross-wise to the VW bus, blocking its exit. The car pulled up across the garage door. Men came tumbling out of both and sealed off the house as if they knew what they were doing, and the bloke in charge led the rest of them into the house with Bo-bo. Every man jack of them carried a machine-pistol and a truncheon.

'Oh dear,' said A. D. Carr, 'This could be bad news for Martin Donner.'

But it wasn't. We watched and waited for about an hour, then the tough dandy came out, followed by the Communist heavies, followed by the blokes with machine-pistols and clubs. Last of all came Bo-bo and Guardi. They were doing all the talking: the trouble was that no-one seemed to be listening. The bloke in command motioned the heavies into the VW bus, and three of the riot police got in with them: one to drive, and two to point their pistols.

'Are they all on the bus?' I asked Dave.

'All except the four originals.'

The commander turned on Bo-bo and Guardi and spoke. They were silent till he finished, then began again at once. He got into the car and drove off in mid-sentence. The VW bus followed, and the riot police brought up the rear. Bo-bo and Guardi walked after them and locked the gate: they were still talking.

'What d'you reckon?' said Dave.

'I reckon the cops are breaking it up,' I said. 'Sending the Montagus and Capulets back to their own backyards.'

'Spoilsports,' said Dave.

'Then why did he leave our four behind?' A.D. asked.

'Good heavens,' said Dave. 'You don't suppose

the Fabulous Four got involved with nasty rough work like fighting? They haven't left the house since that VW arrived – and I bet they can prove it.'

Later on I copped the news on the car radio. The police had taken strong measures to avert further incidents. Sending them home with a slapped wrist, I thought, and probably the Fascists too, but without proper proof what else could they do?

I'd brought sandwiches and wine and San Pelegrino, and we ate and worked out the next move. There was only one. To keep on watching. I left the others to it and drove to a call-box and phoned the hotel. We were delayed in Verona I said. We might not be back till Sunday. The desk told me Signor Baxter hadn't got back either and I said that was OK. He was with us. Business. The desk didn't give me any arguments. We'd paid in advance...

When I got back Dave was explaining to A. D. the finer points of a Colt Python 357 Magnum. 'It isn't just that it'll go through steel plate,' he was saying. 'It's the psychological effect. Did you ever see such a mean-looking bastard?'

And indeed it is a big, nasty-looking gun.

I drew first watch and A.D. relieved me at three; and I slept as best I could on the hard earth. At nine I drove into Verona, and had a shave at a barber's, then did some shopping: a jumbo-size vacuum flask I had filled with coffee at a café, paper plates, knives, milk, bread, butter, ham, cheese and marmalade at a supermarket, and a couple of Japanese replicas of 357 Magnums. They didn't have the Colt Python: just the Smith and Wesson Combat Magnum but the Smith and Wessons looked every bit as nasty. When I got back I was welcome, no doubt of it. The coffee and food saw to that. A. D. was pleased with his replica too, but Dave fretted because it wasn't real.

'I couldn't hit anything if it were,' said A. D. Carr. The long day wore on, then around tea-time we got a bit of excitement. Bruno came out and went into the garage, reappeared in the BMW.

'Oh good, he's better,' said Dave. I wondered what was good about it.

Then the others appeared, carrying suitcases.

'What now?' said A.D.

'We stop them,' I said. 'They don't leave.' I turned to Dave. 'You tell us how.'

And then the phone rang inside the house, and all four went inside.

'That makes it easier,' said Dave. From the hide he produced a rotting mattress he'd found where we parked the car, and jammed it over the golden spear points that tipped the railings. A.D. gave him a hand, and Dave went over with the flowing grace of a cat; A.D. was about as graceful as a gorilla, but he was fast. When it was my turn I nearly stuck, but the other two lifted me down, we went up the driveway at the trot. All three of us carried Magnums, and only two of us were bluffing.

They made it easier still by all huddling round the phone in the study. Guardi held the receiver, naturally, but the other three were listening hard. He was yelling.

'No,' he said. 'For once you do what the pigs tell you to do. Stay where you are, and keep out of trouble... Why? Because I'm telling you, that's why. Also I'm setting up something much better. If we go on like this we'll take too many casualties. Be patient. We'll make the Fascisti wish they'd never been born. I promise you... Fine, fine. Just don't call me again for a while... OK... OK... *Ciao*.'

Dave walked in so quietly that Emilia actually looked up before she knew he was there. She gasped aloud.

*'Buona sera,'* said Dave. The other three looked up, incredulous, and A.D. and I walked in to flank Dave on each side.

'Don't try any tricks,' I said in Italian. 'Don't even move.'

'Bloody Fascists,' said Guardi. 'You're bluffing.'

Bruno, poor fellow, believed him, and took off like a rocket, heading straight for A. D. Carr. A.D. dropped the Magnum on a chair, steadied him with a left, then used a right cross that spun Bruno halfway across the room and as he did so Bo-bo grabbed for her handbag. Dave shot it out of her hand. The bullet went on through the leather and slammed into the wall.

'We're not bluffing,' I said. A.D. licked his knuckles then picked up his toy gun.

'Up against the wall,' said Dave.

Guardi made no move. 'You're not Italian,' he said. 'You're not one of those Lombardy Fascists.'

Dave said in English, 'That doesn't mean I won't shoot if you don't move.'

They moved all right. They thought Dave meant it. I think he did, too. Dave made them stand, palms touching the wall, and searched them, men and women alike. It was as impersonal as it was degrading. I wondered how many times he'd done it in Belfast. Guardi had a Walther PP3 automatic, a lot of money, including a fistful of Donner's US dollars, and credit cards. Bruno, who looked far from well, also had a Walther, a cosh and not nearly so much money. All Bo-bo's stuff was in her handbag: a Beretta 32, a much more ladylike gun than the Walther, money (no dollars), credit cards, make-up. Emilia had only money and make-up, and enough grass to blow the minds of all four. Each of them also carried cigarettes and a lighter, but the cigarettes were just smokes, the lighters just for lighting them, not poison darts or gas guns. While Dave went on with the searching I pocketed the Beretta and A.D. took one Walther, tucked the other into Dave's pocket.

'See if you can find some rope,' said Dave, and A.D. went off. Guardi turned his head to say, 'I don't know what you think you're doing, but I'm warning you–'

Dave slammed him with the barrel of the gun along the side of the head, hard enough to make his knees buckle. 'We look to our front,' he said. 'We speak when we are spoken to.'

They stood in silence until A.D. came back with some clothes line. They tested its breaking strain, then I chopped it into lengths with the Swiss Army knife and we sat them in chairs, then trussed them up like Christmas turkeys. I'd promised we'd deliver them alive, and they were a tricky lot, the Fabulous Four, even sexy little Emilia. When it was done I ran the car back into the garage, came back and joined A. D. and Dave in watching them. The silence bothered them: it

273

was alien to them. They were afraid of it.

'Who was on the phone?' I said at last.

Guardi was so relieved at the sound of a voice he answered at once.

'Friends in Padua. The pigs took them away from here. You'd better be careful. They might come back.'

Dave said, 'Somebody's asking for a belting,' and Guardi was silent.

'They won't come back,' I said. 'You told them to stay where they are. And you're the leader. I heard you say so.'

He gave up then, and we gave them some more silence. This time it was Bo-bo who cracked.

'You were fools not to wear masks,' she said. 'I shall remember your faces, believe me.'

'It makes no difference,' I said.

'Of course it does—'

'No difference at all,' said A. D. Carr.

She was silent then. The next question was obvious, but she was too afraid to ask it. Emilia had a try instead.

'Please,' she said, 'what do you want?'

'We don't want anything,' I said. 'The man who wants things won't be here till tomorrow.'

'And who is he?' Guardi asked.

'Martin Donner,' I said.

Emilia said at once, 'I didn't want to be mixed up in that. I liked her. I didn't want to hurt her. Honestly.'

'Shut up,' said Guardi. 'Just shut up, will you?'

'That's good advice,' I said. 'Don't waste your breath on me.'

Dave said, 'I think I'll take a bath.'

'Go right ahead,' I said. 'I want to take a look around myself.' I turned to A.D. 'You can cope all right?'

'Be a pleasure,' said A.D. Carr.

There was an armoury, there had to be, and I found it in the wine cellar. Wine racks were lined up against what looked like a wall, but part of the racks swung away if you held them right, and there they all were: sawn-off pump-action shotguns, machine-pistols, an Uzi machine gun, even a rocket launcher from Brno: Israel and Czechoslovakia. Either side of the Iron Curtain. Those geezers upstairs weren't fussy so long as somebody dropped when you pulled the trigger … I made a selection and stuck them in a Gucci bag someone had thoughtfully left handy.

I went upstairs to their rooms, went through their papers. Italians, like most Europeans, are far more fussy about papers than we are. Passports, identity cards, driving licences. All sorts. Guiseppina known as Bo-bo was a Contessa. Contessa Guiseppina de Calvi. Addresses in Rome, the Abruzzi, and, of course, Sirmione. Age twenty-eight. Quite a mature student. She was down as doing post-graduate research in politics, which was ironic. Bruno Silva wasn't down as anything. Age twenty-five, no job and no prospects. Not any more. Emilia Orsino, twenty-two, was studying languages. So far she knew five. She'd need to be eloquent in all of them.

I took all the keys I could find and went down to the room where Dave had set fire to the papers. What he'd burned was mostly rubbish. The important stuff was in locked drawers. The list of names was a big one, whittled down to a short list of three: a very rich, and from what I'd heard, very nasty industrialist, an Arab ambassador from the Emirates; and a cardinal. Against each was the figure 2: two thousand million lire, I guessed. Six thousand million in all: say three million quid. Give or take. It would cost a bit to finance, but then they'd got a bit. They'd got three-quarters of a million dollars.

I put it all back nice and tidy, the way I found it, for the police, then went outside, put the Gucci bag in the Lancia's boot and went back to the others. Dave had already joined them.

'Now,' I said. 'Tell us about Mrs Donner.' The temperature dropped by ten degrees.

'You know we lifted her,' Emilia said at last.

The others looked as if they could kill her: all except Bruno. He was having trouble looking like anything.

'Well?' Guardi said.

'Bruno doesn't look well,' I said, and indeed he didn't. He looked unconscious. A.D. must have really belted him a good one.

'Bruno looks awful,' Bo-bo said.

'I wish I could help him,' I said. 'I mean nobody should die before their time.'

Bo-bo was silent at that: maybe she was thinking of Jane.

I went over to him. He wasn't tied by the ropes: he hung inside them. Poor Bruno... The only member of the proletariat present, and he was out cold. I turned to A.D.

'He seems to have withdrawn from reality,' I said.

'Who wouldn't?' said A.D. and came to stand beside Bruno, to slap his face, rhythmically, left after right. Nothing brutal: just inevitable.

Emilia said, 'That is torture,' and Guardi said, 'Shut up.'

After maybe forty blows Bruno opened his eyes once more.

'Now,' I said, 'do we go on being nice? Or would you rather we got nasty?'

'Oh for God's sake,' said Guardi. 'Just tell us how we get out of this and how much it's going to cost.' And at once he looked happier. Red Commando or not, he was the kind of bloke who believes that whatever you want, all you have to do is put a price on it. Way he was brought up, I suppose.

'Well now,' I said. 'This could be an expensive business.'

'Well of course,' he said. It didn't bother him a bit. He was still a rich kid, with a rich kid's evaluation of what he was worth.

I went up to Bruno. He was trying to look as if he didn't understand a word, and failing miserably.

'You speak English,' I said. Not a question; a statement.

'Yes,' he said.

'You want to die, is that it?' I asked him. He didn't answer. Of course not. His eyes rolled towards Guardi. He was waiting to be told what to say. But Guardi had his own problems.

'Don't you believe you're going to die?' I said. 'Haven't you worked that out yet?'

Bruno still kept twisting his head toward Guardi.

'He can't help you,' I said. 'Not this time. It's up to you, Bruno. You'd better tell us.'

'No!' It was Guardi, using the kind of voice that cracks windows.

I shrugged. 'Suit yourselves,' I said, and looked at my watch. 'By tomorrow it won't make any difference.'

'Why won't it?' Bo-bo said.

'Because you'll all be dead,' I told her.

There was silence for about three minutes, then Emilia began to cry.

Bruno said, 'I don't understand this. I think maybe I'm being cheated here.'

'Bruno, be quiet,' Guardi said.

'Why should I?' said Bruno.

'Because I'm telling you to,' said Guardi. 'Now be quiet or I'll–'

'Or you'll what?' said Bruno. 'What can you do, sweetie? Let me live?'

I think it was only at that moment that Guardi really began to believe that he might die. For a moment he looked at Bruno with horror, then he made a huge effort. His voice became gentle.

'Bruno ... Caro,' he said. 'You know what we mean to each other.'

And then suddenly it wasn't a play any longer.

'We don't mean a damn thing,' said Bruno. 'You're a good lay, but I've found better in Venice–'

Guardi jumped inside his bonds as if Bruno had jabbed a pin in him, but all Bruno did was turn to me.

'Ask your questions,' he said and I did, and he gave me the answers. Emilia got into the act, too.

But not Bo-bo and not Guardi. Guardi even tried to shut them up, until A.D. went and stood beside him, then he was quiet. When they'd done I went to make coffee and sandwiches. I offered the prisoners some as well, but they weren't hungry. While I was absent Guardi had been doing some thinking. He told me so.

'What about?' I said.

'Money.'

'You mentioned that before,' I said.

'This is *real* money.'

'For what?'

'Just to let us go.'

'How much?' I said.

Three-quarters of a million dollars.'

'Oh that money,' I said. 'But it isn't yours to give.'

'But I know where it is,' he said.

'So do I,' I said. 'Under the basil plant.'

Again he made that jerking movement inside his bonds, but this time it was despair. Their last chance had gone and he knew it.

'There's something else there,' I said.

'Her head,' said Bo-bo. 'That rich bitch's head.'

She too knew that their last chance had gone, but it only made her more defiant.

'Somebody hurt her,' I said. 'Hurt her badly. The marks are still there.'

'Bo-bo did it,' said Bruno. 'Bo-bo and Emilia.' A.D. had to fight hard to stay still.

'I didn't,' Emilia said.

'You thought it was fun,' said Bruno.

'She didn't look so pretty when we'd finished,' Bo-bo said.

279

'Turn you down, did she?' said A.D. She spat at him.

And that's the way we passed the time. Interrogation: bribery: begging: defiance. Again we took it in turns to sleep. Our prisoners never closed their eyes. With so little time left, they didn't want to waste any time in sleeping... Early on Saturday afternoon I made more sandwiches, more coffee.

'How much time have we got?' Guardi asked.

I looked at my watch. 'Maybe a couple of hours if the plane's on time.'

'I could do with a smoke,' Guardi said. 'A real smoke.'

'Oh yes. *Please,*' said Emilia.

Last request, I thought. The prisoner always gets a cigarette before he faces the firing squad, but it doesn't usually have hash in it... I untied Emilia. She seemed to be OC marijuana and in any case she'd be the least trouble. But even she looked as if she'd leg it at one point, till Dave put the Magnum on her. After that she got busy breaking up tailor-made cigarettes, mixing them with hash, rolling new cigarettes with the mixture. She was generous with the hash, I noticed, but it would be their last one after all. When she'd done I tied her up again, and let them have one hand free to smoke. They sucked at those cigarettes as if they could keep them alive.

I turned to my gallant band.

'You still want to hand them over to Donner?' I said.

Dave said, 'Nothing's changed,' and A.D. said, 'Not a damn thing.'

Donner was to say he would be at the rendezvous (a map reference) by putting an ad in the small ads column of the *Verona Arena*. All he had to write was ABC, followed by the date and time of the meeting, and then XYZ, so it would read ABC 21721 XYZ. He'd done just that.

'But what I don't know,' Donner continued, 'is that it's Guardi who's put in the ad. He's going to pull another kidnap – on me this time – and kick off with a quarter of a million to replace the quarter he's already spent, then slap a ransom on top of that. And me – I'm such an innocent I go along with all the garbage. Also I want to get the ones who did what they did to my wife.' I believed him. 'Only this time I bring along my good friends Mr Black and Mr White, and when it comes to the shoot out Guardi and his pals are outclassed, believe me. They all die, only one of them lives just long enough to tell me where – where Jane's remains are, so I can bury her properly. That way I find my money, too. Any questions?'

'Did you bring the quarter million?' I asked.

'Of course,' said Donner. 'It's the first thing the cops will ask for. They're human aren't they? They enjoy looking at money.'

'Did a messenger really deliver a letter to you?'

'Sure,' said Donner. 'We've got witnesses.'

'And did you use the messenger service?'

'You think I'm dumb, Mr Hogget? I had a guy dress up in a phony uniform – a guy I can trust. When I phoned the messenger service they didn't know a thing about it. Any more questions?'

'No,' I said. 'You've covered everything. Congratulations.'

'I'll need their guns,' said Donner.

'Emilia doesn't have one.'

'Let's have yours,' he said.

'Gladly,' I said. 'But it's a fake.'

He took it from me; gawped at it. 'Well I'll be damned,' he said. 'Did you all use fake guns?'

'One's real,' I said.

'Get it,' said Donner. 'And the other three.' Even his requests were commands.

Of course Dave jibbed, but in the end he handed over, first wiping it clear of prints. I wiped the others, too – we'd handled them – and took them to Donner in Bo-bo's handbag.

'Why the drag act?' said Donner, looking at the handbag.

'I wiped the prints off,' I said. 'We'd handled all those guns.'

'Smartass,' said Donner, but he was impressed. The bullet hole in the bag impressed him too.

'Somebody did that with a Colt Python? Nice shooting... Where's the bullet?'

'In the wall,' I said. 'Whoever owns the gun must have been careless.'

Donner nodded. 'It's all corroboration,' he said. 'Shows it's their gun. No problem.' He passed the bag to Black. 'What are you going to do now, the three of you?'

'My friends fly home tonight,' I said, lying in a forthright, manly sort of way. 'I'm staying in Italy a while.' That at least was true.

'You got a reason?'

'I've been travelling too much,' I said. 'London – Paris – Venice – London – New York – New York – London – Rome. And all in a week. It's time I dawdled a bit. Acted like a tourist.'

'Suppose you're asked why you flew to New York and back?'

'A client asked me to find a picture. He'd heard it was in New York and I went to see. It turned out to be a false alarm.'

'You can prove that?'

'If I have to.' Horry Lumley has no money, but he looks as if he has, and he'll always lie for me at a price.

'Great,' he said. 'I guess that's it, Mr Hogget.'

I hesitated. In spite of everything, he'd shown some feeling for his wife.

'Mr Donner,' I said at last, 'your wife's remains are where I said they are, *and* the money. But if you want to check – I'd send somebody else. It's – it's a pretty sickening sight.'

'Yeah,' he said. 'OK Black and White will check.' He turned to them. 'But that's all you do. Put everything back as it was.' He returned to me. 'Put your guys on the plane,' he said, 'and leave the rest to us. We take over now. Enjoy your vacation. You've earned it.'

And that had to do instead of goodbye. Just stay out of my way, and a cheque for a hundred thousand dollars.

I collected my merry men, and we went out the back way. When I ushered them into the Lancia A.D. baulked.

'My bike's back there,' he said.

'So's the Fiat,' said Dave.

'Later,' I said. 'To oblige me.' They grumbled, but they got in. Dave went on grumbling about the loss of his Colt Python.

'Look in the Gucci bag on the floor,' I said.

Dave unzipped it and found he was looking at a machine pistol, two sawn-off shotguns, three Smith and Wesson .357 Magnums, only for real this time, and enough ammunition for each.

'Jesus,' he said. 'Won't they be missed?'

'A drop in the bucket,' I said. 'Those geezers were getting ready for a war.'

We reached the secondary road that would take us to the autostrada.

'Put the bag back on the floor,' I said. Dave did so, and three minutes later we had company, a red Alfa-Romeo that could stay with the Lancia no matter how hard I tried, so I didn't try at all.

'Don't look round,' I said, 'but we've got company. Just as well we didn't collect the rest of the transport. I told Donner you were going by plane.'

'I'm worried about my bike,' A.D. said. 'I don't like leaving it.'

'You can pick it up at nine,' I said. 'And the Fiat.'

'Suppose Donner's there?' said Dave.

'He won't be,' I said, and told them the scenario.

'Crafty bastard,' said Dave.

We went back to the hotel and Dave packed. All A.D.'s gear was in the panniers of his motor-bike so I had to lend him a case of mine to make things look right. Then I paid for the extra nights for Dave and A.D., and kept mine on for that night only. It would be nice to sleep in that bed. I'd paid enough for the privilege...

All the way to Marco Polo airport we had company. Dave and A.D. took out their suitcases and I got out with them, shook them by the hand

and thanked them for all their help as if it was all for real. In my game you never know. Maybe the geezer watching us could lip read.

Dave said, 'So long, old son,' and A.D. nodded, and they went into the airport. I got back in the car. This was the tricky bit. Supposing he had orders to see Dave and A.D. into the departure lounge? But the only orders he had were to stay close to me. I took him back to Riva del Garda, for a dinner at the Ristorante Cesare that wasn't sandwiches, then back to the hotel for an early night's kip after I'd phoned Uncle Pietro.

That was for me, you understand. The poor geezer who was tailing me would have to sit up and keep watch in case I decided to sneak off at some terrible hour like three in the morning. Still, he had a chance to catch up on his sleep when the relief man took over. That was at nine-thirty, when I paid my last bill and finally left the Hotel du Lac.

I spotted him on the autostrada. He was driving another Alfa-Romeo, a blue one this time, which was foolish even if it was a different colour... Spotting him was no bother. All I did was get into the fast lane and go, which meant he had to do the same, and when I went back in the slow lane, he had to as well. Simple

I took him to Verona. It's a useful town if you're being tailed. Lots of winding streets in the old town, blind alleys, unexpected turn-offs. And I knew it well, too. My mother had taken me there often enough and I blessed her for it.

I lost him in the Corso Cavour. There's a turn-off there that leads to a jumble of houses that must have been condemned in Julius Caesar's time. The turn-off's at the end of a road that curves like a bradawl, so my tail wasn't in sight of me when I turned off. The ruin of a path I was on looked like a dead-end, but there's a gap if you know where to look for it. The Lancia didn't like it and I told it I was sorry and was glad Dave wasn't with me. But we made a good road at last, about a mile from where I'd lost the Alfa. I never saw it again.

I stopped at a bookshop and then went on to Uncle Pietro's favourite café. He was waiting for me, oozing questions he knew I wouldn't answer. At the same time he was almost crying with relief because I had phoned up and made an appointment first, even though my aunt had gone to visit a cousin and Claudia was at the market. He handed over the keys to his chalet without a blink, because he knew in his bones there was something in it for him. Something big.

Then it was back on the autostrada, but heading northeast this time. I was going to Bolzano, where my army was waiting for me.

It was handy enough for the Austrian border, but that wasn't why I was going there. It was also the last place Jane had been before she died.

It used to be called Bosen, which is its German name, and, a lot of people there will tell you, its correct one. It's in the South Tyrol, which used to be part of Austria, but Italy grabbed it after the First World War, and managed to hang on to it. The old town is German, and looks as if it was built to a design by the Brothers Grimm; all sharply pitched roofs and curlicued eaves, and a long colonnade of ancient shops.

That was where I'd arranged to meet the army – in a bar, the sort of bar tourists use. They were tourists themselves if anybody asked: not that I thought anybody would. We were a good fifty miles from Linz. They would ask there, all right... Our reunion was cheerful, largely because A.D. had got his bike back and now Dave had his Lancia. I had no feelings of love, or even friendship, for the Fiat. It was a car and it went and that was it.

'Has anybody heard anything?' I said. 'Your car radio needs fixing, Dave.'

He handed me a copy of the *Corriere della Sera*. Early edition. So it had made the nationals. 'Millionaire American in Gun Drama', I read. 'Donner and His Bodyguard Avenge Wife's Murder'. 'Four Red Terrorists Killed'. I went on to the smaller print. He'd followed the scenario to the letter. Bo-bo was the one who lived long enough to tell where his wife's head was, and the money. It didn't surprise me that she'd been chosen. She was the head torturer.

'It's been on the radio, too,' said Dave.

'And television.'

'There's hardly been anything else on,' said Dave.

'It's big stuff,' I said. 'Has Donner said what he's going to do now?'

'He gave one interview,' said Dave, 'then announced he was suffering from nervous exhaustion and was going to rest. He didn't say where. The media men are going frantic. They can't find him.'

I won't have to, I thought. Not this time. Not if this caper works.

'You still want us to go through with it?' A.D. asked.

'What ... yes,' I said. 'I can't make you – now you know what you're up against.'

'I'm beginning to see why you acquired that arsenal,' A.D. said. 'You know it's funny...'

Sometimes you could die, I'd said to Dave. But not this time. Not out loud.

'By funny I mean odd,' A.D. said. 'I've been remembering my time in the ring,' he said. 'It was your asking me about it that triggered me off. I hadn't thought about boxing for years... It was the money that got me into it initially. Not very large sums by your standards, minuscule by Donner's, but enormous by mine. And quick. No more than an hour's work at most... And then I began to analyse what I was doing when I fought. *I had to win.* That was the one thought uppermost. I had to win, to the extent that if I looked like losing I fouled. Mostly I got away with it because I'm quick. Of course it didn't go down well with other boxers, but that didn't worry me. They didn't like me anyway. I read books and I hit hard. To their minds the two things didn't gel...

'Then I tried to sort out what was going on below the surface, so to speak, while all this urge towards winning went on. There were two things. First there was fear – not of losing. I refused to ac-knowledge that possibility – fear of pain, of being hurt, even of brain damage. Even – in a remote way – of death. Boxers are occasionally killed in action so to speak... But with the fear there was what I can only describe as a sort of exaltation, a delight as intense as really successful love-making.'

He turned to Dave. 'Tell me,' he said. 'Was being in the Paras like that?'

'There were times,' said Dave, 'when it was exactly like that.'

A.D. turned back to me. 'I was never in the army,' he said. 'I've often regretted it. Maybe this will prove an adequate substitute. Let's see.'

It was a hell of a roundabout way to say yes, but yes it had been. I tried not to show my relief.

'And you, Dave?'

'Well of course,' he said, then after a pause: We're mates, aren't we?'

'We'd better get moving then,' I said. 'Oh – just one thing A.D. Do you speak German? Just in case we have to talk our way out of anything?'

I knew Dave had a bit, on account of being stationed in Germany, but his accent's terrible as he'd be the first to admit, and all I can manage is my weird Italian.

'Pretty well,' A.D. said. 'I lived there for a couple of years.'

'You have been around haven't you?' said Dave.

'Don't get me started,' A.D. said. 'I want to save it for my autobiography.'

I took out Donner's cheque because I like handling money. This time, rather too late, I looked at it properly.

'The rotten bastard,' I said.

'What's wrong?' said Dave.

'He's post-dated the cheque,' I said. 'I can't cash this for a month.'

'So he's on to us?'

291

I thought of Lenora Buell. 'I don't think so,' I said. 'Just careful with his money. Let's go.'

First we went to Uncle Pietro's chalet, which is up the mountain-slope a couple of miles out of town. Quiet but cosy. Tyrolean as hell, but all mod cons inside. The army loved it. We dumped all the gear there we thought we wouldn't need, then I bought another vehicle. It was getting to be a habit. This time it was a camper: one of those vans that thinks it's a house on wheels: bunks and table and chairs and a butane-gas stove. I bought it from a sort of bandit who presided over an acre of used vehicles, and beat him down because I paid in American dollars. From the look in his eye he wasn't going to do anything as banal as put it through the books, which suited me fine. We parked it round the corner from the hotel and I went back for the zip-bag with the guns and added Donner's expense money, then shoved the bag into the house on wheels.

'You're now both treasurer and armourer,' I said to Dave.

'It's just a knack,' said Dave. 'Where am I going?'

'Linz,' I said. 'There's a restaurant there called Die Alt Tyrol–'

'How on earth do you know?' A.D. said.

'It's in the Michelin Red Guide to Austria,' I said, 'which is why I bought one in Verona. Meet us there.' I turned to A.D. 'You and I will go on the bike, God help us. They know for certain about the Lancia and they may know about the Fiat. But the bike they don't know a thing about – at least I hope not.'

292

'But don't you want them to know you're in Linz?' said Dave.

'I also want to get there,' I said. 'So mind how you drive.'

The motorway from Bolzano to Linz contains some beautiful scenery: mountains with peaks so white they gleamed in the sun; pine forests, lakes of pure unsullied blue, streams that really were crystal clear. But I didn't see much. This was because my eyes were tight shut most of the way. A.D. knew only one way to drive, and that was as fast as possible.

We passed Dave almost as soon as we'd cleared the town, then the road began to unwind like a tape on fast forward, until we passed the frontier post. That was a doddle really. Both the Italians and the Austrians waved us through as soon as they saw the British passports. Tourists, the wave said. They've spent all their lire, now they're going to start chucking away their schillings. Now the pound's revived we're welcome everywhere.

Linz is a nice little town, respectable, hard-working: a few pretty buildings and a sensational backdrop of mountains. We stopped at a stationer's, and I sent A.D. in to buy some maps. Kaiserinstrasse was on the edge of town and we headed straight for it.

It was a new road, lined with big new properties. Dr Neumann's was by far the biggest; a building so white as to look antiseptic, spare and geometric in design, with a garden around it that was mostly lawn and trees, and the kind of fence even I could cope with. That was all I got for the moment, because A.D. kept on going as per instructions, but it was all I needed. We went on till we reached a turn-off, and returned to town by a different road, found a café across the street from the Alt Tyrol restaurant, and waited for Dave and drank beer.

'That caravan thing's so slow,' said A.D.

'It's also roomy,' I said. 'We need room. And if we bring this off we won't be in a hurry anyway.'

'I hate dawdling,' A. D. said.

'You've already proved that,' I said.

Dave arrived at last and parked in the square and we went over to meet him and had lunch in the restaurant. The other two told me it was good, but I was too scared to eat.

Suddenly it was time to go and I paid the bill. A. D. rode his bike out of town and I rode with Dave. Just before Kaiserinstrasse A. D. was waiting for us. We loaded the bike in the camper, parked in a lay-by and set off to walk. Dave had the binoculars with him. We worked our way to the back of Kaiserinstrasse which was meadowland speckled with large, melancholy cows. Dave dropped behind a hillock of grass and we joined him. Slowly, patiently, he surveyed the ground. At last he said, 'Nobody watching.' That bothered me.

'Want me to come with you?' Dave asked.

'No,' I said. I lied. 'You and A.D. go and see if anybody's watching the front of the house.'

'Right,' said Dave, and tapped me lightly on the biceps. 'See you soon.'

I wished I had his confidence, but I was committed. I had to go. Getting in was easy as it happened. Nobody in their right mind breaks into a psychiatric clinic after all, which is what this was. All I did was worm my way to where a copper beech obscured part of the fence; climb the fence – wooden pickets five feet tall, not a problem if you were careful – and I was in. There was a path to the front of the house, and I followed it. On the front lawn the patients were foregathering, just as Dr Gregory had told me they did. The obvious loonies had an area to themselves, and a couple of heavyweight nurses to keep an eye on things, but the rest just sat in the sunshine or strolled, singly or in groups. The women wore summer dresses, the men were in shirts and slacks. So was I. I willed myself to move. I didn't bother to look crazy. There was no need. I *was* crazy or I wouldn't be there. Gudrun Müller was sitting in the sun. She looked far better than her photograph: nice, even tan, the needle-marks faded to tiny scars, and she'd put on just enough weight. I went to her.

'Hi,' I said.

She looked up and smiled.

'Hi... You're new here aren't you?'

'Just arrived,' I said.

'It's not too bad. Honestly it isn't. You're British?' I nodded.

'Why are you here? Do you mind my asking?'

'Not at all,' I said. 'I'm here to see you.'

She looked at me as if I belonged with the crowd with the muscular nurses. 'You've got to be kidding,' she said.

'No,' I said. 'You're Gudrun Müller. You were helped by a woman called Jane Donner.'

'You get away from me,' she said.

'If you yell I'll be arrested and I swear to God

I'll tell the lot. Do you want that?'

She stared at me, appalled. 'No! I don't want that,' she said at last.

'Jane helped you?'

'Yes.'

'Paid for your cure here?'

'Yes.'

'You know she's dead?'

'I cried all night,' she said.

I made my voice gentle, soothing, as if I was doing the voice-over in a cough-mixture ad.

'You know how Jane died?' I said.

'Oh yes,' she said.

'I'm after the ones who did that to her,' I said.

'It won't bring her back to life,' she said. 'Nothing will.'

'You can help me,' I said.

'Please!' Her voice was loud, too loud. She looked about her. Nobody was bothered. In that neat, precise garden nobody was bothered by anything but themselves. 'Please,' she said again, more softly: 'I've been ill ... I'm only just cured.'

'Miss Müller,' I said. 'I understand all that – but what I'm asking is such a small thing. Just do it for me and I'll never bother you again. I promise.'

I gave her my best smile: all open, boyish charm. I hated myself. She sighed. 'What is it you want?'

'Jane helped you escape from the flower-shop? – the one that was a cover for dope-peddling?'

'So you know it all,' she said.

'Who ran the flower-shop, Miss Müller? Who? That's all I want from you. Just a name.'

She didn't answer for a while: she was too busy

thinking. 'If I tell you,' she said at last. 'I'll have to get out of here.'

'Does he know where you are?'

'Of course not,' she said. 'But if I tell you – you'll use it won't you? And then he could be on to me. I'll have to go away. The trouble is I have no money.'

'I have,' I said. 'Can you get out of here?'

'I'm just about cured,' she said again. 'I'm a trusty, I can do as I please.'

'Meet me later,' I said, 'and I'll give you twenty thousand dollars if you give me a name.'

'OK,' she said.

'Where will we meet?'

'You know the Café Metternich?' It was where A.D. and I had waited for Dave. 'I'll ring you there in an hour.'

I went back to my army. Dave had spotted a look-out further up the main road, watching from a car parked by an empty house. It was a blue Alfa-Romeo Giulia. At first I felt relieved because a hunch was right, then I felt scared because I had to take more chances, and lastly I left angry, because once again I realized I wasn't being taken just for a mug – I mean I often try to get taken for one: sometimes I don't even have to try – but this lot had me taped for a supermug, and that really did annoy me.

We went into the camper and examined the arsenal. 'What d'you fancy?' said Dave.

I picked up the pump-action shotgun. It wasn't sawn down to pistol size, like some you see, just a foot or so off the barrel and a few inches off the butt. 'This,' I said. 'It's the only one I'd have any

297

chance with.'

'You'll have to get in awfully close,' Dave said.

'I'll *be* awfully close,' I said. 'They'll see to that.'

'Maybe I'd better have one as well,' said A.D.

'You never fired a gun?'

'I had a Daisy air-rifle when I was a kid,' A.D. said. 'I was hopeless.'

Dave sighed and handed him a shotgun, then turned to me. 'You're just going to turn up waving that thing?' he said.

'It'll be in the zip-bag,' I said. The one that's supposed to contain the money.'

Dave loaded the shotguns for us so that we wouldn't make a mess of it and disgrace him.

'Remember,' I said, 'the one I call Mr Gandhi mustn't be touched.'

'You've already told us that ninety-three times,' said Dave.

'Just remember it,' I said.

We drove back into town and nursed a cautious brandy apiece, then I sent A.D. off to buy a flask. Bang on time the phone rang and mine host called me to it. Goody sounded nervous but then she would sound nervous. She was taking a big risk.

'Have you got the money?' she said.

'Yes,' I said. 'Twenty thousand.'

'Take the Salzburg road in an hour from now,' she said. 'There's a turn-off on your left just after a village called Grossheim. Two kilometres on. Follow it till you come to a ruined farmstead. I'll be there waiting for you. Come alone, Mr Hogget.'

'There's only me,' I said and hung up, madder than ever. Not just twit of the year: twit of the century.

We went back to the camper and looked at the map. An easy place to find. 'We'll be off then,' said Dave, and reached for the spare helmet. 'If the opposition's there already we'll come back and they'll have to try again. Give us half an hour. If we're not back by then – do what the lady said.' I opened my mouth. 'And don't tell us again about Mr Gandhi.' I shut my mouth, and Dave grinned and punched me on the shoulder. 'You'll be OK,' he said. 'You just do the talking. Leave the rest to us.'

A.D. shook my hand. 'I still haven't got you,' he said. 'You're fascinating.'

Then my army took off on the motor-bike, and I had one more brandy, with coffee this time. The half-hour came and went, and it was time to go.

# 17

More picturesque landscape, gaunt, white mountains, lush, green valleys, ancient villages, churches with onion domes, and still I didn't see them. This time my eyes were open all right, but I was too scared... The village of Grossheim had a particularly beautiful church, I remember, what they call Baroque. I did see that one because I had to wait for the lights to change and it was bang in front of me. The main door was carved, I remember, all saints I supposed, and the Blessed Virgin with her Child. For a moment I wanted to go in and pray, which was something I hadn't done since mum died. But I knew if I got out of that van I'd never get back in again, and the lights changed and I drove on, kept an eye on the milometer for the two kilometres, and sure enough there was the turn off. The road was only a cart-track; the camper hated it. And it was a long cart-track: the ruined farm was well back from the main road: any bangs, even the loud ones, would not be heard.

The farmhouse itself looked like the kind of place where Dracula might spend his summer holidays. Dark and eerie, with a strong suggestion of fungus about it. No sign of a motor-bike, which was as it should be; only Goody Müller in her cute summer dress. A few tatty sheds surrounded the farmhouse. One of them must have her car in it. Was I supposed to be daft enough to think she'd walked? I climbed out of the camper and she came to me at a run.

'Let's get inside,' she said. 'I'm scared somebody may be watching us.'

Somebody was, but I wasn't supposed to know. 'Watching us? Here?'

'I was followed,' she said. 'I know I was. That's why I put my car in the shed.'

That's better, Fräulein Müller, I thought, as she took my arm and dragged me into the farmhouse. We went into the living-room.

It was even worse inside than out. Completely bare, most of the ceiling collapsed, wooden beams half-exposed, two battered doors half-open, and there *was* fungus at that. On the walls. There was also someone with whose face I was familiar: a slim, smooth-looking sort of man, about forty, hands open by his sides.

'Why hullo, Mr Gandhi,' I said. 'What on earth are you doing here?'

'My name isn't Gandhi,' said the man.

'Maybe not,' I said, looking cunning, 'but you own the flower-shop.' I turned to Goody Müller. 'You said you'd come alone. What's wrong? I brought the money. Look.' My hand dipped into the zip-bag.

From behind me a voice said. 'Drop it, bud,' and I went raving mad. It's the only explanation. I began to swing round even before whoever it was had finished speaking, my left hand holding the barrel of the gun inside the bag, cuddling it to me, my right hand on the trigger and I blasted off even before I could see whether he had a weapon or not. But he did. A Colt Commander automatic which he didn't get to use. The shotgun boomed like a cannon and he was dead: just so much ugly meat. Oh Jane, Jane, the things I did for you.

Vaguely I was aware of the abrupt clatter of another weapon, and Dave's voice saying 'Hey you. Gandhi-ji. Drop it.' And all the time Goody Müller was screaming – I wanted to vomit, but I knew that if I did I was finished, so I turned round instead. Two more men lay dead, each beside one of the half-open doors. Mr Gandhi stood stock still, a .38 revolver at his feet, looking upwards. I looked upwards too. Dave and A.D. stood balanced on the roof beams: Dave with a machine-pistol, A.D. with a shotgun.

'Put your gun on the swami, Ron,' said Dave. I was happy to oblige, and Dave leaped down. A.D. followed.

Dave walked up to Goody Müller and hit her backhanded so that she staggered across the room, but the screaming stopped.

'For God's sake,' I said.

'For God's sake nothing,' said Dave. 'She was going to have you killed... And while we're on the subject – just what in the hell did you think you were playing at?'

'I got mad,' I said.

'You very nearly got dead,' said Dave. 'Still we've got your guru.' He reached out, stiff-armed the slim, smooth man until he stood beside Goody.

'We'll start with your name,' he said.

'I'm not afraid of you,' said Gandhi.

'Of course not,' said Dave. 'You're afraid of him.'

He nodded at A.D. and I looked myself. I don't know how our prisoner felt about him, but I was bloody terrified. A.D. stepped forward.

'It's like this,' he said. 'I was rather a friend of Jane Donner's. I don't like the way she died.'

'I didn't do that,' said Gandhi.

'You interrupt me again and I start now,' said A.D. 'Otherwise you may have a chance. Listen and listen well. I used to be a boxer but I gave it up because I was always fouling. Now... Either you tell us what we want to know or you and I go a few rounds together. Bare knuckle. There won't be any nonsense about my winning by a knock-out, of course. Every time I knock you out you'll be brought round till I do it again... What's your name, you bastard?'

'Gian Battista Morelli,' said the smooth, slim man.

'Back up against the wall,' said Dave. 'Shoulders touch the wall. Stand to attention. Let's see how smart you are.'

It's a very painful way to stand for any length of time, but then it's supposed to be.

A.D. said, 'I'd like a word with you outside.'

I looked at Goody Müller. She hadn't moved since Dave had hit her. We went outside.

'I've come to the conclusion I'll never make a soldier,' A.D. said.

'You saved my life,' I said.

'No,' A.D. said. 'I wanted to save your life. I like you. But when the time came, I couldn't pull the trigger. Dave killed mine as well.' He paused for a moment. 'Dave doesn't care. About taking life I mean. He doesn't care at all. You want to watch that.' Another pause. 'After you'd killed you weren't sick. Didn't vomit, I mean.'

'No,' I said.

'I'm afraid I'm going to have to.'

I left him to it and went back inside, put Goody behind one of the decrepit old doors into what was either a very small room or a very large cupboard.

'Mr Morelli wants to tell you things,' Dave said.

'I hope so,' I said. 'Our friend's waiting outside warming up for the main event.'

Morelli turned as green as A.D.

'Just ask your questions,' he said. 'Please.'

I asked them, and out it all came. He got a little coy about where Donner was staying, but A.D. came in at that moment. He looked pale, but that could have been the lust to maim. Certainly Morelli thought so.

'Venice,' he said. 'On the Grand Canal. Palazzo Boldini.'

'Good man,' A.D. said. Then suddenly his fist moved no more than six inches, a low, hard, dirty punch, and Morelli made a sound like wet cement hitting concrete, sank to his knees, clutched his stomach.

'I did that for two reasons,' A.D. said. 'One was Jane Donner. The other was to give you the merest glimmer of an idea what will happen to you if you tell us lies.'

I went into the other room or cupboard or whatever it was, and talked to Goody. She was quite convinced she was going to die, and hence very forthcoming. As much as she knew tallied precisely with what Morelli had told us, so I took her back into the living-room. Morelli was on his feet again, but he looked far from well. I said so.

'He can't travel in that state,' I said. 'Give him a drink.'

Dave passed him the flask, and he grabbed it and gulped, then said: 'Travel where?'

I turned to Goody, whose eyes saw only the flask.

I said: 'I'm forgetting my manners. It should have been ladies first. Excuse me, please.' She downed the stuff as fast as Morelli.

I'll say this for Dr Gregory. Whatever the stuff was he'd prescribed for me, it was quick. They were out cold in three minutes.

'We'll need a spade,' I said.

'There's a toolshed full of them,' said Dave, and so we buried the dead beneath the broken floorboards of a barn: a nasty business. There was also the matter of an Opel Kapitan parked in what had once been the stables. If I could find things I reckoned I could lose them too, so I drove it further up the track to a spot where the meadowland ended, and soil that was mostly grit began, a spot where rusting cans were heaped on the rusting remains of agricultural machinery. No wonder the farm had gone bust. I added the Opel to the collection, and set fire to it. Nobody knew and nobody cared.

When I got back Dave had turned round the camper, A.D. had gone to collect his bike, head back to Bolzano, and forget about murder by putting his own life at risk... The camper had twin divan beds. We took out the mattresses and replaced them with Morelli and Müller, put cushions back on top, then I started using my brains again and we took the mattresses to the still burning Opel, added them to the bonfire. If I'd thought about it earlier we could have taken them in the car and saved ourselves a walk.

We drove back to Italy. No problem for us: two carefree holidaymakers who couldn't wait to get at the Chianti and the signorinas, but I was a bit worried about A.D. He made it through. Border-guards never seem to bother with motor-bikes the way they do with cars, not unless the riders look like Hell's Angels. We met up with him at Bolzano, and I took one look at him and sent him to bed, then went out to a booth to phone Uncle Pietro. He got a bit shirty about a long drive at that time of night, but when I told him why he changed his mind.

He reached the chalet about midnight, but I

had coffee ready, and in any case he'd had a hundred and fifty kilometres to drive and think about nothing but what was in it for Uncle Pietro. I told him the whole story, and if he didn't rub his hands he was using all his will-power not to.

'And you can prove all this?' he said.

'Of course.'

'Tommaso,' Uncle Pietro said, 'always you are my favourite nephew. What must I do?'

'Go to the police,' I said. 'Tell them you can deliver.'

'Suppose they say no?'

'They won't dare to risk saying no,' I said. 'And anyway – a smart politician like you must have a senior policeman he can talk to?'

I looked at Uncle Pietro's face and knew at once what he was thinking: a) because he was a good and caring pappa he knew he could get Adriana off whatever hooks there were; and b) he really would be a politician. Not just a leader-writer. With a coup like this behind him who knew where it would all end? He'd be a deputy at least. And even as a journalist he had the exclusive of the century...

'It will be very good for the policeman too,' I said, and I knew I'd got him.

About then Goody Müller and Morelli woke up with headaches like hangovers and Dave gave them coffee and I took Goody Müller into the living-room. Her fear was hurting more than the headache.

'Why did you do it?' I said. 'Wasn't Jane good to you?'

'She was the best thing that ever happened to

me,' Goody Müller said.

'Why then?'

'You've never been an addict, Mr–?'

'Hogget,' I said. 'Ron Hogget... No. I never have.'

'Then maybe you won't understand. Gian Battista found me in Dr Neumann's place just a few days ago. When I was cured. He warned me you might be coming. How he knew I don't know–'

'I do,' I said. 'Go on.'

'I was to let him know if you came... Set you up... Like I did...Or else he'd give me heroin again. By force. Make me an addict again... Then cut off the supply... I couldn't go through a cure twice... It's not possible... Can you believe that?'

I thought of Dr Gregory's pictures.

'Yes,' I said. 'I can believe it ... I've got bad news for you.'

She shrugged. 'Is there any other kind?'

'Morelli will get off,' I said.

'I thought you'd kill him,' she said. 'That flower-shop – I only worked there. Honest.'

'Sure,' I said. 'You and Arthur Hoyt and a couple of goons for the rough work. But not any more. Hoyt's dead.'

'*Arthur?*'

'A man called Sokolny killed him about the same time he killed Sokolny. Morelli set that up, too. Oh – and he put another girl in the shop in your place. Even called her Goody Müller – and got away with it for months. How could he do that?'

'Because the only regular customers we ever had were junkies,' Goody said at once. 'If he'd told them King Kong was Goody Müller they'd have

307

said sure. Of course – or else no more dream dust. But please – Mr ... why is he going to get away with it?'

'Because I need to nail his boss. The one behind the whole operation.'

'It wasn't Gian Battista?' I shook my head. 'Who then?'

When I told her she cried out loud. It was heartrending. But I calmed her down at last, and took her back to the others. Her chin came up: she was all right again. She went up to A.D.

'Forgive the coy approach,' she said. 'But haven't we met somewhere before?'

'You slept on my floor once,' said A.D.

I left them with their memories and went outside to think. Uncle Pietro would have to stay and keep an eye on them while the army and me went calling, but that was OK too. During the war Uncle Pietro had been in the Resistance: he knew far more about guns than I did.

Surprise, I thought. The element of surprise. Don't give him time to think, cook up a story; just get there and hit him with the facts or as many as it was safe to use. So after breakfast Dave tied up Goody and Morelli, and we left Uncle Pietro happily swinging a Colt Python 357 Magnum by its trigger-guard and making phone calls... Piazzale Roma yet again, and then I thought, we'll do the thing in style, and hired a gondola to take us to the Palazzo Boldini. The gondolier said it was empty – in Venice gondolieri know everything; at least they think they do – but I told him to take us there anyway and he did because we were paying.

The approach by water is always the best to a

Venetian palazzo, and this one was in first-rate nick: the water steps in good repair, the mooring posts painted in spirals like barbers' poles of red and gold, bright and gleaming, the huge doors gleaming too in red outlined with gold. It was an elegant house, but it looked very closed indeed. I leaned on the bell-push while the vaporetti swished by, taking their loads of tourists to the Academia and San Marco, and I pushed till my thumb was sore and watched the churning waters.

But a manservant came at last. I heard him coming. Footsteps on marble floors, then the rattle of what sounded like a hundred bolts and locks and chains. Then at last the postern door set inside the big one opened, and I saw him, a big geezer, clumsy-looking for a manservant, in black trousers, white shirt, bow-tie, and a sort of sleeved waistcoat of red and gold. He was standing in profile to us, so that only his left arm was showing.

I said in Italian, 'Nobody's going to shoot anybody, so don't bother hiding your gun. Just go and tell Mr Donner that Mr Hogget is here. We'll wait.'

The door slammed, locks, bolts and chains went on again. The thorough type... We sat on the steps and waited. I wished we'd brought a pack of cards to show how nonchalant we were, but we got in at last, past a hallway with furniture and statuary shrouded in dust-sheets, up the finest staircase I ever saw outside an MGM musical, along a corridor, until at last we reached a room where the furniture was visible: elegant, gilded furniture with cushions of golden silk, buttoned in scarlet. But Donner was standing to meet us, and Mr Black and Mr White were standing too, one on each side of him, their hands close to their pants' waistband.

'Why, Mr Hogget,' Donner said. 'You're limping.' I was, too. 'Been in an accident?'

'I've been in a fight,' I said. 'But that was yesterday. Today we talk. And I'll tell you why. We've got Morelli and Goody Müller.'

Donner was too much of a realist to waste time in stupid denials.

'I was afraid you might,' he said.

'So now we talk about it. Only first we lock your servants up, then my team and your team check each for guns.'

'You're calling the shots, Mr Hogget?'

'Indeed I am,' I said. 'You see Morelli and Goody Müller have talked.'

'They weren't alone,' Donner said.

'They are now,' I said. 'Except for guards of course.'

Donner sighed and turned to White.

'Lock Carlo and the rest of them up somewhere,' he said.

I said to Carlo, 'Leave your gun here before you go,' and Carlo looked at Donner, who nodded. Carlo put his gun on a table.

I said to A.D., 'Go with Mr White. He might just get careless and forget to turn the lock.'

While they were gone, Dave frisked Black and Donner frisked me, then vice-versa. We had all carried guns, and we stored them on the table alongside Carlo's. Then A.D. and Mr White came back, and they frisked each other. Two more guns. I stored the whole lot in a vast commode painted scarlet and gold.

'Now we can talk,' I said.

'You talk,' said Donner. 'I'll listen.'

I sat, and motioned to the others to do the same.

'Your father-in-law doesn't like you,' I said.

'Well isn't that just too bad,' Black said, then Donner looked at him and he wilted.

'He never did like you,' I said. 'That's why he went to a lot of trouble to find out what you were up to in Vietnam.'

'And what was I up to in Nam, Mr Hogget, apart from fighting for my country and winning the Distinguished Service Cross?'

'You were trafficking in heroin, Mr Donner.'

'Trafficking!' He mimicked my accent. 'Stop being so goddam British, Say what you mean.'

'You were selling heroin to your fellow-soldiers, and so not only impeding your country's war effort but also ruining their lives. You did this on a huge scale. As master-sergeant in a supply depot you had the best opportunity there was. You're a clever man, an ingenious man. Your capacity for work is enormous... You made a million, Mr Donner. At least.'

'You can prove this?'

'Morelli can... He was one of your assistants for nearly three years... Gian Battista Morelli also known as John B. Morrell. Born in Reggio, Italy. Emigrated with his parents to New York when he was three years old. Now a US citizen. Did a three-year hitch in Vietnam. Transport sergeant... He was OC Transport for you, too. He tells me you never did pay him enough for the risks he took.'

I thought Donner might rise to that one, but he was holding himself in check. He stayed silent.

'To get back to Dr Gregory,' I said.

'He's the one who dislikes me.'

'One of thousands,' I said. 'He's done a lot of work on drug addiction.'

'So I heard.'

'It was your wife who told you,' Donner was silent. 'He was able to get a look at a lot of records – the position he was in. Photographs too. He sent them to your wife.'

'I think you're lying,' said Donner.

'You mean she told you she destroyed them? Somebody told me once they thought Jane Donner expected too much of people… She loved you, you know. Even Dr Gregory admits that. But she expected a lot of you, too. Was it too much? Did she expect you to give money to the men you'd destroyed? Was that it?'

'There are no photographs,' said Donner.

'She told you she'd destroyed them and you believed her. She loved you, after all. She wouldn't lie to you. Nor did she… Only she didn't tell you all the truth, either. She destroyed the photographs, but she put them on microfilm first. She kept the microfilm.'

'Where? Where did she keep it?'

'The apartment in Paris. The same place where you planted the evidence that led me to Guardi and his Red Commando.'

'Where I planted–Why in hell would I do that?'

'All in good time. Let me just finish with Dr

312

Gregory first.'

'You do that. I'm bored with him.'

This time Black and White risked a laugh.

'You had plans for him, too. A car accident... Due to happen while you were in Italy being a hero, so how could it be your fault? Only Dr Gregory's in a clinic in Florida having a checkup. There's nothing wrong with him, but by the time they find that out you and your pals will be in prison.'

'For what?'

'Murdering your wife.'

'You're crazy,' said Donner. 'Guardi murdered my wife. You fingered him for us. You should know.'

'You set it up,' I said. 'Set Guardi up too, come to that.'

'Why?' he said. 'Why should I?'

'Because you couldn't be sure she wouldn't talk about those photographs. That she wouldn't go to her father and ask to be shown them again–'

'I don't believe you've got the microfilm either,' he said.

'You will when you see it in court,' I said, and then he believed me. 'At first you didn't think of killing her,' I said. 'I don't know why. Maybe you had a fondness for her—'

'She was my *wife*,' he said. 'I loved her.'

And in a weird way perhaps he did. It didn't stop him, though.

'You saw she was drawn to Frank Sokolny. You had one of your boys ask around – and that led to Mickey Wood, and he led you to your old pal Morelli.'

'I don't remember anybody of that name.'

'He remembers you,' I said. 'Oh boy, does he... Anyway, you now had a hold on Sokolny – Mickey Wood – so you make Sokolny your wife's keeper. While *Honeyfall* was in rehearsal he was with her all the time – reporting back to Morelli, who reported to you... You're sure you don't remember any Morellis?' No answer. 'Then your wife came over to Europe and met somebody else.' I deliberately didn't look at A.D. 'Somebody you couldn't make into your spy as you'd made Sokolny.'

'She did say something about a writer she was keeping,' Donner said. 'It was her business.'

'Only because you couldn't make it yours,' I said. 'She even tried to send you a voice tape to get you back.' I mimicked her voice. 'What's Jane done to upset you?' I said.

He grimaced. 'So why didn't she send it?'

'We can never know,' I said. 'But we can guess... And you were a busy man. The CIA's blue-eyed boy. Business never better and you were just on the brink of getting a huge defence contract. And your wife knew it. More money. More restitution. You knew perfectly well that your business couldn't stand a drug scandal – especially with your wife as star witness against you. You set up the kidnapping by Guardi.'

'How could I do that?'

'You couldn't. Morelli could and did. He comes from a long line of Mafiosi. They have their contacts with Red activists. They have contacts with everybody... So they dredged up Guardi for you and he was delighted to oblige. A blow against capitalism.'

'It cost me a million.'

'You got most of it back.'

'Because you found it. Why would I hire you if I'd done it myself?'

'To keep Dr Gregory quiet. He was beginning to suspect – was also beginning to talk. So you hired me – because you thought I was stupid. Smart enough to find an Athenian deodrachm – OK. You didn't want a complete idiot – but nowhere near smart enough to find your wife's real killer. Just about able to find Guardi – after you planted evidence for me to find. Somebody slipped up there, Mr Donner – forgot to plant it before I went back to Paris.'

'Nuts,' said Donner. 'You were attacked in Paris just after you found that address for Guardi. You were always being attacked according to you. Would I do that?'

'Of course,' I said. 'In New York you wanted to get rid of me – away from the flower-shop, back to Europe and the Reds. So you scared me off.'

'And in Paris?'

'You rushed things a bit, using the Ritz's type-writer, planting Guardi's address so soon after we talked, so you arranged a fake attack to make me think of other things.'

'*Fake?* A guy was killed.'

'You should have thought of that,' I said. 'Who planted Guardi's name in the flat? Mr Black? Mr White?' No answer. I stood and thought how much I hated Mr Donner. All those threats on my life had scared the daylights out of me, but at least I'd stood up and faced them, and that had made me feel pretty good – till Morelli had told me it had all been faked... Time to hit back.

'Never mind,' I said. 'It'll all come out in court.'

By now nothing Donner could say would make his two heavies smile. His face told me nothing: theirs were showing the strain.

'Then Mickey Wood got greedy,' I said. 'His habit was expensive, and he no longer had your wife to sponge off. He'd tried blackmail before – I found a list of names of blokes he'd got money from. Now he was ready to give it another try. He and Sokolny had figured out there was something wrong with the Guardi story. Sokolny wanted to keep quiet about it. But not Mickey. Mickey wanted money – so you had him killed.'

'Who says?'

'Morelli.'

Donner shrugged. 'It's always Morelli,' he said.

'And Gudrun Müller.'

'Their word against mine. Anyway Goody Müller's in New York.'

'The second one is.'

'There's only one.'

'It's no good,' I said. 'Goody's not an addict any more. Jane had her cured. She makes sense. She'll be believed.'

'What can she say?'

'That she was a pusher who lived with Morelli. That she'd even gone with Morelli to Riva del Garda.'

'So she was in on it?' Donner said.

'Don't be daft,' I said. 'She went to Riva del Garda because Morelli liked having her around – but not when he was talking business. She was a junky, Mr Donner. Did you ever trust any of

316

your junkies?'

His head jerked then. That one got to him.

'He took her to restaurants and places when he relaxed. That's how she got that book of matches from the Ristorante Cesare that Mickey Wood got hold of.'

'How did he do that?' Donner asked.

'By asking for a light,' I said. 'Anyway – if Goody had known anyone was out to hurt Mrs Donner she'd have acted at once. Mrs Donner saved her life.'

'So she still doesn't know?' said Donner.

I remembered that terrible cry she had given when I had told her. Maybe while she was still on the needle she might have wondered, but now she knew.

'Oh yes,' I said. 'I told her. That's why she's talking so much. She'd sooner kill you – but as she can't she's talking.'

'Doesn't she hate Morelli too?'

'She hates your whole world,' I said. 'But you're the one she wants on the rack. I told her it had to be you or Morelli. She couldn't have both – and she chose you. It didn't take a second.'

All the same I thought, if I were Gian Battista Morelli I'd take good care not to stay in the same town as Goody Müller from now on. If it were me I wouldn't stay in the same country.

'So what you're saying is I had Wood killed because I'd heard you were on to him.' I nodded. 'Who would have told me that?'

'Sokolny told Morelli,' I said. 'Not meaning to, poor devil. And Morelli told you.'

'And I suppose I had Sokolny taken care of

317

too?' said Donner.

'Certainly,' I said. 'All he wanted to do was stay quiet, but you couldn't believe that, could you? Of course he had to die.'

Again silence, again a sense of strain among the heavies, then Black cleared his throat, and Donner looked at him. Just that. It was enough.

More silence, then at last Donner said, 'You said I liked my wife... If I did, would I let them do – that to her?'

'Do what?' I said. 'Torture her face or cut her head off?'

He swallowed. I was getting to him. 'Any of it,' he said at last.

I crossed my left leg over my right. My guess was it would happen any moment now.

'You wouldn't know,' I said. 'You wouldn't know they would do that – and you wouldn't know they wouldn't, if you follow me. But you should have known. They'd had enough publicity. You should have known they were a bunch of psychopaths. Morelli should have told you. Usually those nuts revel in publicity. Video-tapes, masked interviews, big, big headlines. It's what you expected, wasn't it, Mr Donner? But you didn't get it. Did they tell you why?'

No answer. Not a word.

'Because they'd been hired by a capitalist – been made tools of the capitalist system. Oh, they did it all right. They'll oblige the Mafia if it helps the fund-raising – and they needed cash to set up their next big one. But that particular kidnap – your wife's – was not ideologically correct. That's what they told me. So they treated it like a job – just

318

another chore – and when it was over they had their fun with Jane Donner – which wasn't in the contract, then they killed her, then they cut her head off to show their contempt for every capitalist alive. When you hire psychopaths, Mr Donner, you shouldn't be surprised if they behave like psychopaths.'

He didn't look at either Black or White, yet some kind of signal must have been given because they went at Dave and A.D. like missiles leaving a launching pad, and while they were doing it Donner headed for the commode that held the guns: and while he was doing that I pulled up my left trouser leg and took out the Bernadelli I'd lifted from Guardi's cellar. It was strapped in place by surgical tape and yanking it free hurt like hell but I did it.

'Donner!' I yelled.

He looked at the Bernadelli and stood still. He was perhaps three feet from the commode. It could as well have been three miles. I was nearly crazy with rage and fear and he knew it. He stood still.

'Sit on the lid and watch the fight,' I said, and he did just that. I stood beside him, the Bernadelli nosing into his ribs.

On the face of it, Black and White had had a good idea trying to jump Dave and A.D. They were both hard men, both experienced street fighters: how were they to know that their opponents were both harder and even more experienced, and desperate for an outlet for their nervous tension? Dave hit whoever it was that was up against him with his elbow or his fist or the edge of his hand or foot: A.D. just punched low and dirty. Both methods caused pain. The best thing that happened to Black and White all day was that they finally became unconscious... And just as they did there was more banging on the door. I went downstairs to admit Uncle Pietro and about half the Italian Security Police.

# 18

Three days later Dave and I were on our way home in the Lancia. A.D. had already gone on that homicidal bike of his. He'd refused all my offers of money except for expenses.

'It was an experience,' he said. 'Maybe I should have refused it, ethically speaking, but it may help my writing. Besides – all this publicity may send my price up a bit... So long, Ron. You're the hardest of the lot of us, did you know that? That's why I couldn't get you. You hide it so well – how hard you are. Come on over to the Bush and drink rum some time.' Then the bike crashed like heavy artillery and he was gone.

There was an awful lot of publicity. It began with Uncle Pietro taking pictures as soon as he got inside the place: but that was OK. He took flattering shots of all the senior policemen – and from there it just snowballed. Press, radio, TV. And the same story over and over, not to mention telling it to the coppers. But in the end they let us go. So I phoned Melanie but she was out and I thought I'd surprise her and off we went... Austria, Switzerland, Germany, France. And the Lancia smooth as silk. An overnight stop in Grenoble, then on to Boulogne and the Hovercraft. We didn't talk much. There didn't seem much left to say. Just outside Paris Dave asked me: 'What about those geezers we killed? The ones in Austria?'

'What about them?'

'Won't Donner tell the cops they've disappeared?'

'How can he?' I said. 'The way he tells it, Donner doesn't even know they exist. He doesn't even know Morelli exists.'

'Oh,' said Dave, and then: 'But Morelli's a drug trafficker. That's going to look bad when he's called as a witness.'

'Morelli is not a drug trafficker,' I said. 'The way Morelli tells it he's a nice, innocent florist whose girlfriend had a habit and because of that Morelli went along with what Donner told them both to do.'

'Who thought that one out?' said Dave.

'I did,' I said.

Dave risked a look at me as he drove. He seemed far less sure of me than he'd been before we left England.

'Goody Müller,' he said.

'What about her?'

'How did Morelli make her do what he told her? Or was it Donner?'

'Donner thought of it,' I said. 'Morelli would have done it.'

'Done what?'

'Goody was cured. Jane put up money, but it

was Goody who found the will-power. She was off the stuff. No longer an addict. It nearly killed her, but she felt great. Like coming out of prison.'

'So?'

'So Morelli told her – on Donner's instructions – that if she didn't play along she'd be injected with heroin by force until she became an addict again. Nobody ever got cured of heroin twice.'

'What a pair of bastards,' said Dave.

'They're not the only ones,' I said.

We by-passed Paris and went on to Boulogne. The only reason we weren't bothered was because the Italian police had let it be known we were still in Venice and we'd been lucky at passport control... On the Hovercraft Dave drunk lager and I had a g and t and bought Melanie a bottle of Diorissima on account of I'd forgotten to get her anything in Italy. Dave still had nothing to say, and I didn't bother him, just waited. We were halfway between Dover and London when he breathed in deep and I knew that was it, so I got in first.

'Melanie will be that glad to see us,' I said.

'If you don't mind, Ron,' he said, 'I'll just drop you off and carry on to my place. I'm whacked.'

'But I do mind,' I said, 'and anyway, I reckon Melanie's entitled.'

'Entitled to what?'

'To choose between us,' I said. He kept on driving.

'How long have you known?' he said.

'Since I phoned her from New York when I took the deodrachm,' I said. 'I heard a match strike, but she said she wasn't smoking. She'd never lie to me. And somehow I knew it was you.'

'That was the first time,' he said.

'Then there was your bookmark,' I said.

'Bookmark?'

'Very sexy,' I said. 'Typical of you. Sexy and scholarly. A Christian Dior nylon. Only it wasn't. It was a Hong Kong imitation. I bought Melanie half a dozen pairs last time I was in Kowloon...'

'It didn't mean anything,' said Dave.

'Try telling my old man that,' I said. 'He must have seen you together. Busting to tell me he was. But if he did he couldn't collect from Melanie. So he told Anna Maria and collected from her instead. You an' all, I expect.'

'Yeah,' said Dave.

'Well it can't go on like that,' I said. 'Melanie'll just have to make her mind up which of us she wants.' No answer. 'I told her about you and Adriana,' I said.

'Oh,' said Dave, and then: 'I like Adriana.'

'Too bad,' I said. 'Well you can't have her. Not if Melanie wants you.'

'Who says?'

'Well, I do, of course,' I said. 'I can do it too. All I'll have to do is have a word with Uncle Pietro. You haven't a hope, Dave boy.'

'I don't know that Melanie wants me. I don't know that I want her all that much,' Dave said. For a tiny moment only I could have killed him.

'You should have thought of that before,' I said. 'Look out for the turn-off for the West End.'

We finished the journey in silence. There didn't seem anything left to say. When we got to the house there were no lights on and I told myself it was summer time, not properly dark, but Melanie always loved drawn curtains and every lamp burning money. And true enough there was a note, bang in the middle of the kitchen table. I picked it up and read it, and passed it to Dave. He was entitled, too.

'Gone home to mother,' he said.

'That's about the size of it.'

'Are you going to fetch her?'

'No,' I said. 'If she's gone to mother she'll never come back. I know Melanie – *and* her mother. You going to go there?'

'No,' said Dave.

'You want to go and see Adriana?'

'If you wouldn't mind,' said Dave.

'You can drive me over there. I want to see my sister.'

Slip her the price of a mink I thought. The one Melanie was going to get... Not now.

And blow me when I arrived who should be there but the dear old dad, smashed out of his mind, so naturally Adriana knew all about Dave and Melanie, and the one bright spot in Anna Maria's life was that her Sydney was out playing bowls.

'Good to see you, son,' said my dad.

'It isn't mutual,' I said.

'How's wedded bliss?'

'You're too late,' I said. 'I know all about it.'

'Do you?' he said, getting tearful. 'Do you? So now you know what it's like being abandoned by a loved one. Your nearest and dearest.'

'So will you in a minute,' I said. 'You got money from our Anna Maria. Give it back.'

He just stood there swaying.

'You're telling yourself I wouldn't hit my own father, and maybe I wouldn't. But I warned you before. I can have it done.'

My father put a tenner on the table.

'That's the lot?' I said, and he nodded.

'Now get out,' I said.

'Don't worry,' he said, 'I wouldn't demean – I wouldn't demean—'

He was too drunk even to finish his sentence, but he went, and Anna Maria burst into tears. We're fond of each other, my sister and I. That's why I gave her the money for the mink, and soon we were drinking Orvieto together, and she stopped crying.

Dave didn't do much good with Adriana. She wasn't all that bothered about Melanie – it wasn't that – the trouble was she'd had a phone call from Uncle Pietro. The daughter of a future deputy had to look a bit further than a mini-cab driver. I took him to dinner to cheer him up. The Dorchester.

'I didn't think you'd buy me even a hamburger,' he said. 'But this–' and for once he could find nothing to say about food. I thought of Jane Donner, then I thought of Lenora Buell. 'Maybe there were faults on all three sides,' I said. 'Anyway we've both lost her. And you're a hell of a good minder.'

'All the same,' said Dave, 'this dinner'll cost you a bomb. Suppose Donner does stop that cheque?'

'That's my boy,' I said. Learning to think constructively. He's left it a bit late, though. 'Of course he'll stop it,' I said. That's why he post-dated it. So he could stop it if I found out.'

'Then how—'

'I cheated on expenses,' I said, 'plus I took a whack out of the ransom money. Don't worry, Dave. I can pay for the dinner. And there's a bonus.'

Plus there's a cashmere jacket, and there's also a Turner oil, I thought. And I know a bloke in Antwerp who'll forge me a beautiful provenance – a deed of gift giving it to Ms Milligan, all nicely written on Jane's own writing-paper and signed Jane Donner of which I'd kept a few samples. Cost me ten grand, the bloke in Antwerp would, but the Turner was worth three hundred grand at least, and everything that was left Ms Milligan and I would split down the middle. But I didn't tell Dave any of that. A born worrier is Dave.

Over coffee and brandy Dave said, 'It all got ... sort of personal with you, didn't it, Ron?'

I didn't bother acting stupid, not with him.

'It did,' I said. 'I got to know her, you see,' I said. 'Really know her. She was as real to me as you are.'

'You – fell in love with her?'

'No sense in that,' I said.

'No sense in love,' said Dave. He must have been thinking of Melanie. 'You said they don't execute murderers in Italy,' Dave said.

'Not any more,' I said. 'They get life.'

'Donner should hang,' said Dave.

'He might get off,' I said.

'*What?*'

The idea obviously hadn't crossed Dave's mind, but it had mine.

'He'll have the best lawyers money can buy,' I

said. 'The best witnesses money can buy an' all. Of course he might get off.' I sipped brandy, then coffee. 'It makes no difference.'

'You can't mean that.'

'But I do,' I said, 'because starting tomorrow I'm going to take lessons on how to shoot a gun, and if Donner gets off I'm going to kill him.'

The publishers hope that this book has given you enjoyable reading. Large Print Books are especially designed to be as easy to see and hold as possible. If you wish a complete list of our books please ask at your local library or write directly to:

**Magna Large Print Books**
Magna House, Long Preston,
Skipton, North Yorkshire.
BD23 4ND

This Large Print Book for the partially sighted, who cannot read normal print, is published under the auspices of

## THE ULVERSCROFT FOUNDATION

### THE ULVERSCROFT FOUNDATION

... we hope that you have enjoyed this Large Print Book. Please think for a moment about those people who have worse eyesight problems than you ... and are unable to even read or enjoy Large Print, without great difficulty.

You can help them by sending a donation, large or small to:

**The Ulverscroft Foundation,
1, The Green, Bradgate Road,
Anstey, Leicestershire, LE7 7FU,
England.**
or request a copy of our brochure for more details.

The Foundation will use all your help to assist those people who are handicapped by various sight problems and need special attention.

Thank you very much for your help.